NEVER SO PROUD

A WWII Action Thriller

John Wingate

SAPERE
BOOKS

NEVER SO PROUD

Published by Sapere Books.

20 Windermere Drive, Leeds, England, LS17 7UZ,
United Kingdom

saperebooks.com

ISBN: 978-1-80055-343-9

I have never felt prouder of the Mediterranean Fleet.

It is perhaps even now not realised how nearly the breaking point was reached, but that these men struggled through is the measure of their achievement. I trust that it will not lightly be forgotten.

It takes the Navy three years to build a new ship. It will take three hundred to build a new tradition. The evacuation will continue.

Extracts from the Dispatches of
ADMIRAL SIR ANDREW CUNNINGHAM

JOHN WINGATE

FOREWORD

To be able to present a factual account of the incidents recorded in this book is a privilege undeserved by the author. However, the late Admiral of the Fleet, Viscount Cunningham of Hyndhope, K.T., G.C.B., O.M., D.S.O., encouraged me with these words shortly before he died:

I don't doubt that the youth of the country knows little of what the Navy did for the country during the late war; the tendency is to forget all about it as a nasty dream and with little about it worth remembering.

While you are writing these stories of naval operations, I would ask you to look into the evacuation of Greece and the operations round the evacuation of Crete. In my opinion (as I hope I showed in my despatch) the wonderful spirit of the sailors, both of the Navy and the Merchant Navy, is an example never surpassed by fortitude and tenacity when nearly dead-beat.

In order to record satisfactorily the drama of those terrible ten days in May 1941, the author required the first-hand experiences of those who took part. That these men who commanded, and those who valiantly followed, gave so freely of their time and intellect, is an honour keenly sensed by the author.

Only three of the major characters are fictional: Sub-Lieutnant Tanner, Midshipman (A) Brander, and Leutnant Hermann Maeck. Through them the reader will fight alongside the actual men who waged the battle.

I wish to thank all those who have written of their experiences: those who fought in Crete, from the British family throughout the world, whether they served as soldiers, Royal Marines, airmen or sailors. Without their anecdotes, this story would have lost its flavour. My apologies are humbly offered to those many unsung heroes whose deeds I have inadvertently overlooked.

Finally, it is impossible to express adequately our debt to those brave Captains who, being in the thick of action, have generously recalled their experiences. In particular I must mention:

Royal Marines
Major-General R. W. Madoc, C.B., D.S.O., O.B.E., R.M.
H.M.S. *Ajax*
Admiral Sir Desmond McCarthy, K.C.B., D.s.O. *and Bar.*
H.M.S. Decoy
Lieutenant-Commander A. G. Prideaux, R.N.V.R.
H.M.S. *Dido*
Admiral Sir Henry McCall, K.C.V.O., K.B.E., C.B., D.S.O.
H.M.S. *Formidable*
The late Admiral Sir Denis Boyd, K.C.B., C.B.E., D.S.C.
H.M.S. *Hotspur*
Commander R. H. Hodgkinson, D.s.c., *and Bar,* R.N.
H.M.S. *Jackal*
Commander T. V. G. Phillips, D.s.c., *and Bar,* R.N.
H.M.S. *Kashmir* H.M.S. *Kelly*
Captain H. A. King, C.B.E., D.s.O., R.N. Admiral of the Fleet, The Earl Mountbatten of Burma, K.G., P.C., G.C.B., G.C.S.I., G.C.I.E., G.C.V.O., D.S.O.
Captain M. E. Butler-Bowdon, O.B.E., R.N. (*Kelly*'s Navigation Officer).
H.M.S. Orton
Commander P. Cole, D.s.c., R.N.

The late Mr Alec Wright, Chief Engineer, British Broadcasting Corporation.

I wish also to thank Lieutenant-Commander P. K. Kemp, R.N., Head of the Naval Historical Department, and Lieutenant-Colonel W. B. R. Neave-Hill, Head of The Army Department Library; Commander N. P. E. Whitestone, Naval Correspondent of the *Daily Telegraph;* Vice-Admiral Sir Aubrey Mansergh, K.B.E., C.B., D.S.C., Editor of The *Naval Review* and Captain G. A. French, C.B.E., who was Assistant Director of Plans in 1941; the Editor of *Live Letters,* Mr Robert Balmforth of the *Daily Mirror,* and Major Robert Master-Curtis, Royal Marines, who gave invaluable assistance.

My gratitude is also due to those authors who have written so fully upon this episode in our history. Particularly, I should like to mention:

The Mediterranean and Middle East by Major-General I. S. O. Playfair and Others (H.M.S.O.)

Greece, Crete and Syria by Gavin Long (Australian War Memorial)

Daedalus Returned, Crete 1941 by Baron von Heydte (Hutchinson)

Airborne Invasion by John Hetherington (R. Schnidler)

To conclude, I must stress that any views or opinions expressed in this book are my own and do not necessarily represent those of anyone else.

JOHN WINGATE

CHAPTER 1

Six-foot-two, lean and gangling, Sub-Lieutenant Bill Tanner of the Royal Navy coiled himself deeper into the slit trench as the stick of bombs whistled over the top of him. He shielded his gaunt face from the debris that was spattering upon his tin hat. When the bombers had swung away across the northern edge of Maleme airfield, Bill gingerly raised his tousled head above the lip of the trench. He was surprised by another tin helmet less than a yard away; it also was tentatively testing the lull. Its occupant slowly searched the horizon, then turned towards Bill.

'Don't overplay this courage lark, Brandy,' Tanner said, his grey eyes smiling. 'They might give you a medal.'

'Brandy' Brander, Midshipman (A) and Tanner's observer, did not deign to reply. A burly youth of eighteen, he was almost as broad as he was tall. His brown eyes were like a spaniel's as they turned dispassionately towards the sea.

'109s this time, O Valiant One,' Brandy muttered.

Once again the two men flattened themselves as three Messerschmitts hurtled across Maleme airfield. Bill watched the spurts of dust where the bullets kicked up the dirt: the fire was concentrated upon the only occupied aircraft shelter, less than fifty yards away. Inside this sandbagged shelter nestled their Fulmar, the only Fleet Air Arm aircraft remaining on the island of Crete. During yesterday's bombing, the Fulmar had been damaged whilst refuelling for its flight back to Alexandria.

Tanner was the 'sprog' pilot of the squadron — the youngest and most junior — so had been last in the queue. General Freyberg had reluctantly ordered all fighters back to Egypt, because the few that remained were being decimated by this incessant bombing. A shattered aircraft on the ground was useless: better to live and fight another day.

As Tanner watched the German fighters sweeping across the huts, he noticed the Fulmar mechanics waving frantically and holding up their thumbs. Bill and Brandy scrambled from their trenches; Tanner's long strides outpaced Brander's twinkling steps as they raced each other across the stony ground, but they were beaten by their Squadron Commander, who had sprinted from one of the surviving huts.

'All right?' Commander George Beale panted, nodding at the oil-smeared sergeant. 'Air-worthy?'

'She'll hold together, sir.'

Beale turned to his two fliers. 'Take off,' he barked.

'Aye, aye, sir.'

Tanner and Brander saluted. They jumped for the wing and scrambled into their Fulmar. The hood of the cockpit slammed over their heads and suddenly it was very quiet.

As the handlers turned the fighter towards the field, Tanner automatically went through his drill. The muscles in his face set taut, the skin drawn like parchment across the fine cheekbones. His eyes were the grey of a winter sea, ruthless and cold in their determination. The engine exploded into life and he gave her the gun; no time for fancy stuff now. He held up his thumb; he saw George Beale's rugged face peering up at him, saw the arm swing down.

'Chocks away!'

The fighter started rolling out of its pen, then quickly gathered way, bumping and lurching on to the bomb-scarred field. There was no wind, so Bill opened immediately to full throttle. He felt the tail lift.

'Bandits! Right ahead!' Brandy shouted down the intercom.

The Fulmar was racing down the runway. A stick of bombs erupted directly ahead, and Bill felt her lurch as one wheel clipped the edge of a bomb crater. He hauled her up suddenly, clear of those fatal traps; he'd worry later about the opposition. The aircraft's Merlin engine roared, the prop glinting in the rays of the new dawn. Suddenly she was airborne... As she gained height, he banked steeply to check his bearings.

Down below, the handlers were scrambling like ants across the yellow dust. In the centre, motionless, stood George Beale in his khaki shorts. He was looking upwards and saluting. Bill waggled his wingtips momentarily in reply, then concentrated upon the fight ahead.

Bill glanced above him. He *must* gain height to avoid being bounced. God, how slow these Fulmars were! Thank heavens the sun was not yet high enough to blind him. He looked down at the sea over which he was now streaking; he glimpsed the white ribbon of surf curling along the beaches of the north coast of Crete, then squinted upwards again. He could scarcely believe his eyes.

The blue of the northern horizon was blotted out by a black armada of approaching aircraft.

'Jeepers!' he heard Brandy yelling. 'Alarm, right ahead!'

Bill did not reply immediately. This explained the morning's colossal bombing. He'd need to gain more height before attacking.

Crete was a fortress manned by exhausted and ill-armed troops who had recently been scraped together after the evacuation of Greece. The garrison had been expecting this invasion for days. The weeks of makeshift and frenzied preparations against invasion were now over, and the long-awaited German attack on Crete was beginning with their first airborne assault in history.

Bill swallowed and tried to ignore his fear. 'I'm high enough, Brandy,' he called through the intercom. 'All set?'

'Yep.'

'Tally-ho!'

Tanner shoved the stick forwards, and down went the fighter's nose. He glanced in his mirror: no sign of MEs, even with cloud at 8,000 feet. His stomach had turned to water, for he knew this would be his last flight. One naval fighter, designed to operate from aircraft carriers, versus this Luftwaffe Air Armada. All he could do was to get in amongst those lumbering JU 52s before he was blasted out of the air. At least he'd have the satisfaction of knowing that he'd be taking some of those German paratroopers with him.

The leading gliders were now barely two miles from the Akrotiri peninsula. Bill could easily distinguish them: lines of JU 52s, with their slender gliders strung out astern on tow lines, like children's kites. Their escorts of ME 109s had already passed over the coast; Bill could see them shooting up the gun positions.

He glanced at his altimeter as the scream of his dive began to deafen him: 4,000, 3,500, 3,000 feet... He must select the densest group and tear it apart. Even once he had run out of ammo, he should be able to force the JUs into a shambles.

'I'm taking that bunch right ahead, Brandy,' he called out. 'You watch the gliders.'

Suddenly the Fulmar was on top of the nearest flight. Bill could clearly distinguish the black crosses emblazoned upon the corrugated sides of the Junkers. The first transport drifted across his sights. He dragged the Fulmar round and squeezed the firing button. Sweeping by, he banked steeply to port. The Brownings chattered, and he watched his tracer slicing diagonally through the Junker's fuselage. He saw the pilot's helmeted head slump over the controls. A glider to starboard dipped suddenly, then fell like a stone, its tail flapping beneath it like matchwood: its dead weight was dragging down its parent transport. Paratroops spilled through the gash in the glider's fuselage.

Tanner's target, spiralling downwards and dragging its glider with it, slid beneath the Fulmar's belly. Bill made a tight turn to port, straightened, jinked, and there — on the end of his nose — flew another covey of transports. He had already missed the leader, so he steadied on its glider. As he pressed the firing button, he heard Brandy yelling behind him. Bill peered in his mirror.

Three yellow snouts were growing larger with every second.

Weaving in the blue cone behind him, the Messerschmitts were diving for the kill. Bill lingered a split second for his fire to scythe through the glider. He saw it disintegrate; he glimpsed the human torches leaping from the flaming fuselage. Then he pulled away.

He glanced again in his mirror. The nose of a 109 now filled it completely: Goering's crack squadron. Bill wrenched frenziedly at his stick, but he knew he was too late. He saw the fabric of the enemy's wings shatter suddenly, and then the puff of smoke as the guns spoke.

The Fulmar shuddered as the bullets struck. As the 109 sailed on down beneath him, he heard Brandy yelling defiance through the intercom. Then, miraculously, the bullets ceased as the MEs suddenly broke away. At that moment the engine spluttered, coughed, and then began to vibrate hideously.

Bill saw the blue sky beneath him as he fell out of the top of his roll. Smoke was streaming from the engine. The aircraft was bound to catch fire; he did not relish the prospect of being fried to become a 'flamer'. He wrestled with her until, using the speed of his dive, he was able to control her long enough to level off.

'Bale out, Brandy!'

Bill banked steeply, then, his heart hammering inside him, he waited an eternity for the dumpy figure of his observer to tumble out of the tight turn. *Thank God!* — there he went, a jumble of arms and legs, falling, spiralling downwards towards those fishing boats. A white mushroom of silk appeared, then the speck vanished astern of the Fulmar's tail.

Bill gently nursed the dying Fulmar out of her turn and dragged her nose seawards. He steadied on 330 degrees, then watched his instruments: 2,400 feet and steady at 135 knots. He sighed as he realised the engine was still functioning well enough to keep him above stalling speed, but the oil pressure was falling…

He glanced round the horizon and released the hood lever. *God be praised!* Directly ahead of him, he could see the gleam of sunlight upon the wet sides of warships on the horizon. They were British cruisers, with their destroyers on either bow; the ships were steaming westwards at full speed, their bow waves creaming white in the dawn. Bill eased the Fulmar round to 320 degrees. If he could ditch alongside them, he would have a chance.

It was at this instant that a gob of black smoke spurted from the engine. Flames began to lick along the cowling. He pulled back the stick as the heat began to engulf him.

Bill slammed back the hood. The Fulmar rolled slowly to port, then, as she stood momentarily on her tail, the young pilot leapt clear of his doomed fighter. The slipstream caught him, knocking the breath from his lungs. He tore at his ripcord as the sea swirled up to meet him.

CHAPTER 2

No Quarter

'Achtung!'

Leutnant Hermann Maeck's head jerked upwards as the red warning light snapped on: five minutes to the 'drop'.

He remained motionless, the only man among the paratroopers not to check the final adjustments of his equipment. Maeck was a stranger in this platoon: he'd endured a silent twenty minutes since taking off from Catania. The normal professional soldier mistrusted a fifth-columnist: for Maeck was a trained S.S. agent, dressed in Cretan peasant's clothes. His sardonic grin had not endeared him to his companions. He was proud of belonging to the elite of the Nazi Stormtroopers and, strangely, his arrogance showed in his eyes and the slant of his prominent cheekbones. The stubble on his chin was blond; he had not shaved for days. His hair was flaxen beneath the old cap he wore. Only of average height, he was wiry, broad and tough; his eyes were blue, and on the rare occasions when he did smile, his teeth were startlingly white, a shining gold-filled tooth emphasising his clean-cut appearance.

'Prepare to jump.'

Maeck yawned, then rose from his seat and snapped the hook of his parachute to the static line running centrally down the roof of the fuselage. His face was contemptuous as he lined up in the queue: he had been ordered to jump in the middle of

Heydte's platoons so that he would be less identifiable amongst the mass of floating chutes.

'Ready to jump!'

For the first time, Maeck felt fear. He glanced at his watch: 0713. The door was open now and the slipstream sucked the air from his lungs. Astern, their glider was swaying at the end of its tow rope; below, he glimpsed a white ribbon of surf sliding beneath the bouncing wing. Next, the yellow and green of the fields and olive groves; peasants looking up, waving, then scuttling away. A dusty road, then, suddenly, the black bursts as the flak exploded below them. The Junkers swayed and lurched, then banked drunkenly to port. The roar of the engines died.

'*Achtung! Achtung! Spitfeuer...!*' someone was yelling.

Maeck glanced outwards to where an enormous paratrooper was pointing. He was Max Schmelling, the world heavyweight boxer, and he was showing no fear. In the doorway was framed the end-on view of a British fighter diving from out of the sun.

'Go!'

The first paratroopers jumped. Maeck followed, leaping outwards and forwards as the slipstream caught him. The chute opened, the force jerking the air from his lungs. Then, as he swung like a pendulum, he watched with horror the transport that had been carrying him. Already flames were licking along the Junkers, the glider astern of it a crumpled thing, plunging to its doom on the end of its tow rope. Men were tumbling from the glider's shell; some, whose parachutes were tangled in the splintered woodwork, were plummeting earthwards, ensnared by the lines of their chutes; others had jumped regardless, to escape the inferno, and were hurtling to their messy deaths.

Maeck turned his head away. This was not the party they had been expecting. Where was the umbrella of Messerschmitts?

Above the bedlam exploding above his head, above the screams of men shot in their harness at the end of their swaying chutes, he caught sight of three yellow-nosed 109s. Their guns were blazing as they chased the impudent English fighter. Maeck cheered exultantly as the earth came up to meet him. A few feet more, and he might yet reach the shelter of those olive trees.

Maeck loosened the automatic strapped beneath his smock and tensed himself for the impact. He looked down at the crumpled white parachutes already on the ground. They seemed so still, like broken moths around a lantern.

The ground rushed up to meet him, and he grunted as he hit the soil of Crete.

'Yellow warning!'

Sergeant Hooker bellowed the command he had received from his troop officer, Lieutenant Corbett. The order was merely a repetition, because 'A' troop of 234 Battery, Heavy A.A., had been manning their four 3.7-inch guns since dawn: they had been carrying out this ritual for the past ten days. Hooker watched his gunners scrambling to their mountings.

'Red warning!' yelled the communication number.

'What is it?' snapped the sergeant.

'Stukas.'

'Give me a height,' shouted Corbett from the command post.

'Eight five hundred…'

'Take the centre one.'

'New height, six five hundred… target coming in…'

'Switch on… one-nine-o, four one hundred… X barrage, black out… FIRE!'

Hooker's spirits soared as his guns roared. At last! At last the waiting was over. Here came the swine in their hordes, the northern sky thick with the black beggars, the sky throbbing with the roar of enemy engines. Hooker grabbed his binoculars. Tier upon tier flew the enemy planes, hundreds of them silhouetted against the northern sky. In the van were the weaving fighters: Junkers 88s, the twin-engined ME 110s, and the swift, manoeuvrable, single-engined 109s. Behind them, in perfect formation and stacked up like a pack of cards, lumbered the JU 52s, the troop-carriers with their loads that the Crete garrison had been expecting for so long. Hooker watched them circle over Maleme airfield, away to the westward, while others broke away and headed for Canea, straight for his 'A' troop. As he watched, the guns of 'B' troop opened up from their position on the Akrotiri peninsula, 400 feet above Souda Bay.

Hooker swung round. Amidst the pandemonium of the flak above their heads, multicoloured clouds had suddenly blossomed. From the parachutes swung the grey-green of German paratroopers; already they were barely three hundred feet above the heads of the gunners. The paratroopers were firing from their hips with automatic weapons as they fell.

'God!' breathed Hooker, mesmerised for a split second by the astonishing spectacle. He picked up his rifle, slammed the bolt shut, sank to his knee and started firing 'rapid'. He had no need to shout; his gunners had followed suit. Propping their rifles on the gun mountings, every soldier was blazing away at the exposed paratroopers now swinging down atop the battery.

'It's now or never, boys,' Lieutenant Corbett shouted, emptying his revolver into a German swinging less than fifty feet above him. Then suddenly, devastatingly quickly, 'A' troop was surrounded.

'To the guns!' yelled Corbett. 'Take the platoons with you, Sergeant!'

Hooker heard the order as he slammed home another magazine. Scarlet with rage at the lack of weapons — six rifles between 140 men, and only six pistol rounds for each officer — Hooker tore towards the guns. There he could rally them and hold out.

He dropped behind a gun wheel; heard Corbett's whistle; watched the gunners rallying around the mounting; saw four paratroopers plump into the ground less than ten feet from Corbett. The Lieutenant, his revolver useless now, hurled it at the nearest Hun, then charged with his bare fists. Three soldiers tore after their officer as the paratroopers crumpled on to the soil. They landed on top of the struggling enemy and throttled them with their bare hands.

'Here, Sarge!'

Hooker looked round. Seven gunners, with one rifle between them, stood breathlessly by his side.

'Spread out in a semi-circle and don't let the beggars concentrate,' Hooper shouted. 'Grab weapons off the dead.' He started to dash towards a pile of yellow silk. He was about to spring when the body moved.

In that instant a stick grenade was lobbed amongst the motionless soldiers. Hooker stopped in his tracks. He turned. Time stood still, eternity ticking away, the gunners mesmerised by the evil thing.

Hooker knew what he must do. With all the power of his legs he sprang towards the grenade; as he landed upon the crinkled bomb he saw the red soil opening between his feet. Then he knew no more.

CHAPTER 3

Battle for the Airfields

The fishing boat which had plucked Midshipman (A) Brander from the sea had declined to follow the smoking Fulmar into the Aegean. Instead, Brandy was landed on the beach of the fishing village of Ay Marina, three miles west of Canea. He couldn't blame the Cretan skipper. It was not fear of the bedlam, both in the air and ashore, that dissuaded the fisherman: fuel was now unobtainable.

Brandy was already drying off from his ditching. His watch still ticked, and was showing 0920. He'd better stop fussing about Bill Tanner, who was a good pilot. When Brandy had last seen the Fulmar, the fighter seemed to be once more under control, though emitting black smoke. If Bill was continuing seawards, he was doing so intentionally: he had probably sighted a destroyer returning from the nightly Aegean patrol.

Brandy stamped in his squelching shoes and began his walk westwards along the Maleme road, which hugged the coast. He must find his Squadron Commander and report Tanner's loss. He began loping down the road, still unconscious of the racket above him.

He had hardly travelled a hundred yards when he heard the ME 109s. He flattened himself as they sprayed the road with their machine guns. Bullets whipped up the dust around him, then he saw the MEs winging down the road. They were soaring upwards again to gain height before swooping on the airfield.

He got up, dusted himself off and resumed his trek westwards. All about him the air was thick with shell bursts, and westwards of Maleme a speckle of parachutes was floating downwards. Around the hills of Alikianon, he could see the troop transports lumbering in a large sweep towards Galatos. Their gliders were being slipped, and he watched them disappearing from sight behind the olive groves.

Passing through the New Zealand 5th Brigade in Platanias, Brandy reached Pirgos at half past ten. All was confusion as the bombs rained down upon the little town, but by now Brandy had learned when to run. Bent double, he dodged from building to building, an eye and ear continually cocked skywards.

He heard someone shouting at him to clear the line of fire. As he jumped into a broken doorway, a Bren opened up behind a wall to his right. He looked up as the JU 52s flew over at 300 feet, the black crosses showing clearly against the white panels on their wings. Brandy gasped as he watched the Germans leaping from their doors. They spilled out in clutches, both from the transports and from the gliders being towed: great hawks were the gliders, beautifully proportioned in their slender lines.

Brandy realised suddenly that the drop was right on top of the houses near which he stood. White and blue, yellow and green parachutes suddenly billowed two hundred feet above him. He threw up the rifle he'd picked up off a dead Kiwi he'd passed on the road. He loaded and closed the bolt.

He'd never shot a man before. Now he deliberately lined up the 'V' of his backsight with the foresight: a grey-green German was swinging above, the parachute harness trussed between his legs. Brandy saw the horror on the white face; saw the paratrooper loosening the grenade at his hip. As the man fumbled, Brandy squeezed the trigger.

He did not wait to see the result, but re-cocked and aimed at the next dangling Hun. There was no time to waste. These were the precious seconds in which the defenders had the sky-invaders at their mercy. The man was growing larger at every second, but he slumped limply as the Bren on Brandy's right stuttered again.

Suddenly the paratroopers were all around them, but this New Zealand platoon of the 21st Battalion gave no quarter.

As the Germans landed on the flat roofs of the little white houses, the Kiwis shot the paratroopers down as they struggled to slip from their harnesses. There was a crash, and Brandy heard something slithering down the wall to his left. As he spun round to empty his rifle into the paratrooper, Brandy saw the blood spurting from him. Although his eyes were open, the man was very dead.

Brandy looked towards the street on his right, whence emanated blood-curdling screams. A bunch of New Zealanders had trapped five paratroopers in a cul-de-sac. The Kiwis were fixing bayonets. As the Germans began to open up with their automatic weapons, the New Zealanders charged. The steel flashed in the sun. The screams ceased. The Kiwis, several of their comrades now motionless amongst the crumpled corpses, rushed back down the street to mop up other pockets. Brandy ran after them. Apart from isolated groups of Germans moving along the drains by the side of the streets, the New Zealanders had soon cleared Pirgos.

The Midshipman forged on through the staccato bursts of fire, but it was noon before he reached the eastern edge of Maleme airfield and found he could progress no further.

The battle for Maleme was working up to a savagery that would never be forgotten. From the trench into which Brandy had jumped, and which he shared with a group of New Zealanders, he could watch the airfield below him.

'How goes it, Kiwi?' Brandy asked the corporal on his right, during the brief lull. 'Why can't I go on?'

The New Zealander was from the 28th (Maori) Battalion of Brigadier Puttick's New Zealand Division. He had the open look of the Kiwi, but his tired, freckled face had lost the serene gaze typical of his countrymen. He looked dead beat.

'Look for yourself,' he said. 'We've had to withdraw from the western edge of the field.' He pointed with his right hand, while his left arm still cradled his rifle. 'Look at them,' he moaned in disgust. 'The Hun doesn't give a damn for his losses.'

Brandy watched another JU 52 flopping down through the flak; it was landing on the airfield which, littered with the wreck of crashed planes, now resembled a junk yard. The transport was levelling up miraculously through the barrage hurled at it; suddenly the plane dipped to pancake on to the airfield. There was a cloud of dust, and the Junkers up-ended on its nose, then toppled over sideways.

Brandy marvelled at the accuracy of the New Zealand gunners firing from the higher slopes to the eastward. A couple of ranging shots and then the transport was bracketed. But it was too late: the German troops were already pouring from the plane and dashing for the safety of the perimeter. Some hurled themselves flat and started firing at the gun emplacements. The corporal next to Brandy picked up his rifle, squinted along the sights, then opened rapid fire. Two scuttling infantrymen tumbled over like ninepins.

'Still they come; they don't mind how many they lose,' the corporal complained. 'They're chucking in reinforcements regardless.' He slammed another magazine into his rifle. 'Excuse me, sir…'

Maleme, Brandy knew, was now the key in this battle for Crete. If the Kiwis were forced from the airfield, the enemy would hurl in air reinforcements from Greece. Maleme was vital.

The corporal turned towards Brandy.

'They've been dropping from the sky since the dawn bombing stopped,' he said quietly. 'The first paratroopers landed amongst the 22nd Battalion on the western edge of the field. Down there…' He pointed towards the dried-out river bed of the Tavronitis. 'Then the transport planes came, towing their gliders. The beggars landed their gliders behind a blanket of dirt and smoke. We didn't realise, because at that moment six hundred paratroopers were landing amongst us.' The corporal's eyes were glazed with fatigue and there was a hopelessness in his voice.

'They came at us across the river, dodging behind the pillars of the bridge. They charged then, straight into Lieutenant Sinclair's platoon, while he was holding that wide front over there.' The corporal's hand stretched out along 1,500 yards of Maleme airfield. 'The Stukas are going for the guns. Every time the bombers come over, there's one less A.A. gun.' He smiled grimly, but Brandy saw the pain behind the man's eyes.

'What's happening now?' Brander asked. 'I'm trying to find Commander Beale.'

'You won't get through, sir,' the corporal said. 'You'll have to wait until we recapture the western end of the airfield.'

'When will that be?'

'When we sort out this mess.' The corporal looked away, across the airfield. 'Shouldn't be too long, sir.'

Brander felt the uncertainty in the soldier's voice. Another six hours would decide the issue.

Twenty miles to the east of Souda Bay lay the small harbour of Retimo; forty miles eastward of Retimo, the largest town in Crete, Heraklion, supported 43,000 Cretans by the commerce of its magnificent harbour. This was the port for Knossos, the ancient capital of the Minoan civilisation. Between Canea, Retimo, and Heraklion stretched the fertile plains from which cereals, olives and vines are cultivated.

By the end of April 1941, the peaceful life of the descendants of the first Minoan dynasty of 6,000 B.C. had become unsettled: the British had begun to build airfields at Canea, Retimo and Heraklion.

At half-past four during the afternoon of Tuesday the 20th of May 1941, Petty Officer Telegraphist Alec 'Shiner' Wright, Royal Naval Reserve, was peering out of a cave dug out of the rocky side of a hill overlooking a wadi — a dried-out watercourse — above Heraklion. He did not obtrude his sturdy frame from the shadows of this one-time shepherd's cave and his khaki shirt and shorts melted well into the background.

'Here come more of the baskets!' he shouted, before dipping back into the shadows. 'Hey, Smithy, are you in touch with Alex yet?'

The tall, black-haired P.O.Tel. Wright turned his back contemptuously upon the advancing swarm of Heinkel 113s. Since noon they had been plastering Heraklion. From this cave Wright had watched the remorseless destruction of the town, and now the port was little more than rubble. The two

Gladiators had been forced to return to Alexandria. Despite their gallantry against all odds, despite being reduced to flying colander, despite being unable to land on the pot-holed airfield, they had still tried to hold off the Luftwaffe. Now they had been ordered back to Egypt, and there remained only the one brave little Spitfire. Alec Wright had watched her last flight that morning: she had chased the Luftwaffe until she was out of fuel. When finally she landed, the waiting ME 109s pounced and tore her to shreds on the field.

'Yeah, Shiner, in touch with Alex, loud and clear.'

Alec Wright was lucky to have Petty Officer Smith of the Mobile Naval Base Defence Organisation. Though he was a crazy cuss, Smithy knew his stuff; he had been in Crete since the B.D.O. had landed three weeks earlier. His task was to sort things out initially and to form the nucleus of a base for the garrison.

'What about a cuppa?' Smith shouted from the darkness. 'Shall I nip out and get one?'

Shiner peeped out into the wadi. 'O.K. — there's nothing about. Scoot!'

The P.O.Tel. felt worried as he watched Smithy nipping along the ten yards and into the cave next door. The ME 109s had been strafing them all morning, roaring down the wadi, their guns blazing at anything that moved, their wing tips less than forty feet from the entrance to the cave. He could look down on them and could even recognise the same pilots, helmeted and ruthless in their cockpits, searching for anything that moved.

Shiner lit another cigarette. The heat was beginning to diminish now, but heaven alone knew what would happen next.

He grinned to himself he as remembered the last few days. On the 15th of May (years ago, it seemed) he'd been whistled out of *Illustrious* and told to report to *Fiji* within the hour. (Though he hadn't known it at the time, they'd got the wrong Wright!) He'd just had time to grab his camera and gear before six hours later, at 0400 in the morning, he was dumped on the jetty in Heraklion. It wasn't until he saw *Fiji*'s silhouette disappearing that he realised he'd left half his personal gear aboard, and some of it was valuable. No matter, he'd retrieve it later: he'd been busy enough setting up his W/T station that night. 'Wright,' they'd said, 'Wright, you are to set up a W/T link between Crete and Alex. Do what you can to help the Army.'

Alec had smiled then. He was the only radar expert in the Middle East, so they must have needed him badly for Crete. He was virtually a law unto himself, anyway: one of the first B.B.C. television engineers, he'd been 'in' on radar since its birth. The Navy had snapped him up, and there he was, the only Naval Radar expert in the Middle East.

He'd got through to Alexandria by early dawn on that first day. They had camouflaged their aerial by substituting it with an old telegraph pole, and now they had a crackling signal through to Alex. At the traditional time, 0900, they had dusted off their white shorts, shirts and white solar-'bowlers', and marched off proudly to the Army H.Q. They were ushered before the Officer Commanding, Brigadier Chappel. Alec Wright was proud of his efforts and felt pleased with himself.

'In contact with Alexandria,' he reported briskly, slicing off a salute. 'If there's anything the Army wants, sir, you have only to ask for it. We're in touch with Alexandria.' He lifted his eyebrows and waited for the Brigadier's commendation.

The tough Commanding Officer looked the P.O.Tel. up and down. Then, his eyes flashing, he exploded: 'What the devil d'you mean by that dress?'

Alec Wright smoothed his white shorts and shirt. Admittedly his whites were a trifle soiled, but under the circumstances, surely...

'I'm sorry, sir...

'Sorry, man? Why, you can be seen a mile off in those whites. The Messerschmitts will spot you every time you move. Dammit, we've been lying low for days to conceal our positions!' Chappel's eyes softened suddenly. 'But thanks for the W/T contact. I'll let you know if we want anything. Now, hop it, and draw some khaki from the quartermaster's store.'

That had been two days ago, and now the little W/T station had settled into a routine. With the stew pot in the next cave and the enormous silver ladle which someone had found, Alec Wright had — as usual — organised things well. There was little to do, and no one seemed to want his naval signal station. He watched idly as the pattern bombing started again over the port...

Then he noticed a change in the note of the throbbing aircraft engines overhead. It was fuller, heavier, richer. He looked outwards, then held his breath: a string of Junkers 52s were flying down the wadi, straight towards him. As he ducked into the cave for his rifle he heard the 'Mad Marine' on the hill next door, opening up with his Bofors guns.

As Alec returned to the sunlight his jaw sagged open. From the bellies of the JU 52s spilled bundles of gear and leaping men.

'Parachutists!'

He heard the yells even above the racket that was now splitting his eardrums. Every gun in the wadi had been waiting for this moment; every man was awake. The air was full of flying lead, and sixty per cent of it found its mark. No sooner had the chute opened than its load was swinging lifeless beneath the billowing silk. Then, all around the wadi, the blotches of colour settled: some parachutes held containers, others fighting men, and the battle that ensued was to decide whether each paratrooper could reach the supply container from which he was separated.

Smithy arrived, panting, at Alec's side.

'Take my rifle, Smithy,' Wright shouted. 'I'm going on the air.'

In the shadows of the cave, Petty Officer Wright grabbed the Morse key. No time now for security. He'd whack out the alarm *en clair*. His wrist started flexing along the key:

O-P. O-P. O-P., he tapped; this was the Emergency call. *Enemy parachute troops dropping at Heraklion.* He transmitted the message twice, then switched over to the receiver. It was with immense relief that he received an immediate 'R' from Alex. The outside world now knew the form.

'Wonder how Retimo's getting on?' Alec muttered to himself. He donned the headphones and tuned in to the local frequency. There was little but a disconcerting howl, but as he was shutting down (the enemy had probably already landed on Retimo), he heard an operator on Port Wave repeating a signal from the fleet. Wright tuned in and idly jotted down the message. It was in the SYKO cipher used by the British, so it was not long before he had decoded it:

'From *Rear-Admiral Force A,*' he read aloud. 'To Fiji, Kimberley. *Repeated Vice-Admiral Force D. One. All ships report A.A. ammunition remaining. Two. On completion of refuelling of destroyers from battleships, survivor Sub-Lieutenant Tanner is to be transferred from* Kimberley *to* Fiji *to relieve wounded Walrus pilot. T.O.O. 17.02.'*

Alec Wright shrugged. Force D had been patrolling the Aegean during the night, and must by now have re-joined Rear-Admiral Rawlings with his battle squadron. Evidently some wretched Fleet Air Arm pilot had ditched and been picked up by *Kimberley*, one of Force D's destroyers.

Alec Wright put down the signal. It was unimportant: there was a more immediate battle raging outside his cave. He picked up his rifle. He'd better make certain he won this, his own private war.

CHAPTER 4

Stand To!

Until yesterday morning, Tuesday the 20th of May, when the Germans had dropped from the sky, life for Major Rex Madoc, Royal Marines, had been one of farcical improvisation. With the 23rd Light Anti-Aircraft Battery of the Mobile Naval Base Defence Organisation, a squadron of the 3rd Hussars, a few details from the Black Watch, and a New Zealand band complete with instruments, he and his Royal Marine detachment had been sailed, at a minute's notice from Alex, in a Dutch ship for Crete. At dawn the next day, Wednesday the 14th of May, Madoc had found himself unloading his contingent on to a jetty in the port of Souda Bay. He would never forget the beauty of that morning: the high mountains on the south side of the bay had been mauve in the clear air of dawn, and the low hills to the north washed with the first rays of the sun.

That was an eternity ago. What a paradise the island had seemed then, in spite of the grim reminders on all sides. Poor old *York*! She was sister-ship to the gallant *Exeter* of River Plate fame and, though *York* had always seemed ugly to Rex Madoc, with her square bridge and raked funnels and masts, she had deserved a better fate.

A Greek destroyer was aground on the north side of the Bay and there, beached and listing, lay *York*, her decks awash. She'd been caught napping: the boom had been opened for a ship and not shut again. Through this gap at dawn had crept the

Italian explosive boats; in the low visibility, they had crept up on *York*, who had mistaken them for Cretan boats returning from a night's fishing. The cruiser had opened fire too late, and the brave Italian boats, T.N.T. packed into their bows, had charged full tilt for their target, the crews leaping clear at the last moment. Though *York* was now a hulk, her company had extricated all that was useful and mounted it ashore: wireless transmitting sets, ack-ack guns, including a pom-pom, and vital stores.

The role of his 'Royals' during those first few days had not been exciting: bivouacking under the stars and the olive trees, they had provided working parties and had prepared to take over the searchlight batteries sometime after the 1st of June, when the Army expected the invasion. General Weston, Royal Marines, had been in command of the whole Canea area; Colonel Wills, G.One, commanded Madoc's sector, while the defence of all Crete rested in the hands of General Freyberg, V.C. Things had looked reasonably secure then.

It had been a demoralising week, however. Encamped amongst the olive groves were trigger-happy troops who had been only recently evacuated from Greece. With nothing but their rifles and what they stood in, these men fired at anything that moved or that showed a light in the night — even a lighted match.

It had been a crazy week: his troops had spent it mainly unloading stores that some humourist was grimly dispatching from Alex: an Officers' Library and a complete set of mess utensils, including wine glasses, being among the items. Yesterday, however, the fantasy had been shattered. A horde of German gliders and paratroops had dropped and captured an Ack-Ack position in Canea. This was a non-combatant battalion; the untrained troops could not dislodge the invaders with bare hands, and they possessed only a few rifles between them. Madoc had been given several Matador lorries to lift one of his companies, so he sent his second-in-command, Douglas Scott, to retake the positions. Douglas, after savage fighting, had retaken the gun-site but had caught two bullets in the leg from a Tommy-gun; this would mean sending him out of Crete.

Madoc had then been told to move to a new position at the Monastery. He had established battalion headquarters in a farm near the Monastery, but that Tuesday night he'd been ordered down to a position south of Canea. Here he heard that the Cypriots were looting his Royals' camp, but he could do little about it. He'd been lucky, however, for whilst reconnoitring the indescribable carnage of what had been Scott's battle, he had found an overturned truck. He'd righted it and this was now his transport: at last he could move about.

In the last of Wednesday's twilight, Rex Madoc glanced ruefully at his battered Bedford. He felt exhausted: he'd been on the go since dawn and even now he didn't like his position. His troops were facing south and were much too tightly packed: low-flying fighters at dawn, flying in behind them from the sea, could massacre his men. He had no room in which to manoeuvre either, and Madoc, a large man himself, liked space.

He had just tipped his steel helmet over his eyebrows, the better to scratch the back of his head, when he heard footsteps outside the farm hut which served as his headquarters.

'Major Madoc?' an officer demanded.

'Yes.'

'You're the officer commanding this Royal Marine Company?'

'I am.'

'We're from General Weston and my friend here is the Greek liaison officer.'

Madoc returned the salute. He liked the Greeks. They were courageous and hated the Hun; they'd never give in. He could see the sturdy build of the Greek, but in the darkness could barely distinguish the officer's features.

'We've just received an intelligence report, sir,' the liaison officer said in the peculiar broken English of the Greeks. 'The Germans may attempt tonight to land many troops from the sea.'

Madoc nodded. 'Where?' he asked.

The Greek pointed over the Major's shoulder. 'Anywhere there,' he said, with a sweep of his arm. He saluted and the two emissaries vanished into the night.

Madoc spun round. Two hundred yards away, the surf was lapping upon the sandy beach. It was nearly half past eleven and too dark to reconnoitre. All he could do was warn his northern platoons to guard their rear along the beach. He'd be able to re-dispose at dawn. He'd go and tell his platoon officers now.

He glanced to seaward. It was very dark, but the stars seemed unnaturally bright as they sparkled in Creation's bowl, their reflections gleaming on the blackness of the placid sea. He stepped out of his bug-ridden hut and began feeling his way to the beach. As he did so, he heard a rumble along the northern horizon. Then he saw the flashes of gunfire stabbing the darkness; pinpoints of light and the pencil lines of searchlight beams. Madoc paused for a moment.

'Thank God,' he whispered. 'Lucky the Navy's out there!'

CHAPTER 5

Seaborne Invasion

The night was dark and the sea a glassy calm. Standing at the after-end of the bridge to keep clear of the officers around the binnacle, the tall and angular Sub-Lieutenant, Bill Tanner, felt excitement mounting inside him. Here he was, fully recovered after the morning's ditching, standing watch on *Kimberley*'s bridge with the wind blowing away the remains of his headache. This destroyer was a happy ship, with a fine spirit under her Captain, Lieutenant-Commander J. S. M. Richardson, D.S.O. Bill had been in the water only a few minutes before the destroyer's side had been poppling in the water beside him. Strong hands had dragged him up the scrambling net, then the ward room had taken charge. Hot tea and breakfast had put life into him. Though *Kimberley* and Force D had been bombed all the forenoon and afternoon, he had slept through it and, before he realised it, the destroyers were steaming east again at dusk.

The flotilla, under their Divisional Commander, Commander Tothill, was once more screening Rear-Admiral Glennie's Force D as it swept back into the Aegean, 18 miles north of Crete, on that Wednesday night. *Kimberley was* the second destroyer on the port bow of *Dido*, Glennie's flagship commanded by Captain McCall. The destroyer was steaming at 28 knots through the mirror-like surface of the sea, but was finding difficulty in maintaining her position on her flagship.

Bill Tanner passed a hand through his short mousy hair as he watched the cruisers abeam to starboard. They were a fine sight, even in this darkness: *Dido* in the van, the most modern, with a silhouette much like the new Town class; then *Orion*, Captain Back; and *Ajax*, Captain McCarthy, the two single-funnelled 6-inch cruisers, *Ajax* being fresh from the West Indies after her victory over the *Graf Spee* in the River Plate.

'Port five…'

The Officer of the Watch was altering to the port leg of the zigzag when the Captain suddenly rapped out: 'Alarm bearing red two-o!'

The tension became electric. As so often occurred, it was the Captain who made the first sighting. He was the most attuned to emergency, with an intuition for danger that became a sixth sense. Bill watched Richardson peering through his binoculars, while his officers tried also to pick up the blur that could be the first of the enemy invasion fleet.

Bill could hear the hiss of the bow wave; the reports of 'B' gun's crew as they followed their pointers; and the murmurings from the director control tower behind him as the Gunnery Officer gave his orders. The rigging whined, the halyards slatted against the mast.

'She's a destroyer all right,' the Captain snapped, 'with several smaller objects on either side of her.'

'Trainer… "on".'

'Layer… "on".'

The orders were crackling from the D.C.T.

'Load with H.E.,' Richardson ordered. 'Stand by to illuminate.' Bill heard the Old Man muttering to himself: 'We'll let the cruisers show off with starshell. I'm going in amongst 'em.' He shouted down the voicepipe to the pilot: 'Get off an immediate enemy report, Pilot: *One destroyer, unknown number of unidentified vessels.*'

'Aye, aye, sir,' boomed the pilot. Then a bellow roared from the D.C.T.: 'Ready to open fire, sir!'

'I'm altering to port, Guns. Open fire!'

'Open fire!'

The *ting-ting* of the fire gongs, the long, agonising wait, the — as *Kimberley* steadied with her targets right ahead — A and 'B' guns crashed out. The flashless cordite hardly showed, but it was enough to blind the bridge personnel, who were ducking from the recoil.

'Tell the After Control to stand by Local Control...'

The Snotty, however, was having difficulty in getting through on the telephone. The roar of the guns and the wheel-orders drowned everything.

'Go aft, Tanner, and warn Number One,' the Captain instructed. 'This may develop into a proper melee.'

'Aye, aye, sir.'

In one leap Tanner was through the bridge door and swinging down the ladder. He gained the iron deck abreast the whaler in one glorious slide down the hand-rails, then, oblivious of the wind howling in his ears and of the thunder of the guns, he tore down the upper deck to the after-screen. He saw above him the black finger of 'X' gun slowly traversing from its safety stops; he jumped for the iron ladder and scrambled on to the After Control.

'What's the panic?'

Number One, the hood of his duffel enveloping his head, his hands deep in his pockets, stared nonchalantly down at Tanner. Binoculars hung from the First Lieutenant's neck while beside him stood the Communication Number, a useless telephone receiver in his hand.

'Can't hear a ruddy thing, Tanner. These blasted guns...'
Number One was a Torpedo man.

'Captain says to stand by Local Control with the after guns, sir. He's going in to close quarters.'

The destroyer started to heel to port as she swung to starboard. A searchlight beam stabbed the darkness from the bridge. Bill watched in fascination as the pencil of light searched, checked, hesitated a moment, then steadied on its target. There, suddenly, for the world to see, lay a Greek sailing ship — looking like a caique, with her stunted masts.

The searchlight beam lingered, then swept round to port as *Kimberley* swung. There, naked in the beam, was a small steamer. She was low in the water, very square, and of unknown vintage. She must be the forerunner of many others in a troop convoy. As Bill watched, a Greek ensign was broken out at her mainmast. It was at this moment, too, that *Kimberley*'s first salvoes began to straddle. The range was closing rapidly: it couldn't be more than 3,000 yards now.

Bill glanced astern. The three cruisers had altered their formation to port quarter-line, like half an arrowhead, so that their guns could bear. They had opened 'A arcs', as they were termed, and as Bill watched, *Dido*'s guns blazed, the horizon to starboard flickering from the broadsides. It was an awesome sight and, as the salvoes passed ahead of *Kimberley*, Bill could hear the whine of the shells. Again and again the guns of the cruisers spoke, but now in a rhythmical pattern as a section of their armament fired starshell.

Number One pulled Bill away from beneath the barrel of 'X' gun, which was now bearing: the signalman was acting as communication number for the fire control, while Bill manned the telephone to the bridge.

'That's better.'

Number One was pointing to port. High in the night sky the cruisers' starshell was twinkling like sparklers on Guy Fawkes Night. The magnesium illuminated the scene: dozens of caiques in considerable disarray and, ahead of them, a sleek destroyer, twisting and turning, her bow wave gleaming with phosphorescence. She seemed uncertain of her role — but then, as Bill watched, she turned suddenly towards them, evidently having decided that the best form of defence lay in attack.

'Local Control — Open fire!'

Bill repeated the order at the same instant as the signalman received it on his headset. The First Lieutenant dragged Bill to the open space of the After Control position, on the far side from 'X' gun barrel. From here the ship could be fought and conned, should the bridge be knocked out; from here telegraph orders to the engine room could be transmitted. Being Second-in-Command, the First Lieutenant's Action Station was traditionally in this windy and exposed position on top of the after-screen. From here, if not choked by the funnel fumes, he had a clear view of the horizon, except right ahead. The battle ensign — an unmistakably vast white ensign — flapped and streamed in the wind, above the three occupants huddled in this canvas-screened quadrangle.

Bill twisted away from the blast of 'X' gun. Its barrel jumped backwards in recoil, and from the corner of his eye he watched the smooth drill of the 47-inch crew as they worked around the breech.

'Open fire!'

The flash, the roar of the explosion, the recoil of the gun as it ran back smoothly between the gunners; the breech worker swinging to grab the breech lever; the loader waiting tense, his hand on the loading tray where a shell already lay cradled; the ammunition number crouching behind them as he swung rhythmically to the ready-use locker for the next round: they were like a fantastic ballet, rhythmic in their movements, each working to split-second timing. They had been in action so often of late that they relished the smoothness of their teamwork. As the flash from the next round lit up their faces, Bill sensed their pride of performance. They were utterly engrossed as the mounting traversed beneath the Trainer's hand.

'Shift target!' yelled Number One above the pandemonium. 'Target: caique, red nine-o.'

The Trainer yanked at his handwheel, the mounting swinging crazily as both Layer and Trainer wrestled against the twisting of the destroyer as she tore into the attack.

'Trainer... "on"!'

A second later:

'Layer... "on"!'

'Rapid fire!' from Number One.

The gun spoke again. Two hundred yards away, on the end of the barrel, a wooden caique wallowed motionless, mainsail and mizzen flapping idly in the airless night. She had been abandoned by her Greek crew, some of whom Bill could see leaping over the stern. Even as the 47-inch shells tore through the wooden sides, clusters of German soldiers were aiming rifles from the scuppers. They were brave, but the futility of their action was suddenly borne upon them; they scuttled from the poop, throwing away their guns as they fled. Like puppets on a string they splashed into the sea, which now resembled a maelstrom from the flying metal.

Bill realised suddenly that *Kimberley*'s broadsides were now aimed at the caique. One moment she wallowed there, her Greek ensign fluttering pathetically from her mizzen; the next, her sides spewed open from the broadside tearing into her. Like a pork sausage sliced by a sharp knife, the contents spilled into the black waters. A swarm of screaming soldiers, loaded down with their helmets, arms and accoutrements, slithered in an ant-like stream into the boiling cauldron whose surface was now aflame from the fractured fuel tanks of the caique.

Bill could watch no longer: he crouched over the screen rail to starboard and retched out his insides.

'Shift target… Small steamer, red four-o…'

So the night's slaughter continued. It was horrible, but the guns showed no mercy. Not one German was to land on Crete: even the close-range weapons were firing now. The 0.5s and the four-barrelled pom-pom had joined in as the destroyer, manoeuvring under full rudder, tore into the scattering convoy. Above the team on her After Control, the loom of the funnel glowed red beneath the fighting lights which shone red and green along the yardarms. Through those three hours of butchery the white ensign flapped and streamed above Bill's head; another action was being added to *Kimberley*'s ensign, that vast rectangle of tattered bunting that was always hoisted when *Kimberley* went into battle. Tonight, however, her company could feel nothing but distaste for the task they had to perform.

On the bridge of the 6-inch cruiser, *Ajax*, Captain Desmond McCarthy stood silhouetted like a rock against the glare from the battle now developing to the northward of his ship. He felt certain in his bones that this must be the invasion convoy which it was their job to destroy. Already he sensed that the action might develop into a melee — more the type of fight in which the destroyer boys revelled than the more dignified scrap normally reserved for His Majesty's cruisers. *Dido*, Rear-

Admiral Glennie's flagship, was in the van; *Orion* next, then *Ajax* last in the line. The squadron altered course together towards the enemy as soon as *Kimberley*'s enemy report was received.

Dido opened fire. As she did so, Captain McCarthy glimpsed a grey shape sneaking out from the smokescreen, now less than a mile distant. The torpedo boat was turning full circle to escape *Orion*'s searchlights, but *Ajax*'s 'A' and 'B' turrets succeeded in loosing off a broadside before the turtle-backed torpedo boat re-entered the smoke.

'She's fired torpedoes, sir,' McCarthy heard his Action Officer of the Watch shouting. The Captain was searching for the fall of shot from his first broadside when he saw the tracks: four silver fingers bubbling towards them.

'Hard-a-port…'

Ajax listed as she heeled over, and then, as one torpedo slithered harmlessly by, McCarthy brought his cruiser back to her course. Then suddenly *Ajax* was entering the smokescreen.

The black clouds swirled around the bridge in wads of oily filth. McCarthy lost sight of his fo'c'sle and, coughing and choking, he ducked beneath the lip of his bridge. The cruiser charged blindly through the curtain and, as suddenly, burst through on the far side. There, right ahead and less than two hundred yards distant, was the torpedo boat. She came hurtling towards *Ajax* at thirty knots, a white scar at her stem.

'Open fire!' McCarthy shouted.

He held his breath while the fire gongs ting-tinged behind him. 'A' and 'B' turrets were training as fast as they could; the gun barrels were already depressing and pointing over the fo'c'sle scuppers. Captain McCarthy gripped the binnacle as he waited for the guns to roar.

'Steady,' he shouted down the voicepipe to the Cox'n on the wheel in the conning position below. 'Nothing to port…'

This was a command generally used by destroyer captains, but the Coxswain would know the purport. The enemy was abeam now, less than thirty feet away: the cruiser and the torpedo boat flashed past each other at a relative speed of sixty knots… McCarthy kept his eyes on the compass card… if *Ajax* swung now the collision would be calamitous.

'Why,' he shouted in desperation, 'haven't the guns fired?'

At that moment there was a crash from 'X' and 'Y' turrets and, a second later, shell splashes close on the port quarter.

The Gunnery Officer was yelling down the D.C.T.: 'Captain, sir? She was so close I couldn't depress the guns sufficiently to get on target.'

Ajax shuddered once more as the after turrets sent their parting shots after the enemy wriggling away into the smoke astern.

The D.C.T. spoke up once more:

'Director Layer reports a hit, sir.'

McCarthy grinned: even a gunnery officer could not miss at that range. So close had she been that *Ajax*'s bridge personnel were looking down into the torpedo boat's bridge: her officers had been gazing upwards at the cruiser, their faces frozen in terror as the two ships flashed past one another. A name board on her quarter-deck proclaimed her as the *Lupo*.

'Check, check, check! Train fore and aft. Stand by to open fire…'

McCarthy ducked his head as once again his beautiful ship entered the smoke. He wasn't going to be caught again. He tried to catch sight of his consorts, but *Dido* and *Orion* had disappeared during the last few minutes. He felt fear gripping him after the shock of that near-collision. If *Orion* altered to port now… He gripped the binnacle and braced himself as the smoke began to thin.

'Alarm right ahead, sir.'

A seaman was yelling up from 'B' gun deck, the urgency in his words carrying up to the bridge. McCarthy peered for'd, his eyes streaming from the acrid smoke. 'My God,' he whispered to himself as the smoke suddenly parted. 'What do I do now?'

On the end of his stem hung two ships, less than a cable away. One — a steamer, crammed with German troops — was fine on his port bow; the other, a large caique, was close to starboard of the steamer. *Ajax* was steaming at her maximum speed of thirty-two knots. Her Captain had a split second in which to make his choice.

'Full astern port,' he called down the voicepipe. 'Hard-a-port!' His heart was in his mouth as he waited for the violent trembling that must shake the very frame of his ship. This was an engine manoeuvre which the Commander (E) did not appreciate: the turbines could so easily be stripped. It was a joke not enjoyed in the engine room, but much practised by *Ajax*'s Captain. She spun on her heel, listing heavily as she swung crazily to port. McCarthy, like his Commander-in-Chief, enjoyed handling his cruiser like a destroyer. He enjoyed, too, Cunningham's and Nelson's dicta: *No captain can do very wrong if he places his ship alongside that of the enemy.*

Ajax caught the caique smack amidships. The cruiser shuddered as her bow scythed through the sailing vessel. McCarthy watched the two halves splintering down each side of the fo'c'sle, pieces of timber and lengths of rigging festooning *Ajax*'s sides. He heard the close-range mountings opening up upon the steamer slithering down the port side; he heard the screams of German troops leaping desperately into the water to escape the murderous fire.

'We're going round again to sink what's left, Pilot,' McCarthy said as he conned her into Orton's wake. 'Line ahead and keep your eyes skinned.'

In the darkness, caiques and small steamers were scattering in all directions. As the cruiser swept by, McCarthy heard the screams of men drowning in the wakes. It was an eerie, chilling sound, like the cries of seabirds mewing in the night.

The Damage Control Officer clambered on to the bridge.

'The stem post's a bit bent, sir.'

'Serious?'

'Nothing to worry about, sir. We're not making much water.'

'Good.'

'There's a German rifle sticking out of the crack in the stem post, sir.'

'Oh?'

'A sailor says a German had been on the other end of the rifle: he dropped off quite quickly.'

McCarthy was sickened by this slaughter. They had been at it for an hour and a half already. There couldn't be many ships left, for the destroyers also had been busy.

'Last sweep,' McCarthy called down to the pilot. 'Then we're going home.'

The cruisers were sweeping wide, in line ahead, searching for any ships that might have escaped the carnage. Suddenly a caique appeared from nowhere on a similar course, fine on *Dido*'s port bow. *Orion*'s searchlights caught her squarely in the beam: the vessel seemed apparently abandoned, her only two crew members being in the dinghy which was trailing astern on a painter. At either end sat a Greek, as motionless as a statue. *Dido*'s guns remained silent.

No one moved on *Ajax*'s bridge, all eyes mesmerised by this extraordinary sight. Slowly the caique was being overhauled, and now the two men looked like toys, perched at either end of the dinghy.

'Go on, go on, *Orion*,' McCarthy muttered, beating the bridge with his fist. 'I know it's phoney. Why don't you sink the damned thing?'

Then it was *Ajax*'s turn as the caique swung beneath them, less than a hundred yards away; her decks were deserted.

'I can't murder them,' the Captain murmured to himself, glancing at the motionless Greeks in the dinghy. 'I can't.' He waved to the two Greeks, but they sat stolidly where they were, eyes staring ahead of them. An extraordinary thing... and the caique slipped abaft the beam.

As McCarthy turned back to the binnacle, the sudden chatter of a machine gun rattled from the caique: bullets flattened against *Ajax*'s armour.

Then the night went wild: the after close-range battery opened up under the direction of its Lieutenant, R.N.V.R. His Oerlikons ripped the caique to pieces: German soldiers poured from the hold, crumpling as they reached the deck. The few who escaped leapt over the gunwales to sink quickly in their ponderous equipment beneath the waves.

McCarthy felt nauseated by the butchery. He turned his back and took *Ajax* from the scene of this night's slaughter. As the cruisers disappeared into the night, McCarthy glanced back over his shoulder: the caique was ablaze, the flames licking upwards along her rigging.

No Germans would land from the sea upon Crete that night.

CHAPTER 6

The Barbarians

'Sir?'

Brander swung round. The Midshipman (A) was covered in dirt and dust, his round face grey from the beginnings of a beard. The Kiwi Staffie, who had been moving about the Maleme lines all day, was shouting at him from a ditch.

'Give us a hand, will you? Take a message for us to Brigadier Vasey's H.Q. in Canea and tell him that the 20th Australian battalion must get a move on. Tell him the Maoris here will soon be in position. We can't hold on here much longer. All the telephone lines are down and I can't spare a runner: every soldier who knows how to use a bayonet is needed here.'

Brandy saluted. He smiled and rolled out of his trench as a flight of MEs circled overhead.

'I'll nip as fast as I can, sir.'

'Thanks.'

Brandy disliked leaving the front line, but at least now he had a vital role to play. The situation here at Maleme, the key sector, was desperate. The Germans had poured parachutists into the dried-out Tavronitis river bed on the far side of the airfield. Dodging behind the iron pillars of the bridge, the enemy storm troops had grabbed a firm hold on the perimeter of the aerodrome. The New Zealanders were fighting frenziedly to dislodge their foe, but every hour brought fresh enemy reinforcements from the skies: gliders and troop transports littered the airfield as the Germans poured in their assault troops regardless of losses.

What could be holding up the Australian relief battalion? Lack of transport, probably… Brander pressed on eastwards through the confusion of battle, taking care to freeze when the Messerschmitts were overhead.

Brandy was dodging through the outskirts of Karatsos when a ricochet from a diving 109 struck his left upper arm. Though it was only a flesh wound, he could not stanch the bleeding. An Australian directed him to the hill nearby, on which stood the 7th General Hospital, its red crosses emblazoned boldly on its walls. Brandy hurried towards it.

The Casualty Department resembled a knacker's yard: the stream of wounded was being unloaded from the trucks like butchers' meat, the casualties lying in rows waiting for the hard-pressed surgeons. Brander stepped back as another bearer pushed past him. He felt a fraud amongst these pathetic remains, but he had to stop the bleeding. A half-conscious Australian hopped in, his arm around an orderly, one leg hanging in blood-soaked tatters. The orderly ducked to transfer the weight. He glanced at Brandy. 'What's up with your arm?'

Thus it was that, twenty minutes later, Brandy stood, his hand on his hip, while a surgeon threaded a needle.

'No time for niceties: can you take it, chum?'

'Sure.' Brandy looked away. His black quiff of hair fell over his eyes as he nodded his head.

'Only about four pricks…'

As the needle pierced for the fourth time, Brandy turned his head towards the pandemonium breaking loose at the far end of the reception room. He stood speechless while the surgeon continued his work: a squad of German paratroopers had burst in, Tommy-guns at the ready. They were driving all the walking cases to the wall.

One of the Germans was speaking perfect English. 'Where is the Medical Officer?' he snapped, the grey eyes ruthless beneath his helmet. 'Hurry…' He shoved the barrel of the gun into the orderly's stomach. Winded by the jab, the male nurse jerked his head towards Brandy's surgeon. The Medical Officer was wiping off the remaining blood from Brandy's wound with antiseptic.

'And now,' the surgeon said coolly, rounding upon the German, 'what the devil d'you mean by breaking in here?' His eyes flashed as he stood there in his blood-stained tunic, the needle still in his hand. 'Get out of the hospital! Or are you so barbaric that you ignore the Geneva Convention?'

'I have my orders, *Herr Doktor*,' the German replied, clicking his heels. 'All your patients — those that can walk — are to assemble outside.'

'Your orders, always your blasted orders: that's what you damned Germans always say.' The surgeon hesitated, white with rage behind his muslin mask. 'I will comply under the strongest protest.' He turned to the orderly, who was still gasping from his injury.

'Thompson, muster all the walking casualties outside. Leave the cot-cases where they are.' He turned to Brandy, contemptuously ignoring the brute who stood before him. 'You'd better get a bandage on that when you can…'

While the Germans poured into the wards and manned the windows, the walking casualties lined up outside in the evening sun, ten German guards strutting in front of them. Brander found himself at the head of the column which, stumbling, cursing, and goaded on by its guards, dragged itself away from the hospital and down the Aghya road.

Brander's shirt had stuck to his wound, but although the arm throbbed, the stitches were holding. The bleeding had stopped, and he felt his strength returning. The column of wounded was crawling up a steep hill, on the summit of which Brandy could see the grotesque tombs of a Cretan cemetery. He checked his stride for a moment to help the man behind him. The guard waved his gun and shouted coarsely.

'Come on, chum. Keep going,' said Brandy, ignoring the brute.

Together they struggled on towards the junction with the Canea road. Brandy could see it round the corner barely a hundred yards ahead.

Then, from out of the olive grove on their left, suddenly bounded the khaki figures of Australian troops. Shouting and yelling, they leapt forward, bayonets fixed and firing from the hip. The guard nearest to Brandy crumpled before he could swing round his gun. The Midshipman let go of his charge and swooped for the paratrooper's weapon.

The Australian rescue party faced a terrible dilemma: the Germans had jumped for the shelter of the ditch, on the far side of the road. The wounded prisoners were between the opposing sides, and were caught by the crossfire. Bewildered, the men stood transfixed.

'Get down!' Brandy yelled above the racket. 'Hit the dirt!'

As the men prostrated themselves, bullets whined over their heads. Brandy held his breath while the Australians charged across the road. They leapt over the motionless bodies on the ground, their guns blazing as, yelling and jabbing, they lunged into the crouching enemy.

It was quickly finished. In the sudden stillness Brandy could hear the delirious weeping of a young private.

'You all right, Pommie?' drawled a friendly voice. 'Better come along with us. There's a Field Ambulance just down the road, cobbers.'

For Hermann Maeck, the disillusioned S.S. agent, the events of this second day had not run smoothly. He felt hot, exhausted and frustrated.

Since the parachute drop at dawn yesterday, when they had nearly plummeted into the Aghya Reservoir, Colonel Baron von Heydte's 1st Battalion of the Third Regiment had been pinned down in the prison area on the Galatos road. The fighting had been savage, and Maeck had learnt reluctantly to recognise the Baron's qualities. Colonel Heydte was too human: he had even shared his doubts with Maeck when they had both been huddled in the ditch by the side of an olive grove. Ahead and on the prison hill, the New Zealanders had them pinpointed: the British were firing with all they had.

'Maeck,' said the Colonel between bursts, 'can you run?'

'I can try, Colonel.'

The blue eyes smiled in Heydte's finely chiselled face. Though Heydte was obviously the traditional Army officer type, thought Maeck, he was a reasonable sort of chap. Couldn't help being a Christian, could he — any more than he, Maeck, could avoid being a Nazi? Maeck felt a twinge of shame. He had sneered yesterday morning at those who'd taken their Communion in Greece before taking off, but he'd had to admire Heydte for joining humbly with his troops in their worship. How absurd it all was! Both sides crawling to the same God — how hypocritical could you get? The padre never answered that one.

Maeck stamped out his cigarette in the dirt.

'When we take that damned prison,' Heydte went on, nodding at the building on the hill four hundred yards away, 'you get cracking down to Canea and rouse out the Fifth Column. Confusion amongst civilians in the British rear will ease the pressure here.'

'I'll do that, sir,' Maeck answered. 'But don't fire on us. Remember our password, sir?'

'*Colonel Bock.*'

Maeck saw Heydte grinning beneath the dirt on his face. The German High Command's plans rarely worked out in practice. The Cretan Resistance Group of Fifth Columnists were conspicuous by their absence. No Cretan had identified himself yet as Colonel Bock.

General Student, Heydte had told Maeck, was himself commanding the operation from Greece. The Assault Regiment had been dropped in the west to take Maleme airfield and the hills around it. The Second Regiment would take Retimo, while the First would capture Heraklion. The Third Regiment, of which Heydte's 1st Battalion formed a part, was to capture Canea and Souda Bay. Judging by the building-up at Maleme, it looked as if Student was concentrating on that sector. Troop transports had been dropping all day behind the hills around Maleme. Several were taking off again, so presumably Major-General Meindl had a foothold on the airfield.

'If only we can hold on another few hours,' Heydte had confided, 'the Assault Regiment will gain Maleme, and then Student can pour in reinforcements. That will allow me,' Heydte had continued, 'to extricate my battalion from its precarious finger-hold.'

Lieutenant-General Sussmann's glider-borne shock troops and paratroopers were already exploiting any success: they were spreading quickly over the terrain, already linking up isolated pockets. The ground-to-air canvas signal strips had worked well, and the Luftwaffe had been more than obliging: a gun position to be knocked out here, more ammunition wanted there. Things were progressing remarkably well.

It wasn't until well into the afternoon, however, that Heydte's company finally overwhelmed the prison. Inch by inch they had driven the New Zealanders from the hill, but not until the British were almost surrounded did they finally withdraw. At last Heydte could now overlook the enemy positions. He would redispose rapidly, but first he had to be rid of the encumbrance of these civilian prisoners.

'Maeck!'

'Sir?'

'Clear out this rabble. I can't fight with this scum littering the place.'

So, gibbering and weeping in terror and unrestrained joy, this miserable band of humanity was driven by Maeck behind the shelter of the south side of the hill. The decapitation of one of their number by a British shell hastened the procedure. One of the filthiest of the Cretans had sunk to his knees, gibbering in broken German as he clung to Maeck's boots.

'Get up, you snivelling fool,' Maeck cursed. 'Tell your crew to clear out for the hills — and quick!' He was about to deliver his boot to the base of the prisoner's posterior when he suddenly checked himself. He grabbed the criminal by the neck. 'What are you in for?'

'Murder, sir…'

'Why didn't they shoot you?'

The man hesitated. 'I — well, I was useful to them, sir.'

Maeck grinned suddenly.

'Well, I'll finish the job for them,' he growled, 'if you don't help me. Come on, get up. Show me the way to Canea.'

The wretch did not resemble a murderer as he lay cringing in the dirt. Maeck hauled him to his feet.

'Get cracking, Jo… You'd better worry about me more than you do about the British and Greeks!' Maeck shoved the creature forwards, then followed him.

They left the road when they could advance no further, Jo leading Maeck behind the stone walls of the vineyards. Creeping along the ditches, he cut round to the eastward until he met the eastern extremity of the Greek lines. Maeck had stopped then, undecided on his next move. But when a Greek had thrust a couple of rifles into their hands, and told them to get on with it, there had not been much difficulty in slipping through the enemy lines. This had given Maeck confidence: he would be difficult to identify amongst this motley conglomerate of Greek troops, some even without uniforms. Once behind the British lines, he'd have to think again. Canea would require different tactics.

Maeck and his guide were approaching a hill upon which was perched a cemetery, when they came upon a road junction: one road led to Galatos, the other straight ahea to Canea. As Hermann Maeck crawled stealthily forward, he heard a drone above his head. There, dropping from the sky, was another detachment of paratroops — and they were about to land on his head…

He hauled Jo to his feet. Together they stood motionless, their arms high above their heads. As the first chute whispered less than ten yards above him, Maeck shouted at the white face rushing down towards him:

'Colonel Bock…'

The paratrooper clattered in the dirt; the metal of his harness rang as he slipped from it, and then the parachutist was beside them.

'Deutsch?' the parachutist barked.

'Ja.'

'What are you doing here?'

'S.S.'

'Your job?'

'To spread alarm and confusion amongst the Cretans and the enemy.'

'Why are you in the field, then, with this man?' The paratrooper indicated the grovelling prisoner.

'He's leading me to Canea.'

'Is this the road?'

Thus it was that Hermann Maeck, a smile at the corner of his tight lips, led a detachment of Storm Troopers through the fields. Advancing parallel to the Canea road, the platoon fanned out, only too glad to be directed on their way. To the left and above him, Maeck identified with his map a large hospital block, its red crosses clear for all to see. So far the Luftwaffe seemed to have left it alone.

Maeck was pleased with himself: this latest development was a piece of luck. At this rate he'd soon be able to start his work. Canea couldn't be far ahead. He'd swap identities there: surely the role of a British Army officer would best fit the bill? In the confusion reigning, there must be many a young officer cut off from his battalion.

Maeck stopped in his tracks. Close to the road and under the shade of an olive grove was a group of ambulances, the red crosses glaring conspicuously from the shadows. Half a dozen tents stood between the trucks. A flag, with its red cross on a white ground, drooped from a pole. Maeck crept forward to read on the sides of the trucks the name of the unit:

6th Field Ambulance, New Zealand.

Maeck held up his hand to halt his detachment. He needed a moment to think.

The unit looked busy: a queue of bedraggled soldiers was waiting outside one of the tents. Then suddenly Maeck knew what he must do. To spread alarm and despondency, he could combine his needs with duty.

There was a hard light in his eyes as he rushed forward, his automatic cocked in front of him. It was comforting to hear the paratroopers stumbling after him…

'What do you want?'

A New Zealand medical officer stepped out of the tent from which the head of the casualty queue emanated. About forty-five, Maeck thought; an arrogant type, by the anger showing in the Lieutenant-Colonel's face. Nothing that couldn't be awed.

'Clear your casualties out of the tent,' Maeck said.

'This is a Field Ambulance,' the doctor replied levelly. 'Wounded men are dying while we talk. Now, please go…'

Maeck flushed. Things were not going as he planned. He swung his Tommy-gun towards the queue of prisoners, and the line wavered like wind passing over a cornfield. Maeck grinned.

'I repeat, *Herr Doktor*: get those men out of your tent. I wish to talk to you.'

Maeck felt the eyes of his own countrymen boring into his back. He was being trapped into a ludicrous situation. How could this pig-dog be so stubborn?

He sprayed the ground with a burst of bullets: a whirl of dust kicked up at the feet of the line of walking casualties.

'Get back…'

A youngster had stepped forward from the queue. Though he was in the brown uniform of a soldier, there was an anchor in his cap badge, and the half-wing of a Naval observer on his sleeve. Hermann levelled the smoking barrel at the kid's stomach; he was enjoying this. The youngster halted.

'That's better.' The queue was falling back from the entrance to the tent. 'Now, *Doktor*, shall we enter the tent?'

'That is the operating theatre. I will not allow you inside: a man's life is at stake.'

So simply said, thought Hermann. Such an upright type, this New Zealander with the steady eyes and the grizzled hair. In his blood-spattered tunic, the Lieutenant-Colonel was barring the entrance to the tent.

'Take your men out of my Field Ambulance,' the New Zealander commanded. Slowly and deliberately this time, infuriating in his stubbornness.

Maeck could hear the casualties tittering on his right, while the paratroops behind him were becoming restless. His eyes flared as he stepped forward.

'Stop where you are,' the doctor said quietly. Unarmed, he stood there, his hands still holding a red scalpel by his side, his eyes boring into Maeck's.

'*Himmel!* I've wasted enough time…' Hermann felt the rage mounting inside him. He lifted his automatic weapon as he met the New Zealander's gaze. There was a mixture of contempt and surprise in the doctor's eyes. The trigger softened beneath Maeck's fingers…

The echo of the burst sounded loud in the S.S. man's ears. He grinned broadly as he heard the report reverberating through the olive trees; in the stunned silence he registered a gasp of astonishment from the line of wounded. He kicked out savagely at the young naval flier who had run forward to catch the murdered surgeon.

'Get out of my way…'

The paratroops rushed forward. They drove the wounded back, clear of the crumpled heap on the ground. When the wounded had entered the grove, Maeck ducked inside the tent, dragging the trembling Jo after him.

He was surprised by the gloom, after the sunshine outside. His feet stumbled against something soft. A dead man in a dirty, blood-spattered overall was looking up at him with staring eyes. He must have been the theatre orderly, for his fingers still held a syringe. He lay on his back, but a darker stain on the ground beneath him told Maeck all he needed to know: a ricochet from his first burst must have struck the orderly in the back.

On the stretcher that rested on the table in the middle lay another motionless body, one arm hanging limply over the edge. The upper part of the torso was naked. Maeck looked round quickly. *Ah!* That was what he was looking for: a bundle of clothing heaped in a corner.

Three minutes later a Captain of the Royal Corps of Signals emerged from the tent. He was peering at the identification card which he had extracted from the pocket of his battle-dress tunic. A smile lingered at the corners of his lips as he read the name on the crumpled card:

Mackie, Henry. Date of birth: 1918.

Brander felt all in. Though his wound had dried up, he had found nothing to eat since he had set out on his mission. Now he was further from Canea than when he had started, although he presumed he was still on the right road. He felt numb with shock from the killing of the doctor at the Field Ambulance, and the blood he had lost was making his senses reel.

Sickened by nausea, he had been forced to lie up in one of the vineyards; there he had lain semi-conscious he knew not how long, for it was dark and his watch had stopped. The nausea had passed, but now, in spite of a savage headache, he was hungry. Though he might still be behind the enemy lines — to hell with the Germans! He'd slip down the ditches on either side of the road and find a bite after delivering his message at Army H.Q.

The parapet of a small bridge loomed up in the darkness. Brandy paused, then crept towards it. He stopped, listened for an instant, then slipped down to a dried-out river bed. He jumped as a machine gun stuttered close on his right. Nothing under the bridge... The shingle whispered beneath his feet as he gained the far bank. He heard a twig crackling underfoot. Scared stiff, he froze where he stood, the hairs bristling on the back of his neck...

Suddenly an arm locked around his throat. A knee was forced into the small of his back, a hand slammed across his mouth.

'*April the Fifth...*' a Cockney voice hissed. The hand was removed for a second to allow Brandy to reply to the password.

'Give us a chance, mate,' Brandy gasped. 'I'm a Naval Officer.'

''Struth!' the man behind him muttered. 'You're supposed to reply *Tom Walls*, sir.' The huge man from the darkness released his captive. He had evidently identified Brandy's cap-badge. 'Sorry, sir. You'll be doin' yourself no good if yer wanders about on yer tod like this.'

Brandy turned round, trying to conceal his involuntary trembling. 'Who are you?' he asked. 'No one told me the password.'

Then, from out of the darkness, he saw several figures encircling him. One of them stepped forward. 'What is it, Potter?' the newcomer asked softly, in a cultured English voice.

'Straggler, sir. Says he's an N.O.'

'What's your name?' the squat figure demanded suspiciously.

'Midshipman Brander, sir. Fleet Air Arm.'

There was a momentary silence. Brandy heard the snick of a gun being cocked.

'Rather a long way from your aeroplane, aren't you? Identify yourself.'

'Shot down yesterday,' Brandy said quickly. 'I'm taking a message to Army H.Q. in Canea. Look, here's my identification card.'

Under the light of a blue torch beam, the crumpled card with the blue band across it was scrutinised closely.

'Sorry, chum. But you nearly had it. I'm Lieutenant Moresby,' he added. 'If you hadn't run into us you'd be in big trouble.'

'Can't I get through to Canea?' Brandy asked.

'You're behind the enemy lines. You may join up with us if you like.'

Brandy chuckled. 'I might as well know who you are before I do.'

'We've called ourselves "The Marauders".' There was laughter from the darkness. 'There's ten of us from all units, but most of us are M.N.B.D.O. Take Potter there…' He jabbed in the midriff the man who was holding the Sten. 'He's Potter. Chief Petty Officer Mechanician.'

'Ex-*York*, sir,' the man grunted, introducing himself.

'But what are you doing here?' Brander asked.

'Well, sir, we're playing the Hun at his own game. We're lying low by day behind his lines, and harrying the baskets by night.'

'How'd you get here?' The tension had eased and Brander could see shadowy figures melting into the darkness.

'It's a long story, sir. After the old girl — *York*, I mean, sir — went down, we took her guns ashore. We fired 'em until they were all knocked out. We had nothing to do then, and when the panic started we burnt all the code books and currency.' There was a sad sigh. 'Broke our 'earts seeing all that lot going up, sir. We made our H.Q. in the NAAFI canteen in Souda, and when that became too hot we shifted to our Olive Grove Camp. Pretty grim there, it was.' There were grumbles from the others before he continued:

'Food was difficult, but then we met our Cretans. Twenty of 'em, or thereabouts, who showed us all the tricks.'

There was laughter at this, and then Moresby took up the tale, his voice authoritative in the darkness. 'All sorts joined us: stokers even…' There was much mirth at this. 'But we're mostly B.D.O., with a few bandsmen from the Royals chucked in for luck.'

'They couldna bring their instruments,' a Glasgow voice called. 'Their boots gi'e us enough music as it is.'

'Shut yer mouth,' a deep voice muttered, 'or I'll do yer.'

'We're enjoying ourselves,' Moresby went on. 'At night the Cretans lead us past the Hun lookouts and sentries, and we have a gay old time cutting all their telephone wires. The goats and the shepherds give us cover enough.'

'Tell him about the prisoners, sir.'

'Oh, that? Well, we bagged some of those Jerry paratroopers. They were lost and had joined up with some Stuka aircrew. We rounded them up and bunged them in with some Eyetie prisoners. The gallant Axis allies didn't get on very well together.'

'Hated each other's guts,' Potter explained with relish. 'Good-o.'

Brandy chuckled.

'May I join you, sir?' he asked, turning to Moresby. 'I'm afraid I'm no soldier, though.'

'What the hell d'you think *we* are?' Moresby cracked. 'Join us by all means, but we haven't decided on our maraudings for tonight yet.'

Brandy jumped at the chance. He would no longer be alone. 'Thanks, sir. Why don't we go up and help behind the Kiwis' lines? They need every man up there.'

'What cooks?'

'The Maoris are waiting in Platanias for the New Zealanders. As soon as the Kiwis arrive, they'll both mount an all-out counter-attack to retake Maleme. The Maoris are bursting with impatience.'

Moresby considered a moment. He spoke quietly and slowly: 'If the Kiwis fail, Jerry will have Maleme. He'll be able to land aircraft to his heart's content.' Moresby turned towards his men. 'You know what that means?' he asked, raising his voice slightly.

'Crete will go for a Burton,' Potter replied. 'C'mon, sir. Let's give the Kiwis a hand.'

CHAPTER 7

Black Thursday: Greyhound

'Shell bursts right ahead, sir.'

From his position at the after-end of the bridge, Sub-Lieutenant Tanner noted that it was 1312 by *Fiji*'s chart-table clock. Yesterday Bill had been swung across on a jackstay from *Kimberley* to *Dido*. As *Fiji*'s pilot was sick, Tanner had been transferred to *Fiji* in *Dido*'s Walrus. There had been no chance of flying to date, so Bill had been given the job of Action Recorder. And today, since 1225 when Rear-Admiral Rawlings, in the battleship *Warspite*, had received Rear-Admiral King's signal for support, the battle squadron had been steaming eastwards at 23 knots to meet King's squadron, which was retiring at full speed from the Aegean. This cruiser force (*Naiad* and *Perth*, with the A/A cruisers *Calcutta* and *Carlisle*, and the destroyers *Kandahar*, *Kingston* and *Nubian)* had encountered a daylight caique convoy and dispersed it. *Juno* had been bombed and *Kandahar* had picked up her survivors.

Fiji, flagship of a separate cruiser squadron known as Force B, with *Gloucester*, and their escort of *Greyhound* and *Griffin*, had been patrolling the Aegean north of Canea during the night, but had sighted nothing. While retiring westwards, both cruisers had been superficially damaged by the bombing that had started at dawn. It had been a relief, Bill remembered, to shelter again at 0830 beneath the protection of the battleship's guns. The battle squadron was a majestic sight as it ploughed through the waters of this dangerous Kithera channel.

To the north (much too close, Bill thought) loomed the purple cliffs of Greece. Between this mainland and the most northerly destroyer of the screen, lay the rocky island of Kithera, a brooding, evil thing where it crouched, a shelter for the enemy bombers.

Bill clenched his teeth, the muscles in his gaunt face knotting as his gaze traversed the horizon ahead and to starboard. The line of British cruisers, and the battle squadron's destroyer screens, stretched right across the narrows, between Kithera Island to the north and its sister the islet of Antikythera, to the south. There was little sea-room in which the combined forces could manoeuvre.

Ahead of Rawlings' battle squadron, which was racing to King's rescue, stretched the destroyer screens, widely dispersed against air attack. There too, strung out like a protective necklace, was the third cruiser force, Rear-Admiral Glennie's cruisers from Force D. They had rejoined at 0700 after their successful night action against another caique invasion force. *Dido* was now Glennie's flagship; *Ajax* and *Orion*, *Fiji* and *Gloucester* had formed up at 0830 on Glennie.

Bill glanced astern at the battleships ploughing through the blue of the Aegean. *Warspite* was in the van, her mighty bulk camouflaged in dazzle green and white, her battle ensign streaming proudly at her main. Rear-Admiral Rawlings' flag flew at her foremast. Abeam of her, her younger sister by one year (yet both battleships were over 25 years old) forged *Valiant*, a wall of water white at her blunt stem.

Bunting was still fluttering at the battleships' yardarms. The H.A. ammunition status was being reported to the Admiral: *Gloucester* 18 per cent, *Fiji* 30 per cent, *Dido* 25 per cent, *Orion* 38 per cent, *Ajax* 40 per cent, *Warspite* 60 per cent, *Valiant* 80 per cent. Bill whistled softly: poor old *Gloucester* was, as usual, running low. She was always in the thick of it, particularly since she had rejoined the battle squadron which, as Rawlings had remarked, was serving a useful purpose by attracting enemy aircraft.

Bill Tanner was justifying his existence on *Fiji*'s bridge by recording the minute-by-minute events as she went into action. Officially known as an 'Action Recorder', he was fulfilling a vital function, although — being armed with only a pencil and a file of paper — he did not relish being there as a sitting duck.

He gritted his teeth as he saw the cross-trees of King's Cruiser Squadron appearing up over the eastern horizon, an umbrella of shell bursts clearly heralding the cruisers' position. Bill had grown inured to the cacophony of the guns. Stuka after Stuka screamed from the sky, yet still *Fiji*'s guns kept firing. Now, as Tanner gripped the pencil in his ham-like hand to record yet another attack, the bridge loudspeaker crackled once more:

'From *Fiji* to *Greyhound:* Large caique sighted between Pori and Antikythera Islands. Act independently. Time of origin 1320.'

Bill swivelled his lanky frame round, his glasses to his eyes. There, merged between the islands to the southward, he could see the rectangle of a mainsail. She seemed larger than most, and low in the water: probably full of Germans. The corners of his wide mouth twitched as he watched the destroyer, puffs of smoke at her funnels, turn and race towards her prey.

'Look, sir,' *Fiji*'s Midshipman of the Watch was yelling, 'they're attacking *Warspite*!'

Bill stifled a yawn and glanced again at the clock: 1322.

Warspite, he began to record, *attacked by three ME 109s...* He turned to starboard to watch the fight.

Streaking straight down *Warspite*'s fore and aft line, the Messerschmitts had already penetrated the flagship's barrage, though she was hurling up everything she had. Even at this distance, Bill could hear the rhythmic pounding of her pom-poms.

'They've got her, sir,' the Officer of the Watch called to Captain William-Powlett, who, with binoculars to his eyes, was watching the encounter. One of the bombers, hit by a six-inch shell, disappeared in a puff of smoke. Yet the others held on, pressing home their attacks. Bill saw a black egg spilling from the leading 109's belly.

'I think they'll miss,' *Fiji*'s Captain retorted calmly. 'It's a beautiful attack to watch.'

Warspite was under full port rudder when the bomb struck. There was a flash from her starboard 4-inch and 6-inch batteries, and then a gush of steam and white smoke enveloped the battleship.

'My God,' Bill heard the Officer of the Watch exclaim. 'She's badly hit.'

A silence gripped the impotent watchers on *Fiji*'s bridge. Bill held his breath as the old lady swung out of line: her bows emerged slowly from the smoke and steam as a swarm of Stukas waited, poised above her, for the kill. Then they peeled off for the final act.

Across the water Bill heard the cheering of men's voices: *Warspite*'s guns had not ceased firing for an instant. Still they blazed away, red tongues spitting from their barrels. *Warspite* shook herself, picked up her skirts and, apparently undamaged, resumed her station.

'Good for her,' Captain William-Powlett said. 'But her starboard batteries are knocked out — and so are her boiler room intakes, I reckon, judging by the steam and the white smoke.'

Rear-Admiral King's Squadron was now coming up fast over the horizon, *Naiad*'s signal lanterns working overtime as, being the Senior Officer of the forces present, King took over the command from Rear-Admiral Rawlings.

'It's an impressive sight,' Bill murmured to himself. 'Shall I ever see anything like this again?'

Men sighed with relief as the forces reunited. *Naiad* and *Perth*, *Carlisle* and *Calcutta* wheeled into station ahead of the battleships, *Kandahar* and *Kingston* fitting into the starboard wing of the destroyer screen. The fleet could now concentrate its anti-aircraft fire in these narrows.

Bill watched *Greyhound*. She seemed to be engaging two caiques: the destroyer's guns flashed, then suddenly one of the caiques blew up. She was probably full of Germans and ammunition.

A flight of JU 87Bs, on its way towards the fleet, altered towards *Greyhound*: their wrath raised by the sinking of their comrades, they were obviously intent on revenge. *Greyhound* saw them in time and began to take avoiding action.

She was hampered, however, by lack of sea-room: Pori Island was close to the southward, and she was hemmed in to the northward by the fleet. Weaving under full rudder, she twisted and turned at full speed as she tried to rejoin the battle squadron.

Six 878s, Bill's pencil recorded, *attacking* Greyhound...

The first two Stukas were peeling off now... down they came, vertically, out of the sun. *One*... pull out, the juddering of the flaps, the scream from its siren; *two*... pull out, the egg-shaped bomb toppling on downwards... straight for the weaving destroyer.

There was a flash. Then, where *Greyhound* had been, Bill was horrified to see a column of black smoke spiralling upwards.

'Her magazine...' It was Captain William-Powlett who spoke. The bridge personnel stood rooted to the spot in horror.

'One-eight blue, sir...' The Yeoman's hoarse voice brutally shattered the silence. 'Executive signal.'

The Officer of the Watch bent over the voicepipe.

'Port fifteen...'

Bill dragged his eyes away from the sinking *Greyhound*, who was settling rapidly by the stern. Through his glasses he could see the black dots of her company threshing in the water. Then, as the whole Force, battleships, cruisers and destroyers, turned together to the westward, Bill saw *Kandahar* and *Kingston* streaking from the screen. Bow waves white and wakes boiling, they raced, twisting and weaving towards their stricken comrade.

As they approached the survivors, *Kandahar* and *Kingston* separated on either side of the string of heads in the water. They stopped engines amongst the shocked survivors. The Stukas dived again. Bill saw the swirl as *Kandahar* suddenly went ahead. The 500 lb. bomb plummeted in her wake, the splash throwing up a forty-foot column of spray. The carnage of the explosion amongst the swimming men must have been terrible. Sickened, Bill could not tear his eyes away.

'Look, sir!' the Officer of the Watch shouted. 'They're machine-gunning the survivors!'

Bill couldn't believe his eyes. As the Stukas shuddered out of their dives, the rear-gunners sprayed the swimmers. The bullets were flailing the surface into a maelstrom.

'The destroyers aren't bothering to go ahead now,' *Fiji*'s Captain said. 'They've stopped engines.'

'They're sitting ducks like that,' the Officer of the Watch said softly. 'They haven't a chance, sir.'

Another bunch of 87s was circling above *Kandahar*, a flight of vultures poised to kill. Already its leader was peeling off. *Fiji*'s bridge loudspeaker crackled:

'… to *Fiji*. Give *Kandahar* and *Kingston* A.A. support and stand by *Greyhound* until dark. T.O.O. 1402.'

'Port fifteen,' Captain William-Powlett yelled. 'Course for *Kandahar*?'

The Captain looked grim, but he obviously felt better now that he was going into the thick of it. 'Stand by to open fire,' he snapped. 'Your shooting had better be good, Guns.'

There was a chuckle from the D.C.T. voicepipe. 'The shooting's all right, sir,' a voice boomed, as the for'd mountings crashed into action, 'if we don't run out of ammunition.'

It was then that Bill knew fear. *Fiji*'s swift approach to the scene of *Greyhound*'s disaster was already drawing off the bombers. Bill counted over twelve of them breaking away to form up over *Fiji*. The leader was already steadying up; his wings flipped suddenly and, as the cruiser's flak enveloped him, he peeled off into his dive…

CHAPTER 8

Day of Disaster

Kandahar's mess decks were crowded with *Juno's* survivors, but Commander Geoffrey Robson, D.S.O., had little time to worry: an imperturbable man, he was a born leader and a seaman whom his men trusted. They had all seen much action together, and this was all part of the day's work. Robson's tall figure stood like a rock on the compass platform as he conned his ship to evade the enemy that plunged at them from out of the sun which had, thank God, now passed its zenith.

Kandahar was weaving to starboard under full rudder to avoid six 88s when, at, 1406 Robson watched *Greyhound* cock her bows into the air. He could see her anti-fouling, red like blood, then suddenly she sank in a cloud of steam, stem first.

'Hard-a-port!'

'Hard-a-port, sir,' from the wheelhouse.

'Stop both.'

'Stop both engines, sir?'

The Captain caught the incredulity in the quartermaster's voice, but Robson had to take the way off *Kandahar* or she'd be running down the survivors that now bobbed less than two cables away in the oily water.

'Slow astern both.' He gave the order between compressed lips. It was suicide to stop his ship, if these swine went on attacking while *Kingston* and he continued picking up survivors. *God! Look at those devils swooping across* Kingston*'s stem...*

Six ME 109s were diving upon the pathetic knots of survivors in the water. *Greyhound*'s whaler was in the midst of the turmoil, and two officers were standing up as they tried to haul men into the boat: one was *Greyhound*'s First Lieutenant, Lieutenant Scott, and the other, the Gunner (T), Mr Chase. Robson could see them clearly and he grinned as he remembered the run ashore that the Ward Rooms of *Kingston* and *Kandahar* had shared in Alexandria, such ages ago it seemed.

Scott looked up for a moment, then waved. He turned back to tend the overcrowded whaler, when Robson saw an ME 109 sweeping in low across the water. Scott ignored the evil thing, but a young seaman dived out of the whaler and disappeared. The fighter's guns chattered; the bullets threshed across the surface, then tore into the whaler. Scott slumped across the fallen Gunner (T). By the time the young seaman clambered back into the whaler, all eighteen men were dead. Robson looked away.

'Stop both,' he ordered.

Kandahar had now lost all her way. She wallowed, a sitting duck in the long swell. Her sides were draped with scrambling nets and innumerable heaving lines, whilst, from her guardrails, every man not at the guns hung with arms outstretched to snatch survivors from the water. The point-fives chattered, but, unharmed, the butchers from the sky dropped their bombs amongst the remains of what had been a ship's company. The ME 109s swept *Kandahar*'s decks with machine-gun fire, wheeled, dipped, then swooped again to rake the surface of the sea with their bullets. Time and time again a swimmer, hands outstretched to clutch the line dangling a few feet from his grasp, would be struck in the back from the machine-gun fire. A grunt, a sudden jerk, and the body would slide slowly beneath the surface.

'Hullo, Geoffrey.'

Robson, who was staring 'up sun' to sight the next Stuka, turned towards the voice he recognised.

'Welcome on board,' Robson said. 'You all right?'

Greyhound's Captain, Commander Marshall-A'Deane, D.S.O., D.S.C., was standing there, a bedraggled survivor, dripping puddles on the bridge. His face was grim, but his eyes still twinkled with humour.

'Fine. Thanks for picking us up.' Marshall-A'Deane was already turning towards the ladder, when a fighter streaked overhead. As they flattened themselves, lead spattered against the bridge sides. *Greyhound*'s Captain picked himself up.

'I'll just go and lend a hand, Geoffrey,' he said, 'if you don't mind.' He swung himself down the bridge ladder.

It was *Kingston*'s turn now. Her guns blazed, yet still the planes dived upon her and the men struggling in the water. Three Stukas were hovering like hawks: then, one by one, they peeled off and hurtled down upon their stationary target. They pressed home their attacks, not pulling out until they were 500 feet above the stopped destroyer. Robson watched the black eggs that plummeted on downwards. Then, above the scream from the Stukas' sirens, he heard three distinct cracks as the bombs struck. Three fountains of water spurted upwards, hung there a moment, a white mist blanketing *Kingston*. Slowly the whiteness drifted to the yellow-brown dirt of high-explosive. The film of spray and debris subsided and there lay *Kingston*, rolling violently on top of the swimmers as she wallowed from the near misses.

'Look, sir, port beam…'

The Sub was pointing excitedly to the northward. Unnoticed in the fracas, the cruiser *Gloucester* was less than a mile away and, creaming up astern of her, *Fiji*. Both were brave sights; their six-inch were elevated fully, and their triple ,turrets were blazing away for all they were worth. Already the fire was having its effect, for a group of JU 88s which had been gathering above *Kandahar* suddenly drew away and streaked towards *Gloucester*.

'Thank God they've arrived,' said Robson. 'Now we can get on with the job in hand.' He turned towards the D.C.T., from whence Guns's tin hat protruded contemptuously. 'You look after the baskets now, Guns,' he said. 'I'll get on with picking up survivors.'

Ting… ting…

Guns nodded, his attention distracted by a group of low-flying 109s on the starboard quarter.

So the rescue work continued beneath the merciless attacks from the Luftwaffe, until at 1520 *Kandahar* and *Kingston* finally went ahead, their duty done.

Fiji and *Gloucester*, though they had successfully diverted the heat of the aerial attacks, had drawn a few miles ahead. Robson now settled down to overhaul them but, with all their survivors on board, *Kandahar* and *Kingston* were hard put to it to overhaul the cruisers. *Fiji* and *Gloucester* were now steering south-westwards in an attempt to join up before dark with the battle squadron.

'Alarm red nine-o!' cried the port lookout. A wave of Stukas was peeling off from up-sun.

'Hard-a-port…' Robson ordered wearily, watching the moment of release. He liked to keep the Stukas fine on the bow.

So the game went on, but with this continuous evasive action it would take hours to draw beneath the shelter of the cruisers' umbrella. The attacks were being pressed home even closer now, because the cruisers were conserving their ammunition and were not opening fire until the last moment. The enemy pilots had realised at once that the H.A. ammunition was running out.

Robson glanced at the chart table clock: 1550, an eternity until nightfall. He felt desperately tired: he had been on the bridge now for forty-three hours. He was idly watching *Gloucester* and ruminating upon her wonderful record of staunchness: she had been more consistently bombed than any other ship in the Mediterranean; she had suffered grievously already, but under her gallant Commanding Officer, Captain H. A. Rowley, her happy company had never faltered. *Those Southampton class are the best-looking cruisers we have*, Robson thought, as he watched *Gloucester* steaming at full speed, all guns blazing, her wake a fountain of foaming water. Then, as he watched, he saw a covey of JU 88s pouncing upon the beautiful cruiser.

Robson took little heed of the attack until he suddenly realised that the third 88 was penetrating *Gloucester*'s barrage. There was a yellow flash on the cruiser's upper deck, and then a sheet of flame. Another, then another bomber broke through, and suddenly *Gloucester* was an incandescent torch, aflame from stem to stern.

'My God!' Robson shouted, springing to his feet. 'She's badly hurt.'

Even at this distance he could see that the cruiser's upper deck was a shambles. She was losing way already but still the enemy attacked, ME 109s now, sweeping the tortured ship with machine-gun fire. There were still five hours to go before dark, and the battle had barely begun.

'*Gloucester* sunk,' Bill Tanner recorded at the after-end of *Fiji*'s bridge. '1615. *Fiji* closed wreckage to recover survivors.' He moved to the wings of the cruiser's bridge to stare disconsolately down at the pathetic remains of what a few moments earlier had been proud *Gloucester*. Now only a pall of smoke masked the cruiser's grave; and all around *Fiji* knots of struggling men were threshing in the water beneath a hail of bombs and bullets. Their anguished cries floated up towards *Fiji*'s bridge like the mewing of wild birds.

For Captain William-Powlett this was an agonising moment. Though some twelve hundred men must be here, praying desperately to be picked up, *Fiji* would have to stop in order to rescue them. If she did so, she would lie wallowing there, a sitting duck for the enemy who, like a swarm of angry hornets, was gathering to pounce upon the surviving cruiser. Dare he expose his own ship and her gallant company to certain destruction in order to save *Gloucester*'s survivors? This impossible choice was no new problem these days: the enemy's ruthlessness enforced only one possible decision. Bill Tanner watched the Captain, pipe struck into his mouth, stroll to the far side of *Fiji*'s bridge as he wrestled with the problem. Then he turned to his Executive Officer.

'Drop half our Carley floats and rafts overboard, Commander,' Powlett shouted above the din of the gunfire. 'Tell the survivors to keep together and make to the northward. They should be able to reach Crete or Pori Island, only nine miles away.' He turned to the voicepipe. 'Steer 240 degrees,' he choked. 'Full ahead both.'

Rear-Admiral Rawlings was a large, craggy man. He radiated confidence and stood as firm as a rock on the battleship *Warspite*'s bridge. At 1410 he was watching *Fiji* and *Gloucester* dropping rapidly astern, and a doubt began to cloud his mind. Did Rear-Admiral King realise that *Fiji* and *Gloucester* were seriously short of ammunition?

Rawlings signalled his fears to his senior officer, resulting in King signalling *Fiji* and *Gloucester* to withdraw at discretion, with *Kandahar* and *Kingston* in company.

At 1607 Rawlings glanced again at the two signals in his hand: the first was from *Fiji* reporting the loss and position of *Gloucester* (the pall of smoke was still visible, like a black hand, on the horizon); and stating that *Fiji* had only 5 per cent of ammunition remaining. The second signal was from Rear-Admiral King: he was consulting Rawlings as to whether the battle squadron should return to *Gloucester*'s aid or continue westwards out of trouble.

Rawlings needed time to ponder this terrible problem: to risk further losses through standing by a stricken comrade, or to carry on as a fighting battle unit. He glanced round at his battle squadron as, battered but unbowed, it forged ahead to escape disaster.

Over to the westward was Captain D.5 and his flotilla taking up station in the screen. Captain Lord Louis Mountbatten had steamed from Malta, putting up a U-boat on passage. The 'J' and 'K' fine ships were there too. These modern destroyers — *Kelly*, *Kashmir*, *Kipling*, *Kelvin* and *Jackal* — were the first of the single-funnel boats. With improved boiler design, only two boilers were necessary, so a single funnel sufficed.

Rawlings suddenly made up his mind: it would be a wrong decision to return and support *Gloucester*. He signalled his opinion to Rear-Admiral King.

The air attacks gradually became more intermittent. The lookouts must have been asleep when, at 1645, *Valiant* was struck aft by two medium bombs from an Italian high-level attack. Rawlings groaned as he saw the flashes and the familiar cloud of smoke. Then, through the curtain of debris, there appeared the old battleship, dented but not seriously harmed.

The Admiral's Chief Yeoman of Signals stood at his elbow, a signal pad held before his admiral.

'*From* Fiji,' Rawlings read. '*Kandahar and* Kingston *in company. My position, course and speed: 3050 Cape Elaphonisi 24 miles, 1750, 27 knots. Time of origin 1700.*'

'Thank you, Yeoman.'

Rawlings shoved his cap to the back of his head and sighed with relief. *Fiji* was all right. Only two hours to go before twilight… She must be thirty miles to the eastward. *Warspite* was steering 215 degrees. Rawlings scratched his head. *Better close 'em*, he thought, *just in case.*

He left the bridge and strolled into the Plot, where his Navigating Officer was poring over the A.R.L. Rawlings filled his pipe and then, with his staff officers, he snatched the opportunity to appreciate the situation. At 1800 he ordered an alteration to 180 degrees. He then returned to *Warspite*'s bridge.

Visibility had shut right down. Cloud was low, and although this heralded an early dusk and a dark night, the next hour could be the most hazardous of the day. The attacks had eased off and the lookouts were exhausted. A feeling of relief was in the air, and the men were already beginning to relax.

Sub-Lieutenant Bill Tanner shifted his weight to ease the cramp in his right leg. He had been standing here, at the after-end of *Fiji*'s bridge, for nearly fourteen hours; his face was grey with tiredness and a day's growth of beard. He glanced for the thousandth time at the clock: 1844. The tea and sandwiches ought to be coming round soon. It was good to relax... twenty air attacks during the last four hours, although now they had begun to ease off. The guns had been silent for over an hour: just as well, because there was no more ammunition left. There was a feeling of relief throughout the ship. *Fiji* had repulsed all attacks and had survived fourteen hours of the worst the enemy could do. The battle squadron was over there, only thirty miles to the westward and steering a parallel course. This realisation was comforting, as was the deteriorating visibility which now enfolded them. The Stukas couldn't track them in this, for the cloud base was too low. Bill could hear men singing at their quarters, and occasionally a gust of laughter would drown the murmur of dog-watch gossip. It was incredible what food and an easing of tension could do.

Bill took off his tin hat as the Snotty of the Watch handed him a 'cuppa'. He laid down the board on which he had been recording and, his huge hands folded beneath his chin, he leant across the lip of the bridge to stare out to port. Behind him he heard the Officer of the Watch yarning with the Captain. The sea looked grey and cold and was rising: an unpleasant night for flying, with this cloud sweeping low above their mast-head. There could be no chance now of Bill having to fly *Fiji*'s Walrus, although this was a disappointment after all the trouble of being transferred by Walrus to *Fiji*. However, there it was... His eyes ached with the weight of his eyelids. He shook his head and gazed blindly to port at the thick cloud...

It seemed strange that an aircraft should be flying straight towards him... it looked like a fighter, where it fell out of the grey cloud. He must not doze off again like this... again he shook his head. Then a gob of smoke spurted beneath his imaginary fighter as it started its engine. This ME 109 had a yellow nose. It must have been shadowing from behind the cloud with its engine cut.

'Alarm red-nine-o!' the port lookout yelled, just as Bill also screamed the warning. Then, as the guns spun on their mountings, the ME 109 plunged into its dive.

Bill plainly saw the fighter's machine guns spitting as they sprayed *Fiji*'s upper deck. The pilot's black helmet and pink face were clearly visible in his cockpit as he swooped between the masts; then up and away, as the bomb plunged downwards in its graceful curve. Not a shot had been fired.

Bill was mesmerised by that globular black bomb spinning downwards. He did not hear the desperate orders crackling behind him on the bridge; only the swish of the bomb and the crack of the explosion as it plumped into *Fiji*'s port side amidships. The cruiser shuddered.

The guns were yammering now, as they vainly tried to follow the vanishing ME 109. Then the spray from the explosion drifted across the cruiser's midship section. Bill grabbed his record-board and glanced at the clock.

1846, he scribbled. *Bombed by lone 109. Hit port-side, amidships.*

The howl of the wind in the rigging was decreasing: it was this that first betrayed to Tanner that the cruiser was losing way. Then, quite suddenly, he felt the deck beginning to list beneath his feet.

The howl of the telephones on the bridge was adding to the pandemonium; the safety valves had lifted and the roar of the escaping steam added terror to the chaos. Then, above the bedlam, Bill heard the Captain yelling down the engine-room telephone to the Chief.

'Half speed, Chief?' William-Powlett was shouting above the din. 'Fine. Do your best and let me know the damage.'

Just like a peacetime damage control exercise, thought Bill, as *Fiji,* with a fifteen-degree list to port, slowly gathered way again. By 1915 Bill had recorded that she was making seventeen knots.

Tanner realised then that he was going to drown. The knowledge that he was soon to meet his Maker had a strange effect on him: everything suddenly became three-dimensional, very clear, like a dream, yet somehow remote and unreal. Each sound registered in his ears: the scream of the Stukas, the banging of the guns, the calm voice of the Captain as he dealt with the disaster. The details of *Fiji*'s last moments were registered indelibly on his mind: the Midshipman of the Watch surreptitiously blowing up his Mae West in the corner; the aluminium jug of cocoa slowly sliding across the back of the chart table. It was the clarity of it all that Bill could not understand, but they always said that you saw your whole life before you, didn't they?

Captain William-Powlett was leaning across the Gunnery Officer's voicepipe. Bill saw the light of battle in his Captain's face as, one eye cocked on the circling 87s overhead, he listened to his Gunnery Officer.

'You've run out of H.A. ammunition, Guns?'

'Yes, sir. Right out. There's only starshell and a little practice ammunition left.'

'Use that, then,' the Captain ordered. 'Keep the guns firing.'

It was shortly after this that the list increased and Bill was forced to grasp the bridge-side for support. Then at 1915, a JU 88 sneaked in through the harmless barrage to attack down the fore-and-aft line. Bill saw every detail as the black machine swept directly over him: the black crosses on the white ground, the helmeted pilot, the clean lines of the 88; then the three bombs toppling from its belly.

Bill knew that this was the *coup de grâce*. Though the bombs would miss the bridge, they were bound to hit somewhere. The bridge personnel did not even take cover. The Captain moved imperceptibly to the wings and followed the flight of the bombs. There were three distinct shudders and then, as the 88 swooped up into the cloud, a mushroom of smoke and steam billowed from the intakes of 'A' boiler room.

1912, Tanner recorded, his pencil a-tremble. *Fiji mortally wounded. Captain has ordered Abandon Ship.*

The inclinometer in the corner of the bridge was showing 35 degrees of port list when Bill Tanner was shooed off the bridge by his Captain. The young Sub-Lieutenant ripped the record sheet from the pad and stuffed it in his pocket. He clambered along the starboard wings, down the flag-deck ladder, and then to the upper deck where the hands were mustering in their parts of watches. Their Divisional Officers stood in front of them, as if for normal 'Hands Fall In'.

'We've only six starshells left, mate,' a Seaman Gunner was muttering to his companions, as Bill moved aft.

'Keep silence!'

The Petty Officer of the Main Top Division was having no nonsense, but little could be heard above the roaring of the escaping steam. Bill had never felt so proud as he did at that moment: the discipline of the troops was superb.

Then, as the officers gave their final instructions, she suddenly began to settle.

'Abandon Ship!'

The cry echoed along the whole length of the vessel. Only then did the ranks break, as each man stepped forward to grab some protuberance.

Slowly the ship's side rolled up to meet them, and Bill began slithering up a wall of slippery plating. Next, the barnacles tearing at his hands; then the curses of men fighting their way upwards as the ship rolled down on top of them.

'C'mon, sir,' growled a voice from the bilge-keel, 'grab this…'

It was Petty Officer Cook, Pyles, the man who'd given Bill a cup of tea last night. He was a small man, intelligent, who'd always enjoyed a yarn. Tanner grasped the cook's hand and, knees and legs frenziedly kicking beneath him, he gained the flatter curve of the ship's bottom.

'Thanks,' he gasped.

'Proper pot-mess, ain't it, sir?'

Bill did not reply: a string of ME 109s was streaking towards them, their guns blazing.

'Flatten yourself!' he yelled.

The metal rang where the bullets struck. With a shock Bill felt the wetness of water.

'Time we weren't here, Chief,' he shouted above the pandemonium of men fighting for their lives. 'Get away from the ship…'

He slithered into the water and was surprised at its warmth. His hands stung from the salt in the torn flesh and then a feeling of panic swept over him. He must swim clear or she would roll on top of him.

He glanced back momentarily. A mountain of iron loomed above him, a tangle of ropes and boats' falls swinging like pendulums above the swell. *Fiji*'s bows were already disappearing, and now nothing but her bottom was visible, an expanse of barnacled steel. At her stern her propellers were slowly revolving. Bill then noticed Captain William-Powlett standing on the port bilge-keel. His bald head gleamed grotesquely as he stooped to help an injured man slide into the water.

'Bald as a badger,' a seaman — the relief quartermaster — shouted near Bill. 'Look at the rudder, mates: it's amidships. The skipper's a bleedin' good seaman, right to the end.'

Bill looked round for a Carley float. A destroyer was wheeling amongst the debris, her guns spitting at the murderers now strafing the water. As Bill searched anxiously for something that floated, he saw, ten yards away, a man in difficulties. There was terror in his shouts for help.

'Hold on, chum,' Bill called. He struck out, but, though he was clear of the ship, he was flagging after his long swim. It was then he remembered that *Fiji* had dropped half her Carley floats and rafts for poor old *Gloucester*.

'It's a ruddy long swim,' someone was shouting. 'Gavdo Island is fifty miles east-north-east of us.'

Then the bombs began to rain upon them. At each explosion Bill felt the shock across his abdomen. It was an unpleasant sensation, but he found that if he gripped his hands across his stomach, some of the shock was absorbed.

Half a mile away, a destroyer lay stopped. She was picking up a group of men struggling along her starboard side, when Bill saw three Stukas diving out of the sun. He heard the shriek of the bombs, felt the kick in his guts, and then *Kandahar* disappeared behind a curtain of spray. The mist fell away and the destroyer emerged, her guns still firing, but with a swirl at her stern where her propellers threshed.

'Murdering swine!'

The cries of anger echoed across the water: the survivors shook their fists in blind rage. As Bill reached the drowning men, he heard a calm voice shouting from the darkness.

'Save your breath,' the man was urging. 'Stick together and we'll be all right.'

85

Bill would recognise that voice anywhere. It was his namesake, Padre Tanner. His serenity at this moment was an inspiration to those around him. Bill felt the panic slipping from him, but then he noticed that already the sun was sinking.

'Keep together!' There was urgency in the cries that floated across the water from the knots of men clinging to any debris they could find. As the Luftwaffe strafed them, they would slide beneath the sea and hear underwater the bullets ricocheting off the surface. The fury of the Germans became frenzied as darkness began to rob them of their prey.

'Look, sir!' Leading Writer Malston was shouting from the other side of the locker to which Bill's cluster of men were clinging. 'Reckon Jerry's pretty "chocka" with *Kandahar*...'

The bombers were like a swarm of bees about the destroyer, who was hitting back defiantly with all she had. She was steaming slowly through the group of survivors and, as she closed them, a loudhailer crackled in the gathering dusk.

'Keep close together,' a steady voice commanded, 'I repeat, keep close together. We shall be returning after dark. We shall be returning to pick you up after dark.'

Then *Kandahar* turned slowly away. *Kingston* was already disappearing, her wake white in the twilight: *Kandahar*'s screws threshed as soon as she was clear, the Luftwaffe trailing her as she steamed into the sunset.

'Malta,' Malston said bitterly. 'That's where they're bound.'

'They'll be back,' Bill said.

'They'll never find us,' Pyles retorted.

Across the sea there drifted the chorus of men's voices. Bill could recognise the Padre's anywhere. The strains of 'Roll out the Barrel' echoed jerkily across the black waters.

At 1928 Rear-Admiral Rawlings, now once again in command of the battle squadron because Rear-Admiral King was a few miles to the eastward, received *Kandahar*'s signal reporting that *Fiji* was sinking. At nightfall, Rawlings ordered the two 'V' and 'W's, *Voyager* and *Vendetta*, who were on passage from Alexandria and were to rendezvous at dawn with the battleships, to pick up *Fiji*'s survivors. Then, at 2000, Rawlings passed a *Most Immediate* signal to his Commander-in-Chief, Admiral Sir Andrew Cunningham, reporting the bare details of the massacre. He also included the ammunition state of all his ships, including that of his own flagship, *Warspite*, who had 30 per cent of pom-pom remaining. It was a long and complicated signal by the time it had been encyphered and dispatched.

Rawlings was worried: it would be five hours before *Voyager* and *Vendetta* reached *Fiji*'s position. He glanced at the lean silhouettes of his destroyer screen as they began merging into the twilight. He could spare D.5: Lord Louis could make himself a nuisance at the same time. Rawlings picked up his pencil.

To Captain D.5, repeated D.14, from C.S.7, he scribbled. Kelly, Kashmir, Kipling, *proceed forthwith to recover* Fiji *survivors in position 50' Gavdo 245 degrees. On completion ships are to proceed in accordance with previous orders to patrol Kissamo Bay. T.O.O. 2030.*

The Admiral felt better. Then, as his thoughts whirled upon the tragedies of the past few hours, he was handed a signal from C.-in-C.: *Top Secret and Immediate…* Once again he would have to call upon his destroyers.

He turned to his Flag Lieutenant:

'Tell *Decoy* and *Hero to* break off and proceed to Agia Roumeli to evacuate Important Personages.'

The shaded signal lantern clattered on the flag deck, then over to port a blue light winked in acknowledgement. Two dark shapes slid silently into the dusk.

'That's five destroyers gone,' Rawlings muttered to himself as he refilled his pipe. 'But what about *Gloucester*? I can't abandon her survivors, even though they aren't far from Greece.'

So it was that the residue of Mountbatten's flotilla was detached from the screen. At 2100, as darkness enfolded the squadron and the air attacks ended, *Kelvin* and *Jackal* wheeled out of line and disappeared into the night; they were to help *Gloucester*'s survivors and then proceed to patrol Canea Bay.

Rawlings subsided into his bridge chair. It would be a long night, but the whole force should be able to snatch the sleep for which it craved. He would make his *Night Intentions* signal now: he'd steer 225 degrees all night, then he'd try to thrust from his mind the image of the men drowning at this moment, less than thirty miles to the eastward.

'Must get some sleep,' he muttered, 'or I shan't be able to face the dawn. How many ships shall I have left by this time tomorrow, I wonder?'

CHAPTER 9

Greater Love Hath No Man…

'Nine o'clock, sir…' *Kandahar*'s Officer of the Watch reported. Robson spun round. He had been waiting a long time for this moment.

'Red one-eight,' he barked. He turned to watch the black shape of *Kingston* turning perfectly in his wake. Lieutenant-Commander Somerville was a good seaman.

The Luftwaffe had continued longer than usual with their bombing tonight, but at least Robson had lured them away from *Fiji*'s survivors: and, until now, *Kandahar* and *Kingston* had got away with it. The Germans had gone home for a sleep before they returned at dawn.

A voice was booming up from the Plot voicepipe and Robson leant over the salt-encrusted brass tube.

'Steer o-seven-two, sir.'

It was his Navigating Officer. *Thank God he's competent*, thought Robson. The lives of those poor so-and-sos Robson had left in the water depended upon *Kandahar*'s navigation. The destroyers would have to pick up *Fiji*'s men bang on the nose, because searchlights were out of the question tonight. After all this twisting and turning towards the south-west, it was difficult to keep an accurate D.R. position. Robson prayed that the A.R.L. would not break down tonight: upon the reliability of that clanking machine depended so many lives…

'Course, sir, o-seven-two.'

The Quartermaster's level voice floated up from the wheelhouse. The man was right on course: there would be no mistakes in steering tonight. Robson settled down to the agonising wait. He had increased to thirty knots and he should pick up the black dots in the water about midnight.

'Shake me at 2345.'

'Aye, aye, sir.'

Robson stuffed his hands deep in his duffel pockets, then slumped into his bridge-chair in the corner of the bridge. His head nodded, his mind whirled. God, how he longed for an R.D.F. set. Then oblivion overwhelmed him.

Meanwhile, that afternoon in Heraklion, Captain Henry McCall was leaning over the port wings of *Dido*'s bridge. He felt impatient because this loading, though going well, was taking too long. He'd taken his cruiser alongside early in the afternoon, but he must slip out by 0200 in order to be clear of Kaso by dawn: he didn't relish being caught in those straits again, particularly with the merchant ship he had to escort back to Alexandria: she was packed out with troops.

McCall tried to curb his impatience, but eventually he could contain himself no longer: he threaded his way through the groups of troops who were loading these heavy crates down into *Dido*'s hatchway. The Captain was a large, upstanding figure as he made for the brow, his men standing aside for him. Grizzled and tough, Henry McCall was a strong man who brooked no nonsense. His troops knew exactly where they stood with him.

A crane whirred and a wooden packing case crashed heavily at his feet.

''Struth, mate!' an O.D. exclaimed, as the heavy packing case burst open. 'Roll on me flipping twelve!'

Even under the dim light by which the crane driver was working, the contents were plain to see: a shining heap of golden coins. Bullion, twenty-two tons of it, and mostly of *louis d'or*: all the gold of Greece was being loaded into *Dido*. Several *louis d'or* rolled into the scuppers, and the Ordinary Seaman fell to his knees and scrabbled after them. He grinned at his Captain as he dropped them one by one on to the shining pile.

'And I bet you,' McCall laughed, 'you'll collect a "north-easter" on pay day.' 'North-easter' was slang for an empty pay-packet.

'It fair makes your mouth water, don't it, sir?'

McCall nodded, then clambered down the gangway to the pier alongside which *Dido* was moored. He hurried to call upon the Senior Naval Officer, Captain Portall of the stranded *York*, whose office was further along the pier.

As McCall discussed, in the stuffiness of that wooden shack, the passengers he was to embark for Alexandria, he heard the familiar zoom of diving Stukas. He rushed to the window.

Two 87s were already in their dive. A third was peeling off, while three others hovered astern, waiting to pounce. McCall watched impotently as the hideous machine plunged through *Dido*'s hail of close-range fire. With horror he watched the bombs smother his ship. The bomb splashes leapt upwards and she disappeared behind tall plumes of water. Mesmerised, he watched the curtain of spray and cordite fumes drifting across *Dido*. She must be badly hit; she could not have survived this…

Then, as the mist fell slowly away, there appeared the busy figures of those who were working on the jetty. His men had not heeded the bombs; they were going about their business of roping up the crates as if nothing had happened. Then *Dido* reappeared, apparently untouched. McCall flung open the door and hurried back on board.

An hour later *Dido* slipped, the merchant ship and a destroyer in company. McCall was congratulating himself at the prospect of clearing the Kaso Straits shortly before dawn, when the ship he was escorting broke down.

'Hell's bells!' McCall swore beneath his breath. 'Find out what's wrong, Yeoman.'

The Aldis began to wink its blue light. McCall stared with anxiety at the merchant vessel. Why couldn't the old cow keep up? They were almost out of danger, dammit, and now she had to break down — and here, of all places...

The Captain glanced to the east where, low on the horizon, a sliver of grey slashed the eastern sky. Morning twilight had begun, and already he could pick up the outline of Kaso, where the bombers lurked: the Stukas were less than ten minutes' flying time away. Already the German pilots would be crawling from their pits... Cape Plaka, the easterly tip of Crete, was just visible to the west. *Dido* swung back towards her consort.

'Slow ahead port, half astern starboard,' he snapped. 'Bring me my megaphone. Pilot, close the ship so I can speak with her.'

McCall's anxiety increased: he was troubled by that tub of a ship. There she wallowed, her decks a shambles of wounded and helpless soldiers, while down below she bulged with broken men. McCall had to stand by her, but what a ghastly predicament. *Dido* had nine million pounds sterling on board; how could she linger in a channel where U-boats lurked? And ten minutes away, the Luftwaffe were longing for dawn to break... McCall could contain himself no longer: he waited impatiently for the distance between the ships to diminish...

He heard the poppling of the sea between the two ships' sides as *Dido* drifted down upon the merchant vessel. The silence was uncanny, only the calm tones of *Dido*'s Navigating

Officer disturbing the stillness. The merchant ship's upper deck was crammed with khaki troops, their faces white in the morning light as they stared up at *Dido*'s bridge.

'Can you hear me?' boomed McCall through his megaphone.

'Aye, I can that.' The Master was standing on his bridge and peering up at them.

'If you are not under way within ten minutes, I repeat *ten minutes*, I am coming alongside to disembark all troops. I shall then sink you by torpedo.' McCall's voice had a note of urgency. 'Have you got that?'

'Aye.' The Master waved and bustled back into his wheelhouse. A gust of cheering echoed from the troops in the merchant ship. Ten minutes later she was under way.

Dawn broke fine and clear. *Dido* and her consort were now clear of the Kaso Straits, the destroyer ahead and the cruiser bringing up the rear.

'We're in luck,' McCall was saying. 'We're…'

'Alarm green one-six-o!' the starboard lookout was yelling. 'Formation of high-level aircraft…'

McCall picked them up as his guns began to bark. Six Savoias, and high up. *Should be all right…*

Three minutes later the bombs came whistling down, toppling, spinning in a slow arc, straight for the merchant ship. McCall looked away: a bomb would cause a shambles on her crowded upper deck.

Tall fountains of water leapt upwards, the spray completely concealing the ship which was now forging ahead at full speed. *Dido*'s guns still roared, their shells reaching, like long tentacles, after the retreating bombers. Then, through the vapour, steamed the ancient ship. McCall could see the soldiers wringing the water out of their clothes; they had been drenched from the bomb splashes.

'Yeoman, make to my consort: *Congratulations on your miraculous escape.*'

Dido's lamp clattered, and then the old ship's lantern flashed in reply:

Phew!

'What time is it, sir?'

From the darkness, Bill Tanner heard Pyles's persistent questioning. The cook was on the far side of the grating to which this dwindling band of survivors clung. Tanner had difficulty in distinguishing the man's features. Tanner owned a waterproof wristwatch, and this was their only time-check. Already their immersion seemed an interminable nightmare, for the luminous hands of Bill's watch now glowed at twenty-five minutes past two in the morning.

'Two twenty-five,' Bill answered sharply. He found it difficult to contain his impatience: this question was being asked continually now. He dreaded peering at his watch, for time was running out. When dawn broke, the murderers would return.

'We've been over seven hours in the 'oggin, sir.'

'S'right, mate,' a deep voice chuckled. 'Thought I'd 'a seen enough of this bleedin' stuff already.'

Tanner smiled in the darkness. The speaker was Petty Officer Arnold who, eighteen months previously, had been one of the few survivors from the submarine *Thetis* that had sunk in Liverpool Bay. He was a splendid character.

'Stokers' Mess don't sound all that melodious, do it, Chief?' Malston, a ship's writer, was addressing Chief Petty Officer Taft, the ward-room chef who, as an older man, was near exhaustion.

Across the black waters floated a defiant verse of 'Roll out the Barrel'.

'C'mon, let's give 'em a basinful,' growled Arnold. 'The so-and-sos can't be allowed to get away with it…'

Arnold's deep voice opened and a croaking version of 'London Pride' boomed in retaliation from the grating:

'London Pride, I've got my eyes on you…
London Pride…'

Bill joined in, then those around him added their contributions. Even the young O.D., Bill noticed, was taking part. Edwards was a non-swimmer and only nineteen; the Padre, who was also called Tanner, had delivered him to Bill's care before disappearing again into the darkness to search for other stragglers. 'Take care of him, *Tanner,*' Padre Tanner had gasped. Even in these straits, the Padre had enjoyed the coincidence of their names.

Bill was anxious for Edwards. The lad was delirious: only last week Edwards had heard of the birth of his firstborn, a son, to his wife, a girl of seventeen. His mess had christened the baby by taking Edwards on a run ashore in Alex. The young O.D. kept slipping from the grating; each effort at pulling him back was costing energy, and that was running out.

'Any room, mate?'

There was a splashing behind Bill, and an oil-saturated head bobbed from out of the darkness.

'Sure,' growled Arnold. 'Grab hold.'

The extra weight began to sink the waterlogged grating. Pyles let go and dog-paddled clear. The makeshift raft slowly regained buoyancy.

'Padre's gone,' the newcomer panted. 'Fair wore himself out looking after us.'

There was a long silence while the stranger sought for words.

'How'd it happen?' asked Taft quietly.

'He was striking out towards a Killick who was wounded in the legs.' A 'Killick' was a Leading Seaman. 'We heard the Padre making his way towards the chap when suddenly the splashing stopped. We tried to reach 'im, but he'd gone when we finally got there...' The man's voice choked as he added, ''E was praying for us to the last. 'E was singing as he went.'

From across the black waters floated the strains of the last verse of the naval hymn, those lines that all men knew. In the darkness the hoarse voices were strangely moving...

'O Trinity of love and power,
Thy brethren shield in danger's hour...'

Then through the inky blackness there swelled a crescendo of men's deep voices as they sung to the Padre they had loved:

'From rock and tempest, fire and foe
Protect them wheresoe'er they go,
And ever let there rise to Thee,
Glad hymns of praise from land and sea.'

The hoarse basses faded away into silence. Only the lapping of the water against the grating disturbed the peace. It was Pyles who broke the spell.

'He was truly a saint of a man,' he said.

Somehow, now that their Padre had gone, hope was vanishing with his departed spirit. What was the point of holding on further? The destroyers could not be expected to keep their word... why should they, with dawn but three hours off? Better to go out now, to drown painlessly, than to be sawn in half by the bullets at dawn. So easy to let go and slide silently beneath the surface…

Bill was thrusting away the insidious temptation when suddenly young Edwards pointed westwards. There was hysteria in his voice.

'There they are, sir,' he shouted hoarsely. 'Look, over there, sir.'

Edwards was delirious, but Bill jerked his head round anyway, his heart hammering against his ribs. Then, tears welling in his eyes, he recognised the unmistakable silhouettes of two modern destroyers bearing down upon them.

My God! he thought. *They'll run us down!*

Arnold, however, had kept a boat's box dry on top of the grating. Now he feverishly extracted from the box a torch which he'd guarded for such an emergency. The white light flashed across the darkness. Surely the destroyers couldn't miss this beam?

Bill waited an agonising, interminable minute. He heard the sighs from his group of men as a blue light winked in reply.

'Hold on,' Arnold shouted. 'Don't panic, mates…'

But he was too late. Edwards had already let go and was threshing towards the shapes looming out of the night.

'Come back!' Bill shouted. 'You'll be run down!' Then, as the destroyer went astern, Bill jerked free and struck out after the young seaman.

Tanner remembered the destroyer's side sliding down on top of him; heard the rallying shouts from the seamen on her upper deck. He saw her wake boiling as she went astern, faintly heard Edward's astonished scream as he was sucked under by the propellers, there to be decimated by the swirling blades.

''Old on, mate.'

Heaving lines were plumping across their heads. Seamen were leaping from the destroyer's decks and splashing alongside the survivors to secure the lines around men too weak to help themselves.

'Thanks, chum,' Bill hard Taft gasping. 'You're just in time.' Then they were floundering out of the sea and, torn and bleeding, lying in their own pools of water upon *Kandahar*'s iron deck. Rough hands gently cared for them, hands of survivors already cluttering the upper deck.

'Here, Chief, sippers…'

Bill dimly recognised the Coxswain of *Kandahar*. The burly figure was forcing rum between Taft's lips.

'A-ah,' the Chief grunted. '"Neaters".'

Then, in the confusion, Bill realised slowly that he was safe, plucked from the hungry sea at the last moment. He watched the wounded and the older men being shepherded for'd, there to be turned into the hammocks of *Kandahar*'s mess decks. Bill saw more than one seaman weeping unashamedly at the kindness they were receiving from their rescuers.

Someone threw him a blanket. He stripped and flung his clothes around the base of the funnel. Then he waited there, huddled in his blanket, for his clothes to dry. He felt the destroyer tremble as she once more gathered way.

At that instant there was a cry from the darkness. A man who had been unnoticed was clawing for a heaving line that still dangled from the guard rails. As *Kandahar* slid ahead, the man missed the rope by inches: Bill heard the despair in his cry as he disappeared astern into the night.

Suddenly a short, stocky figure bounded from a group huddled by the first whaler. Throwing off the blanket that enveloped him, he stood there for a moment, gauging the whereabouts of the cries from the darkness. The man wore three gold stripes on the sleeves of his reefer. Poised for a moment upon the top guard-rail, the officer then dived into the inky waters.

Bill sprang towards the side; the wind was blowing into his face, and suddenly it was very dark. He could see nothing in the blackness.

'Who was that?' Bill asked a man who had also rushed to the side.

'*Greyhound*'s Captain, sir,' the man gasped. 'We picked him up when she was sunk.'

'Who are you?' Bill jerked.

'Captain's steward, sir. *Kandahar*.'

'Nip up and tell your Captain.'

But the steward was already scrambling up the bridge ladders. Bill followed him through the screen door and up on to the bridge. *Kandahar*'s Captain was already leaning over the starboard wings, his steward panting by his side as he pointed astern into the darkness.

'Over there, sir…'

Commander Geoffrey Robson could see nothing through his binoculars… only an inky blackness: nothing but the slow lapping of the wavelets against *Kandahar*'s side as she wallowed, stopped, in the swell. Nothing. Damn-all. Silence.

'God, what gallantry!' Commander Marshall A'Deane had always been loved by his troops. Robson could see why.

'Can you see anything, Number One?'

Robson was playing for time. He had turned his ship about to look for his friend. He'd been searching now for ten minutes: if he wasted more time others would drown. God! What a decision to be forced to make. His duty was plain.

'Slow ahead together.'

The destroyer trembled and slowly went ahead.

'That group on the port bow next, Number One.'

'Aye, aye, sir.'

Robson handed back the loudhailer microphone to his First Lieutenant. There was no more need for it now: the gallant Marshall A'Deane had given his life to try to save one of his sailors.

'Stand by to pick up survivors, port side...' It was Number One taking charge again.

'Slow astern both...'

So the rescue work continued through the night. Robson would hear frenzied shouting on one beam; he would turn and manoeuvre cannily towards the cries. This he had to do slowly, for fear of massacring swimmers in his propellers. Then, as he bore down on the invisible survivors, shouts would be heard to port. Ignoring them, a word of encouragement as he swept by, he'd pick up first the original cries from ahead. Stop the ship; rescue the men; then turn in his own length to recover the others... but now nothing: naught save for an accusing silence from the darkness.

By 0230, *Kingston* and he had between them picked up 523 of *Fiji*'s survivors. In the desolation Robson made up his mind.

'Course for the rendezvous with the battle squadron, Pilot?'

'2130, sir.'

'Speed?'

'15 knots, if we are to reach the rendezvous on our 10 tons of fuel.'

'Very good. 15 knots.'

'Aye, aye, sir.'

As the long night brightened with first light, and the twilight merged into dawn, Robson's anxiety became acute. Visibility had shut right down and was now little more than six thousand yards. If he missed Rawlings's Force A.1, *Kingston* and *Kandahar* would be in an awkward predicament: out of fuel and stopped, wallowing, a few miles off Crete: both destroyers packed with survivors — and with no ammunition. (*Kingston* had yesterday evening been firing blanks in a desperate attempt to bluff the Stukas.) Robson longed for the radar that some of the ships now boasted.

Time dragged by. The forenoon watchmen closed up and the morning guns' crews slumped at their mountings, asleep immediately where they fell. Robson forced his eyes to function, dragging them across the horizon to peer through the murk. Why, in God's name did vis. have to be bad, on this of all mornings? The Chief had already reported that his dipsticks were dry: the oil fuel tanks were empty.

'Green one-o, sir…' the Officer of the Watch shouted, unable to conceal the quaver in his voice. 'Destroyer, sir.'

She proved to be the wing ship of the battle squadron's screen. After reporting his presence, Robson received a signal stationing him on the far side. He turned to his Yeoman.

'Make to C.S.7,' he snapped. *'Request permission to refuel alongside you. I shall not reach my position in the screen.'*

Five minutes later *Warspite*, her oil fuel derricks already swung out, loomed down upon the stopped destroyer. A touch 'ahead', and *Kandahar*'s springs snaked across. As the O.F. hoses pulsated from the pressure, Rawling's voice echoed across the twenty-five feet of poppling water.

'Good morning, *Kandahar*, glad you've joined us. We're returning to Alex.'

'Good morning, sir.'

'I'm afraid we may be visited by our old friends,' the confident voice continued. 'If we are, I shall continue fuelling you.' The loud hailer snicked off.

There was a lump in Robson's throat as he replied: 'Thanks very much, sir.'

Even as he laid down the megaphone, *Warspite*'s H.A. guns were opening fire.

The Commander-in-Chief of the Mediterranean Fleet could no longer stand the isolation of his inner office. He had grown to dread the shrill of the telephone and the knock on the door, the summons which brought news of further disaster. The grizzled Scot sprang from his hard, wooden chair and strode into his War Room. He paused a moment to read the signal a young woman was handing him. It was from Rawlings and 'Emergency'. The murmur of voices died away as Admiral Sir Andrew Cunningham glanced at the clock across the room. It was 2330 of Thursday, 22nd May. Surely there could be no further bad news?

'*To C.-in-C. from C.S.7, repeated C.S.15,* he read. *Regret to report…*'

Cunningham winced. *Regret to report,* a phrase which he now detested with a bitter hatred. Once more dread swept through him.

'…Gloucester *and* Fiji *sunk in positions…*'

Cunningham could not believe his eyes as he read the news aloud, so that the plotters could fix the positions upon the huge chart laid out in the middle of the room:

'… Kelly, Kashmir and Kipling *dispatched to recover* Gloucester*'s survivors;* Kelvin *and* Jackal*,* Fiji*'s survivors. On completion 5th D.F. will sweep north of Crete during night. H.A. ammunition remaining is as follows…*'

The Admiral did not hesitate. Instead, he read carefully the impersonal figures which leapt at him from the signal pad.

Warspite headed the list: *4" — 24 per cent, pom-pom, NIL;* Valiant, *4" — 26 per cent, pom-pom, 38 per cent…*

When Cunningham had finished reading the report, his eyes rested on *Warspite*'s ammunition state: *… pom-pom, NIL…*

A.B.C. scratched his head, then looked up, his piercing blue eyes sweeping slowly round the War Room.

'If we leave Force A.1 there, gentlemen,' he said slowly, 'they'll be blown out of the water at dawn. Without ammunition a ship cannot remain afloat.' The Commander-in-Chief turned to his Chief of Staff, Rear-Admiral Sir John Edelsten.

'What have our losses been during the past twelve hours, John?'

The Chief of Staff met his Commander-in-Chief's gaze squarely.

'Two cruisers and a destroyer sunk, sir,' Edelsten replied. 'Two battleships and two cruisers damaged.' There was no need to say more: A.B.C. was thinking, as ever, of his men. *God!* — how he longed to be out there sharing it all with them: the crippling exhaustion, the fear, the horror. Yet here he must remain, cooped up in this damned War Room to direct the Crete operation. It seemed an eternity since the forenoon, when he'd tried to tell his fleet what they already knew: that their Commander-in-Chief was doing all that was possible for them. That morning A.B.C. had signalled: *Stick it out. Navy must not let Army down. No enemy forces must reach Crete by sea.*

Now Rawlings's signal was staring at him from the pink slip in his hand.

…pom-pom, NIL…

A.B.C. was amazed. He knew it was tough out there and that all ships were low on ammunition, but he had not realised the seriousness of the situation. Battleships with no pom-pom ammunition: absurd. He turned to his Chief of Staff.

'John, *Warspite*'s signal decides the issue. Recall immediately all ships to Alexandria.'

Admiral Cunningham could not know that there had been a calligraphic error in the encyphering and decyphering of Rear-Admiral Rawlings's vital signal. *Warspite*, in fact, had sufficient pom-pom ammunition.

Upon such minute errors (three letters of the alphabet) do disasters hinge.

CHAPTER 10

The Butchers

'Open fire!'

Kashmir's Captain, Commander H. A. King, was ready for the JU 88 that swooped out of the rising sun. At first light, a snooper had circled the two destroyers, *Kelly* and *Kashmir*, who were steaming west at full speed through the Kithera Channel to rejoin Rear-Admiral Rawlings in Force A.1. The guns blazed out, dipping and weaving, the twin-engined bomber screaming through the barrage to drop a load of anti-personnel bombs: presumably the 88 had found no British troops ashore. The flying shrapnel hissed in the water where the bombs plunged between the two destroyers.

King glanced at *Kelly*'s wake frothing four hundred yards ahead: 'D'5, Captain Lord Louis Mountbatten, knew how to handle his ship: she was resuming course again, after going 'hard-over' for the 88. *Kelly* was a happy ship, her company respecting their illustrious Captain: already he had been torpedoed in *Kelly* near the island of Sylt off the Danish coast during the invasion of the Low Countries, and again when in *Javelin* off Plymouth; both ships were repaired to fight again.

Kashmir's Captain glanced anxiously over his shoulder: the island of Gavdos, thirteen miles to the northward, was now disappearing below the horizon. *We're lucky to get away with it so far,* he thought, for they'd only cleared Kithera at dawn: too late, because the night's work had been hectic. It had been a strain following *Kelly* at that speed all night. Lord Louis had led them into Canea Bay, where they'd left a large troop-carrying caique burning and sinking. They'd moved up the coast to bombard Maleme airfield: a difficult feat with no proper chart of the aerodrome; *Kelly*'s Navigating Officer had had to deduce the position of the aerodrome from a study of the contours of the hills. However, King, a gunnery specialist, smiled to himself. He hoped that the British troops had been withdrawn well clear of the perimeter. As the destroyers had withdrawn, they'd run across another caique; they had blown her out of the water, but these incidents had swallowed up vital minutes.

'Take her, Officer of the Watch.'

Commander King stepped down from *Kashmir*'s compass platform and subsided on to his bridge seat. This was the moment when sleepiness nearly overwhelmed him: that moment after dawn. *We're damned lucky,* he thought, *to have escaped the attentions of the Stukas so far.*

'Green one-o, sir,' the starboard lookout shouted suddenly. 'Cross-trees above the horizon.'

'Must be *Kipling*,' King murmured, 'waiting for us. Wonder what's happened to her?'

'Put it in the log, Sub,' the Captain said. 'Time 0755.'

As the Sub-Lieutenant dropped to the chart-table, King heard the port lookout:

'Alarm red eight-o! Stukas, just above the land!'

The Captain spun round, shading his eyes with his left hand. Yes, there the perishers were, twenty-four black dots, up-sun, and strung across the sky. Then they seemed to split, a dozen coming for the *Kashmir* and the rest for *Kelly*.

'Hard-a-port,' King shouted. 'Open fire!'

The guns started banging away as she began to heel. King took the first dive-bomber right on the nose, as the Stuka began its dive. It was hurtling downwards, smoke beginning to stream beneath its crooked wings. The gun crews were cheering from somewhere for'd.

'Midships...'

King crouched low over the voicepipe, his eyes squinting upwards at the bomber which was hurtling over 'B' gun.

'Hard-a-starboard!'

'Hard-a-starboard, sir.'

He felt the kick of the stern as the Coxswain reversed the rudder; heard the Stuka's flaps shuddering as she overshot; felt the swish of air as the bomb plunged into the sea close to starboard. He had won that round: he'd driven right in under the 87, forcing it to dive steeper and steeper. That was the secret: force the brutes beyond the vertical.

The second 87 was on its way, its scream weird and terrifying.

'Hard-a-port...'

So the game continued: one eye on his adversaries, the other glued on *Kelly* waltzing between the columns of leaping water that smothered her. Throwing *Kashmir* from side to side, Commander King concentrated upon the next attacker, the third; then the fourth, fifth, sixth... They followed each other at five-second intervals and, what with watching Captain 'D' in *Kelly*, King had no time to follow the bomb. Drenched by the spray of the splashes, he crouched there, concentrating upon the moment when the next Stuka peeled off into its dive; taking *Kashmir* straight towards and under the 87's line of descent, he'd force the bomber to dive on to its back: then, straining his neck, would look for the next one.

'Hard-a-starboard!'

This was where the luck came in... had he swung the stern away from, or into, the bomb's trajectory? Down, down plummeted the black thousand-pounder, bigger now, growing larger at every second: down, down in a slow curve — *God, it's going to hit us...*

He followed the wicked thing, now almost a yard long. It would land on the bridge: he ducked as the monster hurtled by. He held his breath, waiting for the explosion. There was suddenly a tremendous concussion, then silence.

A dreadful noise of tearing metal. *God! The keel's gone. Must have been a delayed action bomb exploding in the boiler room.*

The blue sky was wheeling, spinning above him. As he hit the deck again, the air was knocked from his lungs... He crawled to the side of the bridge and hauled himself upright.

He knew at once that this was the mortal blow: the mast was toppling over the bridge, a crumpled tangle of steel and rigging; a dark rent belched smoke and steam from the for'd edge of the funnel, and there, for'd, the bows were coming up to meet him. He swung aft to see the same horror. Already the midship section was awash and her stern rearing high into the air. Her back was broken. *Kashmir* began to settle by the bow, listing heavily to port, then stopped. His beloved ship was sinking...

'Get those Carley rafts out!' he shouted from the wings. 'She's going, lads.'

The list to port was considerable. King slid over the bridge side and down to 'B' gun deck. He reached the fo'c'sle. As the next Stuka screamed down upon them, its guns raking what still showed of *Kashmir*, he glanced over his shoulder.

Kelly was listing heavily to port, under full starboard rudder. She was a splendid sight, her wake threshing white, her superstructure overhanging the sea where she heeled. Above her the sky was black with Stukas, one in the middle of its dive. *Kelly* was blazing away at it, but the pilot was not to be deterred: he did not release his bomb until he pulled out at mast-head height…

Commander King stepped off *Kashmir*'s fo'c'sle and walked into the sea.

It's going to hit me, the thought flashed through the mind of *Kelly*'s Captain. *There's nothing I can do…*

The tall and upright figure of Lord Louis turned aft as the Stuka roared above his mast-head: *Kelly*'s stern was sweeping across the horizon as, under full starboard rudder, she listed to port. He could see his pom-poms pumping like pistons, the point-fives spitting, their empties spurting from the ejectors… but nothing now could prevent that bomb from striking his ship. It landed on 'X' gun.

Kelly shivered. Lord Louis, fingers gripping the bridge-rail, glimpsed the crimson spurt of flame, saw the gun barrel jerk upwards. He turned towards the bridge to check *Kelly*'s swing to starboard:

'Midships!' he shouted above the racket of the next Stuka zooming downwards. 'Hard-a-port, Pilot.' He glimpsed his Navigating Officer, Lieutenant Maurice Butler-Bowdon, repeating down the voicepipe, and then he turned aft again. *Kelly's list should be coming off now…*

The horizon stopped galloping across his stern as the rudder came amidships. Lord Louis braced his legs against her expected heel to starboard, as the wheel was put hard-over to port. *What's up?* he wondered. *Kelly* was listing more steeply at every second.

'My God!' Lord Louis whispered. 'She's lost stability. She's rolling right over.'

He struggled towards the voicepipe. 'Stop engines,' he snapped.

Within thirty seconds of the direct hit, *Kelly* was turning turtle at over thirty knots, her guns still firing as her Captain had intended.

Commander (E) Michael Evans was the 5th Destroyer Flotilla's Engineer Officer. As he perched halfway through the engine room hatch, he was in fact carrying out his combined duty as *Kelly*'s Chief. He had emerged for a moment to snatch a breather: two E.O.s in an engine room that size was one too many. He was jaded after the night's fun and games; he'd been watching the throttles all night. He preferred not to guess the number of engine movements...

He took off his cap to allow the wind to ruffle his thinning hair. He stuffed the chromium-plated torch, his badge of office, in the hip pocket of his white overalls. He stretched himself, expanding his lungs and deeply inhaling a draught of early-morning air.

He looked up at the blue heavens: *Kelly* and *Kashmir* were lucky to have got through Kithera without attention from the Stukas. At that moment, however, came the commanding note of the alarm rattlers from the shelter of the searchlight platform above his head. He glimpsed *Kashmir* hauling out of line on the port quarter, looked up and saw the first 87 peeling off from a black swarm in the sun. He took off his cap and slithered down the steel rungs of the ladder leading to the gleaming world of his engine room. The pom-poms were already pounding above his head when he reached the plating between the huge circular valves. He was used to this infernal racket.

He grasped the rail which surrounded the port ahead turbine: the ship was listing heavily as the Old Man threw her about. Evans was glad he couldn't hear the so-and-so's from down here: the scream of the turbines saw to that. He glanced at the gauges, below the swinging fanny of barley water. The boiler rooms were just holding their own…

The deck-plates beneath him sprang suddenly, jumping up to meet him. The shock knocked the E.R.A. of the Watch off his feet and, as Evans fell, the whole engine room spun crazily. There was an overwhelming roar of escaping steam, then the sudden scream of turbines running wild… he glanced at the bulkhead emergency self-closing stop-valves on the main steam pipes. Thank God they had shut… As he fought his way up to the bilges which now streamed water and oil upon him, he glimpsed his E.R.A.s wrenching at the main throttles. The crescendo of the turbines was slowly decreasing: at least now the rotors wouldn't disintegrate.

Gasping for breath, Evans glanced about him, his hands bleeding from his frantic scramble upwards. He was standing on the underside of one of the walkways. Some distance below his feet was the deckhead; above his head loomed the huge, domed casings of the turbines.

'You O.K., sir?'

The Warrant Engineer was peering at him, only the brightness of his eyes betraying any emotion. Behind him stood his two E.R.A.s, their bare arms glistening with oil.

'Yes, thanks. You too?'

The Warrant Officer nodded. He was peering at the ship's side.

'Water's just about holding, sir,' he said 'Reckon we're trapped in an air bubble.' Further aft the bodies of two stokers were caught round the shaft: Evans could see the water slowly engulfing them.

'Look, sir — the level's rising.'

The E.R.A. of the Watch had traced the water-line along the ship's side with his finger. The sea had already covered it, and was still gaining. Evans glanced beneath his feet: two round holes glowed luminously from the sunlight that percolated through the surface; those two hatches must now be at least eight feet below the surface. There was no time to waste.

'Take a deep breath, reach the hatches, then swim for the ship's side,' Evans instructed. 'Quick.'

The Warrant Engineer saluted, then, filling his lungs, he dived down towards the bright aperture. The Duty E.R.A. splashed after him. Evans watched the two divers gently swimming, like drifting seaweed, towards the apertures. If they became ensnared now, blocking the hatches...

'Ready?' Evans turned to the remaining E.R.A., who was bleeding profusely from a deep wound in the temple. The white face nodded, then the man hesitantly filled his lungs. Evans watched him plunge, and then, as the water reached his own neck, he inhaled as deeply as his lungs would allow.

It was strangely silent under water. Below him he could see a brown stain from the bleeding E.R.A. and, to the left, the ephemeral circle of light that offered him life. The hatch seemed to be receding, but he'd use up his breath if he kicked too hard. He swung his arms, consciously closing his fingers; he forced himself down, down, down, until suddenly his hands grasped the sides of the ladder. His feet doubled up behind him.

Evans dragged himself deeper until his eardrums ached. He heard a distant singing and then, suddenly, he was through the hatch. He felt the upper deck scraping along his back...

Panic seized him then. *If she's sinking,* he thought, *she's dragging me down with her... God, I must reach the guardrails before she goes... watch out for all the jagged projections, the loose gear; the lips of the torpedo tubes; lucky the canvas dodger hasn't been rigged. I can't last another second… lungs are bursting… Come on, Evans, fight, for God's sake, fight if you want to live.*

A red mist swam before him as he felt the wires of the guard-rails; then he glimpsed above him the translucence of the surface. With one last despairing effort he wriggled beneath the top guard-rail; as his lungs almost collapsed, he kicked frenziedly with his legs, reaching upwards with his hands as he did so.

Sunlight burst suddenly upon him; his lungs sobbed for air. He glanced about him while he lay on his back to recover: the Warrant was there, and the Duty E.R.A. Of the third man, there was no sign.

Maurice Butler-Bowdon, Flotilla Navigating Officer and 'pilot' of *Kelly*, stood alongside his Captain, who was clinging to the distance correction indicator of the Mountbatten station-keeping gear which he had invented. Lord Louis was holding on to the gyro binnacle, and the bridge came up to meet them as the world turned upside down.

As Butler-Bowdon saw the compass climbing above his head, he kicked out and frantically began to clamber past it. The water was suddenly above his head. He struck out frenziedly from beneath the lip of the bridge, as the ship rolled down on top of him. He swam as far as his lungs would allow before breaking surface. A grey mass loomed above him, and all around was the hideous sound of screaming bombers and exploding boilers.

'Swim like hell, Pilot!'

The command rang across the water. As he turned his head, he glimpsed Lord Louis Mountbatten, the last to leave the bridge, striking out not twenty yards away, his face streaked with oil, his hair matted. *Kelly*'s Navigating Officer turned to discover the cause of the horror etched on his Captain's face.

Kelly's keel hung high above the water, less than fifty yards away; and tipped grotesquely into the air were her A-brackets, shafts, and slowly revolving propellers, their blades flashing in the sunlight. Her stern was swinging towards him. He swam away as fast as his clothes and life jacket would allow. He then turned on his back and lay gasping as *Kelly*'s stern swung past him, less than twenty feet away.

'You all right, Pilot?' the Captain hailed. He appeared unperturbed by the terrifying experience of being dragged down through a torrent running at 32 knots. 'Swimming in a tin hat is damned ridiculous,' he added as he took off his helmet and threw it away.

'Yes, thanks. How about you, sir?'

Before Lord Louis could reply, there was a splashing between them as two matted heads broke surface. The larger man, a burly Stoker P.O., shook his head and wiped the oil from his eyes. Owl-like, he peered slowly around him, trying to gain his bearings. Seeing his Captain and Navigating Officer so close on either side of him, he grunted loudly, his teeth gleaming in a smile that broke through his oil-streaked face.

'Amazing how the scum always comes to the top, ain't it, sir?'

Butler-Bowdon ducked. Machine-gun bullets were plummeting into the sea between him and the ship, which was now settling rapidly, stern first.

Lord Louis was feeling naked, and bitterly regretted discarding his tin hat. Torps, who must have walked right round the ship as she turned turtle, was now sitting serenely on her keel, perplexed at what to do next.

As they dog-paddled clear, the scene became heart-rending: *Kelly* was sinking slowly, and, as her bows tilted above the surface, the survivors in the water witnessed the cruellest sight of all. Many men were trapped in the fo'c'sle mess decks. They could not escape through the after-screen door, for it was now deep under water; neither could they wriggle through the scuttles, which were too small. The white faces stared through the open scuttles, too horrified to shout. Someone waved pathetically.

Butler-Bowdon's heart raced. *Kipling* was bearing down rapidly upon them and seemed about to pick up survivors. She was holed in the Reserve Feed Tank, a fortunate position since no water entered the ship. Emerging from a flurry of bomb-splashes and turning under full rudder, she steered straight for *Kelly*, but went astern too late and struck *Kelly*'s upturned hulk a glancing blow.

Butler-Bowdon struck out towards a group of men who were clinging to an overcrowded Carley raft. Lord Louis had got all the wounded into this one raft, and the band of survivors was singing their Captain's choice: 'Roll out the Barrel'. This sole Carley float was filled with wounded, and many men were drowning because their Mae Wests had been punctured by twisted metal.

'Hold on!' someone shouted from above his head. 'Make for the scrambling nets.'

Kipling was drifting down on top of them, her guns blazing as she continued her work of mercy. Lord Louis was towing one of the wounded behind him. As he neared *Kipling*'s side, he sadly slipped his tow. The man was dead.

Fifteen hundred yards away, *Kashmir*'s survivors were also waiting patiently. They had endured three hours, for *Kipling* had made three attempts at rescue. Each time she had been forced by the Stukas to go ahead. *Kipling*'s and *Kelly*'s First Lieutenants were drowned when the boat they were manning at the falls was swamped as *Kipling* was forced to go ahead. When *Kipling* finally closed them, Commander King grabbed the heaving line that plopped into the water next to him.

'Hold on, sir.'

King was covered in oil. He felt sad at losing his signet ring, which had slipped from his oily finger. He could do no more, after the hammering they'd just received from the murdering Stukas: skimming the surface of the sea, their guns blazing, the 87s and ME 109s had systematically butchered the survivors struggling in the water; then, unsatisfied with their efforts, they assaulted *Kipling* while she carried out her rescue work. *Kashmir*'s survivors were now in five Carley rafts and from one of these King watched the bombers contemptuously circling *Kipling*'s blazing guns. The destroyer's point-fives caught one of the Messerschmitts and it disintegrated in a puff of smoke.

Then *Kashmir*'s Captain was standing in his own puddle upon *Kipling*'s deck. A Sub-Lieutenant stood before him, saluting:

'Can you take me up to the Captain?' King asked. 'Bit of a mess, I'm afraid.'

'Captain's compliments, sir. Sorry he couldn't be here to welcome you aboard. Says he's rather busy just at the moment.'

He reached the bridge as *Kipling* finally went ahead. Her Captain, Commander St. Clair Ford, was peering anxiously over the side at the list to starboard. By his side sat Captain Lord Louis Mountbatten, drenched by bomb splashes but still in command of what remained of his Fifth Destroyer Flotilla. On his shoulders alone had rested the decision whether *Kipling* should remain, or attempt to save herself and her company by escaping to the southward. She stayed until the last man had been plucked from the water. It was then 1100, and, as the terrifying list was gradually rectified, *Kipling* worked up to her utmost speed.

There was a lull while the Stukas returned to Scarpanto to re-arm. Then, as expected, they resumed at 1300. Undaunted, *Kipling* fought her way back towards Alex. Although crammed with the equivalent of an extra crew (she had picked up 8 officers and 120 ratings from *Kelly*; 9 officers, 144 ratings from *Kashmir*), *Kipling* weaved and twisted from the Stukas, under the superb handling of her Captain and protected by the unflurried competence of her Gunnery Officer. 83 bombs had been levelled at *Kipling* in forty attacks, yet still she survived, her guns' crews augmented by her extra passengers. Gradually she drew out of the Stukas' range.

She was met the next morning, fifty miles from Alexandria, by *Protector*. *Kipling* had run out of fuel.

CHAPTER 11

The Siege of Heraklion

By the 23rd of May, Heraklion was entirely encircled by the enemy. Yet, from the mouth of his cave in the wadi, Petty Officer Telegraphist Alec Wright had a grandstand view of the battle.

The fighting was now hand-to-hand and consisted of preventing the invaders from reaching their supplies which lay not far from the craters in which the parachutists were pinned. Each man fought his own private battle: the issue was often decided by the bayonet or by cutting-out expeditions at night, when the Germans were stalked in their bomb craters by the Maoris moving like shadows in the dark.

Alec Wright knew that Heraklion might be lost at any moment, even though Brigadier Chappel appeared to have the situation under control. The battle still hinged upon possession of the airfield, for which the Germans appeared to be willing to pay any price.

By nightfall of the 22nd, 950 German corpses had been collected in the British sectors and 300 in the Greek area, but many dead remained where they fell because of exposure to enemy fire. It was Wednesday when Wright heard the enemy were driving women and children before them as they advanced. The Greek Commander had sent the Germans a message that he would kill all prisoners in his hands if they persisted in this barbarity.

These incidents increased the savagery of the fighting. Civilians grabbed rifles from the German corpses that lay rotting in the streets; the Greeks gave no quarter nor accepted it, for this was a fight to the death. However, there were many areas in the town where the indiscriminate fire of the civilians was as great a menace to the British as that of the enemy. Then, when the Messerschmitts roared over the town, their guns spitting at anything that moved, the women and children would shelter with the troops in the slit trenches.

On Wednesday, 23rd, two Matilda tanks arrived from Tymbakion on the south coast, with news that reinforcements of Argyll and Sutherlanders were on the road. During the afternoon, too, Alec Wright watched six Hurricanes from Egypt twisting and flashing in the sunlight as they swept in amongst the enemy aircraft. Unhappily, the naval A.A. guns shot two of them down in flames, the Hurricanes being mistaken for ME 109s. Three of the R.A.F. fighters returned to Egypt, but one landed on the airfield. Later in the afternoon, Wright saw another six Hurricanes tearing into a particularly heavy air attack, but four of the fighters damaged their tail wheels on landing.

'Heard the latest?'

Alec Wright watched 'Knocker' White scrambling along the goat track which led up to the cave. White's voice was echoing across the wadi.

'No,' Alec shouted. 'What's up?'

'Jerry's sent us an ultimatum to surrender.'

Alec Wright was still chuckling when White reached the cave.

'Chappel rejected it outright,' Knocker added breathlessly.

'Should bleeding well hope so,' Wright said, still grinning. 'Who do these Huns think we are?'

'Doesn't make sense,' Knocker replied. 'We're well on top. We've got Jerry licked.'

Wright smiled grimly as he peered down the west wadi towards Heraklion, whence fingers of smoke curled upwards in the heat of noon. In his ultimatum, the German Commander had promised total obliteration of Heraklion: now that the R.A.F. Hurricanes were ineffective, the enemy would keep his word.

Alec Wright turned back into the darkness of the cave. His W/T set was now the only link with the outside world, but the generator was playing up. He'd noticed, down in the quartermaster's stores, a spare that might do. He'd have to nip down the wadi to exchange the generator. He'd be back in twenty minutes. 'Come on, Knocker,' he called. 'Give us a hand.'

The two men waited their opportunity between strafes, then they scuttled from the cave, the defective generator slung between them. Halfway along the track they took shelter from another 109 that was sweeping up the wadi, its bullets kicking up the dirt wherever anything moved: an adventurous chicken seemed somewhat flustered by the dust flying up around her.

'Hullo, Greco! What you doing here?' Alec Wright was surprised to find the old Greek: the ancient had been hanging around more frequently of late. The old fellow was tough: his black eyes flashed defiantly above a grizzled beard, but the German trousers and tunic hung upon him like washing on a scarecrow. His toothless gums grinned as he spread wide his empty hands.

'All right, Greco,' Alec said. 'So you want more grenades?'

The old man nodded slowly.

'Wait here, Greco…'

Alec and Knocker moved onwards when the 109 swung away, the generator scraping along the ground between them as they scrambled down the side of the wadi. They had reached the bottom when Knocker shouted tersely.

'Take cover!'

He jumped clear of the rough track and leapt into a mound of lime that was heaped alongside the road. Alec sprang to the right and pressed himself flat into the ground behind a stone wall. He heard the lead whining as it ricocheted around the cliffs. He glimpsed the leaping line of bullets as they spurted towards him. *Blast!* he thought. *We've left the generator in the open. I suppose the quartermaster will exchange it — providing there's something left of it.* He laughed to himself in the dirt as he recalled the rules of all stores departments.

The ME 109 flashed overhead, so close that Alec could plainly see the pilot grinning behind his firing button: it was the same fellow who had visited them after breakfast.

Wright jumped up and ran across the road for the generator. As he stooped to inspect it, a peculiar figure bore down upon him. The apparition was covered in white lime: clothes, shoes, hair, face, all except its eyes and lips which had remained firmly closed as it lay in the lime heap.

'Knocker!' Alec exploded. 'You look like a perishing black-and-white minstrel!'

Knocker's eyes gleamed from his grey mask. 'You would have looked funnier than me, mate. Look where you've been hiding…' He indicated a dump of hundreds of 5-gallon petrol jerry cans that were stacked where Wright had been sheltering. Alec swallowed.

They stooped for the generator, then trotted down to the stores, past the truck that Alec had 'boned'. This 15-cwt Bedford was used nightly to collect stores, but by dawn it was always returned to the exact spot on which it stood daily. This seemed to fool the enemy, who wasted no bullets on it, thinking it was broken down. This ruse also prevented the enemy from discovering the whereabouts of the stores.

There was no one in the quartermaster's hut, so they helped themselves to a new R.A.F. generator. Then they nipped across the wadi escarpment and began trailing up the path leading to the top. As they reached the crest, two ME 109s streaked towards them from the far end of the wadi.

'Hit the dirt!'

From the corner of his eyes Alec saw the foul things, dipping and weaving below the cliff top. They were approaching nose-on, and Knocker and he were exposed... Alec closed his eyes and prayed.

A furious banging and clattering suddenly erupted from a white tower directly above them on top of the escarpment. It was that Cockney gunner who had mounted an anti-tank rifle in one of the rooms of the tower. The man had brought down two 109s already. His technique was to wait until the Messerschmitt was at zero deflection on the end of the barrel: one shot... *bong!*

One hundred and fifty yards away the leading ME 109 exploded in a yellow sheet of flame. Tail-end Charlie swerved away and bolted out of the wadi.

'Hurrah!' Knocker was yelling exultantly from the dust. 'Good for you, boyo!'

From the tower came the rattling of the breech as the gunner cleared the mechanism, and then a stream of Cockney oaths. Alec felt a lump rising in his throat.

Greco was waiting for them when they reached their cave. His eyes shone as Alec handed over the grenades. Instead of trotting off, however, he pointed to his unshod feet. A toothless grin creased his bearded face.

'You geeve me some Eenglish soldier boots,' he mouthed hesitantly, 'and I breeng you…'

'Yes?' Wright and White asked together.

'One German … *kaput*…' and he drew his finger quickly across his throat.

Alec Wright's mouth hung open.

'How you say?' old Greco continued apologetically. 'Fair exchange, no sweendle…'

'Robbery,' Alec corrected. 'But you've missed the point, Greco. Anyway, we'll see what we can do.'

'When, mastair?'

'Tonight. I'll try the stores again after dark.'

Whistling happily, old Greco slipped off down the path. Half an hour later, according to the gunner manning the anti-tank rifle, the old man was seen picking off isolated pockets of the enemy: in his German field-grey he would walk unconcernedly towards a bomb crater in range of the Germans, then suddenly disappear into an adjacent hole in the ground. From there he would lob a grenade into his neighbour's crater.

During the late afternoon, two new faces visited Alec Wright's cave. The first was a Captain, Royal Navy, the most senior officer yet to take advantage of Alec's stewpot: the silver ladle was used with good effect. The second was a stocky, dark-haired Midshipman from the Fleet Air Arm. 'Where've you come from?' Alec asked.

'Souda,' Brander replied.

'How'd you get here?'

'I'd delivered a message for the pongos to Wavell's H.Q. in Canea. I was at a loose end so went down to Souda.'

Alec raised his bushy eyebrows in query.

'Lieutenant Haig runs the daily provisions in an old trawler. He asked me to give him a hand.'

'Glad to have you,' Alec said. 'How's it going on the Canea front?'

'Disastrous. The Kiwis have been hurled off Maleme, and the whole front is collapsing.'

'Bad as that?'

''Fraid so. The Australians are digging in, but the Germans are encircling behind the hills to the south. The Royal Marines are just about cut off.'

There was a long silence.

'It's murder around Canea,' Brander said. 'It's all hand to hand; the Kiwis are out on their feet.'

Knocker White pushed a bowl into Brandy's hand.

'Have some stew.'

'Thanks, but I've got to go.'

'Why?'

'I'm supposed to return to Souda with Lieutenant Haig in his drifter.'

'Bit late, sir,' Alec said, remembering his manners. 'The drifter shoved off an hour ago.'

The Midshipman raised his black eyebrows. He shrugged his shoulders, like a bear waking from his winter sleep.

'The Captain we had in for dinner told us she'd embarked the two Matilda tanks, just in from Tymbakion. She was down to her gunwales, the Captain said.'

Knocker and Alec Wright exchanged glances.

'You'd better stay with us,' the P.O.Tel invited.

'I'll be in the way.'

'Lord luv-a-duck,' Knocker burst out. 'Short 'anded? Why, you're already on the watch-keeping roster.'

So Brandy joined the little band which, through its wireless transmitter, formed the only link with the outside world.

The evening of the 23rd slipped into dusk and, because visitors always happened to drop in at about supper time, Alec Wright invited them to share the stewpot. They yarned afterwards as they watched sunset fading into twilight.

'You know the Commandos are coming?' Knocker said.

'Hadn't heard,' a sergeant replied. 'We could do with 'em.'

'Where're they landing?' an R.A.F. type asked. 'We're O.K. here.'

'Souda,' Alec Wright said. 'They sound pretty pushed down there. Reckon now Maleme's gone, you pongos are up against it in the Canea area.'

'Garn, Sparks!' the sergeant retorted in disgust. 'You bring us the stuff, mate, and we'll do the rest. Jerry will never take Heraklion, that's for sure.'

'Have you even seen the Commandos at work?' Brander asked. 'Makes my flesh creep.'

'Trained killers,' the sergeant murmured. 'These types from Egypt are a tough bunch.'

'How so?'

'They're armed with small steel bows. I've seen a Commando pierce a sixpence at fifteen yards with those steel darts.'

In the silence Wright could hear the men breathing. The sergeant quickly consolidated his position:

'They have toggled cheese-wires too, for dealing with sentries; and those Commando knives... Ever seen one of those, eh, Shiner?'

Wright rose from his haunches. He wasn't enjoying this conversation, and he had to visit the quartermaster's stores to fetch those boots for old Greco.

'Sharp as a razor; beautifully tempered...' The soldier's words reflected the appreciation of a professional towards his art.

'Aw, stow it, Sarge,' Knocker interrupted. 'Shiner's got to go down to the stores in a minute.'

There was subdued merriment at this.

'What's the joke?' Brander asked.

'The Maoris, sir,' Knocker explained. 'Once it's dark, they come out and play games with the enemy. Jerry's scared of 'em.'

'Them Maoris stalk you in their bare feet,' the sergeant went on. 'They creep up behind you; you don't hear a thing.'

'Germans have been wearing British uniforms,' Knocker explained. 'To identify ourselves at night, we have all cut the shoulder tabs off our tunics. That's the first thing the Maoris feel for…'

It was now pitch dark. Suddenly an eerie scream echoed down the wadi from the German lines. The cave-dwellers froze where they crouched.

'See what I mean?' Knocker continued. 'The Maoris slit their throats.'

'No wonder Jerry's got the wind up,' Brandy said. 'I wouldn't like to be in their shoes.'

'Well, mates,' Alec Wright said, planting his peaked Petty Officer's cap squarely upon his huge head. 'While you beggars enjoy yourselves, I have work to do.'

'Where to, Shiner?'

'I've got to scrounge old Greco his pair of boots.'

'So long, Shiner,' Knocker chuckled. 'Don't forget the Maoris.'

The darkness hit Alec Wright as soon as he quit the cave. He had donned his plimsolls and now he leant against the cliff. He must spend several minutes here to readjust his eyes for night vision, and so he might as well check the Luger he had borrowed from a dead parachutist. He was taking no chances tonight: in the darkness, no-man's land became a limbo of flitting shadows. Only at night could either side move unobserved.

As he waited there, his imagination began to play him tricks; and as he grew colder his teeth began to chatter. 'Blast,' he muttered. 'Why the devil am I so wet? Risking my neck for old Greco's boots...' He was about to return when he realised the shame he'd have to endure on re-entering the cave. He'd never live it down. He shrugged his shoulders and glanced at the luminous dial of his watch. *Better get on with it.* Resolutely he turned his back upon the cave and began to creep down the track to the floor of the wadi.

He moved silently, on the balls of his feet, creeping swiftly along the boulder-strewn track until he reached the 15-cwt truck. He waited there for a moment to regain his breath, listening to the silence of the dead, then crept onwards towards the hut.

It was not difficult to find the boots: the Q.M.'s door was open for all to help themselves, and Alec knew exactly where to look. He grabbed two pairs, knotting the laces together and slinging the boots around his neck. He listened again, crouched low, and slunk back towards the 15-cwt. As he reached the tail-board his foot twisted on a pebble; the stone rattled against a wheel.

Wright stood motionless. It was difficult to hear anything above the thumping of his heart and his deep breathing, but freeze he must, before proceeding. He became aware then that he might not be alone...

He slipped the Luger from its holster and snicked off the safety catch. He jerked his head round... was someone breathing close behind him?

The darkness was tangible, an opaque, clammy thing. Wright turned slowly, his pistol cocked as he peered through the inky blackness. Nothing. He sighed and slipped on the safety catch. He felt a fool now that his knees were trembling, yet he could not dispel the strange sensation of being watched by unseen eyes. A stone rattled on the far side of the truck… Wright went rigid as he fumbled for the safety catch.

'Who is it?'

He listened to his whisper, holding his breath, his heart hammering against his ribs. The stubble was prickling on the back of his neck. God, this was awful; he'd make a rotten pongo…

Someone's knee suddenly crashed into the small of his back; the crook of an arm was flung across his throat and then a hand was fumbling for his shoulder tab…

Alec knew that Death was breathing down his neck. With all his strength he tried to shake himself free, but he was held in a bear-like hug. His assailant's hand tore at his other shoulder. The P.O.Tel opened his mouth to yell before the knife slit his throat… No words would come. Alec was literally speechless with terror. He closed his eyes as he cringed from the cold steel.

His whole life swam giddily before him in this moment of agony; his childhood, the apple orchard they used to raid; his old collie, and the Sunday School teacher…

He felt the Maori's hand sliding across the peak of his cap.

'O.K., Jack,' a gruff voice muttered.

Alec was suddenly released. He stood there trembling, then turned to face his adversary. The Maori had vanished into the night.

CHAPTER 12

The Dam Cracks

During the night of Saturday, 24th May, the fast mine-layer, *Abdiel,* slid alongside the jetty in Souda Bay. Her gangway was run out and 200 Commandos of 'Layforce' (the Special Service Troops under Brigadier Laycock) filed silently ashore. These men were to form the Headquarters and advance party for the main body that were to arrive on the night of 26th/27th of May.

The whirr of the cranes and the clatter of stores being dumped on the jetty added urgency to Abdiel's hurried visit. Bill Tanner stood in his khaki rig beneath Number Two crane: he was busy checking the stores that debouched from *Abdiel*'s innards. He felt stunned by the swiftness of events.

As soon as he'd arrived back in Alex from *Kandahar,* he'd been rekitted and ordered to take passage in *Abdiel,* and to report back to Commander George Beale at Maleme. As soon as he could decently leave this de-storing, he'd press on through Canea towards Maleme to find Commander Beale. Perhaps he'd discover what had happened to Brandy…

'Last load!'

Bill looked upwards at the Lieutenant standing by the guard rails, beneath the leaping shadows of the jib's shaded lantern. The officer waved, the crane whined as it revolved on its mounting, and down swung the final netful of ammunition boxes. To his left Bill saw a party of seamen casting off the steadying lines of the brow, then, as the gangway was being run inboard, four old men staggered up the sloping planks. The veterans seemed dishevelled and on the verge of exhaustion. At that moment a signalman approached Bill.

'Who are they?' Tanner asked.

The signalman nodded towards the gangway.

'Four Greek Cabinet Ministers, sir,' he said. 'Poor baskets.' Then he held out a signal pad for Bill to read. It was a *General* from Admiral Cunningham, the Commander-in-Chief, but it was difficult to read beneath the swinging light of the crane.

The Army is just holding its own against constant reinforcement of airborne enemy troops. We must NOT let them down. At whatever cost to ourselves we must land reinforcements for them and keep the enemy from using the sea. There are indications that enemy resources are stretched to the limit. We can and must outlast them. STICK IT OUT.

Tanner slowly returned the pad to the signalman.

'Thank you, Signalman.'

'All part of the *Abdiel* service, sir.' The young man grinned, then nipped up the gangway as it was being swung inboard.

'Let go back-spring!'

The jetty seemed now to be deserted, so Bill jumped forward to release the wire from the bollard. Then he turned slowly towards the shed which served as N.O.I.C's office.

Inside, two officers were discussing the night's operations. Apparently enemy landings were expected at Sitia, at the eastern end of the island; Captain McCarthy's force of *Ajax* and *Dido*, screened by *Imperial*, *Kimberley* and *Hotspur*, was patrolling out there now, north of Crete. So far, however, no joy.

'Can I get through to Maleme?' Bill asked at length. 'I'm trying to contact Commander Beale.'

'The aviator?' an unshaven Lieutenant-Commander asked with surprise.

'Yes, sir. He's my C.O.'

'The Maleme front is pretty confused, but what's left of the Fleet Air Arm must still be there.'

'Thank you, sir.'

''S all right. Life's pretty depressing here. Heard the latest?'

Bill stifled a yawn: he found it difficult to follow the goings-on ashore. It seemed weeks since he'd taken off from Maleme on that morning of the invasion.

'*Hood*'s been sunk.'

Tanner stood motionless, unable to speak.

'*Hood*'s sunk…'

Bill turned slowly to the tired eyes staring across at him. He couldn't believe the news. The mighty *Hood?*

'*Bismarck* caught her. We don't know any more yet…'

Bill closed the door quietly behind him. He stood for a moment gazing at the dawn.

Sunday. Sunday, the 25th of May. The air was very still, the day hesitating upon another agonising threshold. *Hood* gone… he shook his head and began walking slowly down the Canea road towards Maleme. The ruins of Canea lay smouldering on the right, and, as he approached the Mournies crossroads, he met a Sergeant of the Royal Marines who was returning from the New Zealand Divisional Headquarters. Bill went up to him.

'Can I get through to Maleme?'

The man looked at him, the corners of his mouth twitching.

'Dunno, sir. I'm with Major Madoc's lot at Mournies. We're holding on here by our eyebrows.' The sergeant was obviously in a hurry. 'The Diggers have just found a French 75 and mounted it in our position, but as soon as Jerry saw it he bombed it to bits. Life's like that at the moment... Excuse me, sir.'

The tough veteran saluted and strode off down the road, helmet pulled low over his eyes. Tanner squared his shoulders and moved off down the coastal road towards Maleme. He reached the Galatos fork and flung himself into a ditch as a couple of MEs winged low over his head, their guns spitting at anything that moved.

'Hey, mate, where'd yer think you're going?' a New Zealand voice hailed from the ditch in front of him.

'Maleme. I'm trying to reach my Fleet Air Arm unit.'

There was a pause and then a note of hurt surprise in the Kiwi's reply.

'Where you been the last four days, Pommie?'

'At sea. I'm trying to find my observer.'

The New Zealander whistled as he cautiously poked his head above the ground.

'A naval lootenant was through here yesterday. He'd been sunk three times already, he said?' the Kiwi drawled half-humorously. 'Difficult to believe, ain't it?'

'I believe it,' Bill grinned. 'Been in the drink twice myself.'

'You shoulda stayed at sea, mate. It's ruddy 'ell 'ere.'

Bill Tanner snatched no sleep during that Sunday night of 25th May. The New Zealanders' withdrawal to the new Karatsos line began at 11.30 p.m., and by dawn on Monday 26th they were in position. The troops were utterly exhausted, jaded and hungry, yet still the enemy's pressure round to the southward was relentless. Platoons were hurled in to stop a gap here, to lengthen the line there but, by the time the men had collapsed into their new positions, a hole would appear elsewhere. By noon Bill Tanner found himself alongside the Royal Marine Battalion at Mournies where he met Major Madoc, the Royal Marine officer in charge of that sector of the line. Tall, tough, and a born leader, the man seemed utterly calm in spite of the obvious disintegration along his front. Even as Bill watched, the Australian battalions were preparing to withdraw through the Royal Marines' position.

All that afternoon Bill found himself in action, and by five p.m. he hardly knew how to stand. How these New Zealanders kept going, he could not comprehend: they had been continually in action for six days and nights and most of them had attacked in over twenty bayonet charges.

At 0930 that morning, unknown to the fighting troops, General Freyberg had signalled, in consultation with Captain Morse, the N.O.I.C., to General Wavell in Alexandria:

I regret to have to report that in my opinion the limit of endurance has been reached by the troops under my command here at Souda Bay. No matter what decision is taken by the Commanders-in-Chief, from a military point of view our position here is hopeless. A small, ill-equipped and immobile force such as ours cannot stand up against the concentrated bombing that we have been faced with during the past seven days. I feel that I should tell you that from an administrative point of view the difficulties of extricating this force in full are now insuperable. Provided a decision is reached at once a certain proportion of the force might be embarked. Once this section has been reduced, a reduction of Retimo and Heraklion by the same methods will only be a matter of time. The troops we have, with the exception of the Welsh Regiment and the Commando, are past any offensive action. If you decide, in view of the whole Middle East position, that hours help, we will carry on. I would have to consider how this would be best achieved. Souda Bay may be under fire within 24 hours. Further, casualties have been heavy, and we have lost the majority of our immobile guns.

Abdiel and her escort left Souda that night with 930 walking wounded and unwanted men. But at sea on that tragic Monday the Navy, too, was fighting for its life and for the existence of the Army in Crete.

CHAPTER 13

Desperate Riposte

Rear-Admiral (Air) Sir Denis Boyd glanced at the clock in his darkened bridge aboard the aircraft carrier, *Formidable*. The dimly illuminated hands showed 0330 on this morning of 26th May. With a grunt, he pulled the hood of his duffel closer about his head, strode out on to the wings of his Admiral's flying bridge and peered down at the familiar scene on the carrier's flight deck.

Formidable's Captain, Captain Bisset, had already turned the carrier into the wind preparatory to flying off. The carrier was now steaming at twenty-eight knots and the wind was flailing Denis Boyd's face. At any moment Bisset would be requesting permission to fly off.

Boyd felt uneasy as he peered through the darkness at the force surrounding him. There was the flagship, *Queen Elizabeth*, flying the flag of Rear-Admiral Pridham-Wippell, and astern of her, the other old battleship, *Barham*. Two huge monsters ploughing through the night towards the island of Scarpanto, which now lay a hundred miles north-north-east. Around this Force A.1 were the screening destroyers: Captain Mack (D.14) in *Jervis*, with *Janus*, *Kandahar*, *Nubian*, *Hasty*, *Hereward*, *Voyager* and *Vendetta*.

Boyd smiled to himself. When the Crete business flared up, he had told Andrew Cunningham that he would gladly participate with *Formidable* as soon as the carrier boasted eight operational Fulmar fighters, for, at the start of the Crete battle,

Boyd had only four left capable of combat. Now, just before dawn on this calm Monday morning, *Formidable* was ranging four Albacore T.S.R.s and five Fulmar fighters. How ludicrous they seemed against the Luftwaffe squadrons based on Scarpanto, that hornet's nest in the Kaso Straits!

The strike's target was the island aerodrome where the Junkers were parked in hundreds, waiting for yet another day in which to plaster Crete.

'Ready to fly off, sir.'

It was Bisset. Boyd could understand only too well the man's anxiety and the drawback of having an Admiral breathing down his neck. Boyd had been Captain of Illustrious, and he had been lucky in having Lumley Lyster as his Admiral (Air). Denis Boyd returned Bisset's salute.

'Carry on, please.'

Bisset nodded at his Commander (Flying) and then the blue *Affirmative* glowed from the wing of the bridge. Even from his position on the Admiral's bridge, Boyd was deafened by the roar from the flight deck. The illuminated bat of the Lieutenant-Commander (Flying) flashed downwards. The first Albacore started to inch slowly forwards as the chocks were snatched away.

Boyd watched, heart in his mouth, as once more the drama of a night strike was enacted. The first aircraft had the shortest run. For Boyd, its take-off was always an anxious moment, recalling the agonies of the strike against Taranto. The Albacore was trundling forwards now, its tail up as it gathered speed. Then, just as it reached the round-down, it was suddenly airborne. Boyd pulled his duffel closer around him and sighed with relief. The leader flew off ahead of the carrier and dropped his marker for the remaining three Albacores to form up on him. The Fulmars, being much faster, were to fly off ten minutes later.

In the silence that followed, Boyd returned to his bridge to light his pipe. There was nothing to do now but wait — the worst part of this whole business. His gallant fliers knew the odds they were flying against: if they failed to achieve surprise, their chance of survival was nil. Boyd felt sick at heart: he was asking much of these young men, but they would do their duty, for they knew they were upholding the Army in Crete. *Formidable*'s aircraft were trying to redress the balance, but only Boyd knew the reason his carrier was exposed so close to the Kaso Straits. At dawn she would be within striking distance of the Luftwaffe from Scarpanto; an irresistible target to receive the bombs which otherwise would be aimed upon British soldiers.

Boyd watched the great carrier swinging out of the wind as she resumed course to rejoin the battleships. The Fulmars had flown off now. He'd try to snatch some sleep before the day dawned and before any survivors returned from Scarpanto. Already a silver streak was stealing across the eastern horizon.

'Well, what's the score?'

Rear-Admiral (Air) Boyd was standing with Captain Bisset on *Formidable*'s bridge and was addressing the Squadron Commanders of the Albacores and Fulmars. It was ten minutes past seven and the two men looked tired and hungry as they clambered in their flying rig on to the bridge. Lieutenant-Commander Saunt, the C.O. of the Albacores, spoke first:

'We caught them with their pants down, sir. We destroyed two 88s on the ground and damaged plenty of others. They never had time to take off before the Fulmars got in amongst them.' The Squadron Commander looked across at his comrade-in-arms. Thanks, Jack.'

'How about you, then?' Boyd asked Bruen, the fighters' C.O. 'What did you get?'

'We shot up several C.R.42s, sir, and plenty of Stukas. They never knew what hit 'em.' The Squadron Commander smiled with his eyes. 'We kept going until we ran out of ammunition.'

Boyd grinned. 'Good. Now shake it up and get some breakfast while your machines are being re-fuelled and re-armed.' He glanced at Bisset. 'You've already got some echoes on the plot?'

'Yes, sir,' the Captain replied. 'They're heading this way. I'm closing up at action stations.'

The fliers were already bundling down the bridge ladders as the alarm rattlers sounded. Bisset turned to his Admiral. 'A miracle that they've all returned safely.'

'Thank God,' Boyd replied. 'But we'll need every one of those eight Fulmars before the day's much older.' He paused as he glanced eastwards. 'Fly off the first strike of fighters before re-forming on Q.E.,' he said, referring to the *Queen Elizabeth*, and as soon as Desmond McCarthy's force has taken up station. It's good to have his cruisers with us, although apparently they found nothing last night.' Then Boyd added grimly, 'Every H.A. gun is going to count this forenoon.'

The Admiral turned to watch *Ajax* and *Dido* forming up on the wings of the battleships, while their destroyers, *Napier*, *Kelvin* and *Jackal*, who had recently relieved *Imperial*, *Kimberley* and *Hotspur*, wheeled in astern. The fleet was now in tight anti-aircraft formation, so that the combined fire power of the guns would force up the bombers.

Boyd felt his stomach sinking as he imagined the wrath about to break upon them. He dreaded this waiting, ever since that appalling attack which his beloved *Illustrious* had suffered after Taranto. This premonition of disaster was too real to bear: the sooner the enemy attacked the better.

'Ready to fly off the first fighter patrol, sir,' Bisset reported grimly as he turned towards his Admiral.

'Fly off,' Boyd said. Even as he committed his first four Fulmars, the barrage on the far side of the fleet began to burst in the sky.

'Wish the old girls could do more than 24 knots, sir,' Sub-Lieutenant Phillips grumbled as he watched the massive battleships abeam of them. 'Thank God we're steering south.'

The Sub was Officer of the Watch of the destroyer *Jackal;* light on his feet and with blue eyes, he was carrying on a desultory conversation with his Captain, Lieutenant-Commander R. M. P. Jonas, a reserved man with intelligent and sensitive features.

'Don't complain, Jerry,' Jonas replied. 'We could easily have shared *Kelly*'s and *Kashmir*'s fate, instead of being snugly in Alex harbour last night.'

'Think of *Kimberley, Imperial* and *Hotspur* beating it up ashore tonight, sir; makes me envious.'

'One of the mortal sins,' said Jonas. 'Come on, Sub, you're astern of station.'

Jerry Phillips squinted through his station-keeper at the truck of *Nubian*'s foremast: yes, he was half a cable astern of station in the Tribal's threshing wake. He picked up the engine room phone:

'Up four turns,' he shouted above the scream of bombers overhead.

Behind him he heard the *ting! ting!* of the D.C.T., and once again the guns crashed into action. *Jackal* trembled from the shock as the four-sevens hurled up their ineffectual barrage. He watched with amusement the black puffs where the shells exploded harmlessly below the nearest batch of Stukas.

'Check, check, check!' the Captain shouted suddenly. 'One of our fighters is fouling the range.'

Philips watched two of *Formidable*'s Fulmars tearing into the group of 87s. With guns spitting they twisted and turned, forcing the Stukas to break formation. He heard *Jackal*'s sailors cheering from 'B' gun.

'Good for them!' Jonas yelled. 'My God, they've got guts, those boys.'

'That's the fifteenth dog-fight I've counted so far,' Phillips remarked. 'I've seen four Huns hit anyway, sir.'

'And two shot down,' Jonas added. 'Look at those Fulmars…'

One of the fighters had broken off to streak after a lone JU 88 diving upon *Formidable*. The Fulmar's guns blazed. The 88 dipped as it turned away, black smoke gushing from its port engine, but at that instant three ME 109s pounced upon the Fulmar. There was a bright flash, a lick of flame and the Fulmar plummeted into the sea ahead of *Napier*.

The fleet swept on majestically, leaving *Napier* to search for the pilot. By the time the destroyer had returned, there remained nothing but an oil slick where the fighter had crashed. *Napier* wheeled back into line.

'Poor blighter,' Jonas said. 'He never had a chance.'

By noon, *Formidable*'s eight fighters had each carried out three sorties and fought twenty-four combats. By 1320 only two Fulmars remained, yet still they took off again to fight more than a hundred enemy aircraft. The target for the bombers was, as always, the aircraft carrier, and the Fulmars attacked time and time again, to ward off the attacks from the direction of Scarpanto.

'They're magnificent,' Jonas shouted above the roar of the guns. 'But it can't go on much longer.'

As his words floated away on the wind, *Jackal*'s starboard lookout called from the wings:

'Alarm green one-two-o. Formation of Stukas.'

Phillips glanced upwards along the lookout's bearing: over twenty JU 87s were circling there, having crept up from the direction of the African coast… *Formidable* had not sighted them and was still engaging a small group to the north-eastward.

'Shift target, green one-two-o… Open fire!' the Captain shouted.

Jackal shuddered as the guns blazed, but even as Phillips waited to spot the bursts, the first three Stukas were plummeting down. Too late were *Formidable*'s turrets revolving towards her new assailants; too late did the gun barrels elevate. Even as the pom-poms pounded into action, the first bomb toppled from the belly of the leading Stuka. Even at this distance, Phillips heard the scream of the dive and the shuddering of the Stuka's flaps. The bomb plunged deep into the carrier's flight deck. Those on *Jackal*'s bridge stood aghast for a second, hoping for a miracle… but a black cloud leapt suddenly upwards, streaked with orange flame, and then *Formidable* disappeared in a cloud of dense, oily smoke.

'There's another, sir…'

Phillips was yelling above the racket, for now *Jackal*'s close-range weapons had joined in, the 0-5s drowning all conversation. The last Stuka was pulling out, but her bomb was aimed true. It struck *Formidable*'s 'X' turret, where the accelerator gear was situated. A sheet of flame leapt upwards, and for a moment the carrier disappeared behind her own shroud.

'Alarm red-nine-o...!'

Phillips remembered vaguely registering the cry of the port lookout, but he was fully occupied station-keeping astern of *Nubian*, who was twisting and weaving only a cable and a half ahead. With all her guns blazing, the Tribal was a glorious sight as she heeled to her rudder... Phillips watched her stern swinging and he concentrated upon the boil in the wake where her rudder had moved. He crouched low over the binnacle, coaxing *Jackal* along *Nubian*'s wake: any second now and he'd shove *Jackal*'s wheel over...

The cacophony of battle was distracting, but Phillips remained steady. His job was to conn the ship, and no alarums would deviate him from his concentration. He glimpsed the Captain leaping across his line of sight; he heard him yelling at the port point-five; a shadow flashed across the bridge, and Phillips heard the scream of an aircraft. *Nubian* was swinging clear. Now...

'Starboard ten,' he shouted down the voicepipe, his eyes glued upon *Nubian*'s quarter-deck.

A black shape streaked across his vision: a Junkers 88 in a shallow dive, with its bombs already toppling straight on top of the Tribal's 'Y' gun. There was a yellow flash, and fragments flew off the stricken *Nubian*, like chippings from a lathe. A hole gaped suddenly where her stern had been, but, as the 88 swung away, the bomber was slashed in two by the Tribal's midship pom-pom. A fountain of water spouted where the machine vanished in a seething turmoil of sea.

'Hard-a-starboard...' Jonas shouted. 'I'll take her, Sub.' The Captain leapt to the binnacle as Phillips jumped aside.

Already hoses were being run along *Nubian*'s deck as she lost way. Phillips could see the damage control parties grappling with fires as *Jackal* swung to give A.A. protection. He felt sickened as he saw *Nubian*'s men bundling their dead over the side.

To port, *Formidable* lay stopped, her guns still firing. With her starboard side towards *Jackal*, Phillips could see a vast, yawning cavern running sixty feet down the bows from abaft the cable locker. Men were scrambling like ants in the exposed mess decks but already the damage control teams were subduing the fires. As Phillips watched, the carrier slowly gathered way; then she turned until she was steering the course of the fleet. She was gravely damaged but not sinking: not surprising, with Boyd aboard…

Jackal's guns still blazed as Jonas threw her about to protect their wounded comrade; but *Nubian* was soon under way again and steering by main engines. Signals winked between her and *Jervis*, and five minutes later *Nubian* was steaming at twenty knots. The fleet was altering course to the eastward when *Jervis*'s signal lantern flashed at *Jackal*.

To Jackal, *repeated* Nubian *from D.14*, Phillips read. *Act independently and escort* Nubian *to Alexandria. Force A.1 is remaining in the area tonight.*

Phillips sighed. Already the fleet was drawing the bombers away to the eastward. It would be touch and go whether *Nubian* would reach Alex, but at least *Jackal* could stand by her. Perhaps *Formidable* could also sneak away after dark.

CHAPTER 14

The Flood

Bill Tanner could see that Major Madoc, Royal Marines, was anxious. The temporary lull gained by the New Zealanders' and Australians' glorious charge at '42nd Street' was now exhausted. During all that afternoon and evening, troops had been withdrawing through the Royal Marine lines: Australians, New Zealanders and units from Souda which had become detached; men in groups of two or three, women, children and civilians. Though they were all different, they shared one common denominator: panic, and terror of being caught by the Germans.

Madoc had been told to hold the line at Mournies to allow the Australians and New Zealanders to pass through. The afternoon had been one of total disorganisation, of order and counter-order, until finally all previous commands had been cancelled and the 'Royals' were ordered to remain steady at Mournies. Tanner was happy to be once again amongst the Royal Marines. He felt at home with them, felt he belonged in some strange way; were not the Royals sailors too, and the finest Corps in the world? He was glad to be in Madoc's company. This Royal Marines composite battalion, after acting as a rearguard during the long night of Tuesday, the 27th of May, was the last to disengage.

Madoc had received several conflicting orders: he was to move to Meg Khorafia, the junction east of Souda, where the road forked to the south across the mountains; he was to remain where he was until further orders; if he heard nothing he was to withdraw. Then, half an hour after midnight on the morning of Tuesday the 27th, an Australian liaison officer arrived from Area Headquarters. Breathlessly he told Madoc he was to disengage within the next thirty minutes and to rendezvous at a road junction near Meg Khorafia.

Madoc immediately packed up his headquarters in the battered farmstead, and dispatched runners to his platoon commanders. By 0200 his Royal Marines were on the march along either side of the Canea-Souda road. As they passed the hill on their right, a bomber winged over, illuminating the scene. A flare exploded in its fuselage and suddenly the aircraft was ablaze; it crashed behind the hill and a pall of smoke spiralled upwards. Madoc was thankful that the Luftwaffe refused to operate at night: the enemy could have slaughtered the marching columns.

When Madoc reached the main Souda road he was appalled by the sight that met his eyes: the route was blocked by a stream of fleeing civilians and of soldiers who had lost their units. As the Royals came abreast of Souda, one of Madoc's subalterns came up to Tanner.

'We've got to control this traffic,' he said. 'Nip down to Souda and see if you can organise the civilians. If they keep up this panic, they'll completely block the road.'

'Right you are,' Bill Tanner replied as he turned off the main road. 'I'll do what I can.'

For the first time in two days Bill was on his own. He stood aside for a moment to watch the rabble streaming past him. Old women, young children; old men, and, interspersed amongst them, the khaki splodges of bewildered troops with only one word on their lips: *Sphakia*. Sphakia, the embarkation point where the Navy would be waiting; Sphakia, a tiny fishing village off which, it was said, the ships would be lying — if the enemy bombers did not find them.

The Navy would be there... the Army could depend on the ships, but after the experiences of the recent Greek evacuation, after Norway and Dunkirk, every soldier knew that the Navy could not loiter. They could only fill up and take their human cargoes to Alexandria. A ship could not expand like a concertina, and there were over 20,000 troops in Crete. Hasten, hurry across those beautiful but formidable mountains, overlooking this sweltering plain. Three thousand feet high across the ridge; at night bitterly cold, by day the track unbearably hot. Sphakia... *Sphakia*... Their gaunt faces were set like masks, their eyes staring before them as they hustled along the packed roads.

'Thank God,' Bill murmured to himself, 'thank God the Luftwaffe is asleep. This would be carnage if it were daylight.'

The civilians were moaning as they hurried past, terror in their eyes as they glanced continually over their shoulders at the smouldering ruins of their homes. Bill remembered Madoc mentioning that the German Fifth Column was at work in Canea and Souda. Spreading confusion and panic, the agents soon had the civilians bewailing the terror-bombing.

'Better to endure German rule,' the refugees cried, 'than the awful bombing of Canea.' It was the women who caused the Greeks to break; it was the German agents who persuaded the women to take to the caves in the hills. Bill felt hate in his heart for this ruthless and treacherous enemy.

Fighting against the human tide, Tanner finally reached the jetty in Souda harbour where he paused to gain his bearings. He needed time to think, time to decide how best to control this panic-stricken horde. He peered out at the harbour, empty save for the lighter further down the jetty. Instinctively drawn towards the ship, he strolled towards the Lieutenant impatiently waiting by the brow.

'Hullo, Sub,' the stranger greeted him. 'I'm Haig — lost, beggared and bewildered. Who the hell are you?'

'Sub-Lieutenant Tanner, sir. Same state as you, except I've neither ship nor aircraft.'

'"A"-boy?'

Bill nodded.

'Care for a trip?' Haig enquired. 'I'm just off to Retimo with stores. I could do with some help.'

Tanner smiled and shook his head. 'Sorry. I've got work to do here.'

'Pity. Two trips ago I scrounged a chap called Brander. He was an "A"-boy too. Know him?'

'Brander?'

'Yeah. His pilot had pranged, and he had no aircraft, so he lent me a hand on this provisions run to Heraklion.'

Bill gazed out to sea.

'Good luck, sir,' he said quietly. 'Sorry I can't go along with you. Give the "A"-boy my regards if you see him. I was his pilot.'

Haig jumped aboard. The lines splashed into the dark water. Bill Tanner watched her silhouette melting into the clouds of black smoke swirling across the harbour.

CHAPTER 15

Bitter Decision

Three hundred and eighty miles away to the south-east, the Commanders-in-Chief were imprisoned in their War Room in Alexandria. It was eight o'clock on the morning of Tuesday, the 27th of May. For the tenth time General Sir Archibald Wavell picked up the signal he had yesterday received from Freyberg. One word kept catching the General's eye: *hopeless*. If Freyberg considered the position thus, there could be no gainsaying it: that soldier would never capitulate.

Wavell glanced at his two comrades: Andrew Cunningham, hair grizzled, his piercingly blue eyes anxious for his ships steaming at the limits of endurance off Crete; and Air Marshal Tedder, lean and angular, worn out by the frustration of being unable to provide air cover for his brother services. Yet, Wavell realised, these men never blamed each other: they would co-operate to the limit of their powers, but how could Tedder protect the fleet, and the Army in Crete, if he had no fighters? Once again, the pacifists of eight years ago were to blame: Britons were being butchered out there, thanks to those misguided idiots… Archie Wavell felt sick at heart.

'I'll read it out, Andrew,' he said, glancing at the Admiral. 'Tell me if you disagree on any point.' Then he added: 'Winston won't like this.'

Cunningham smiled sourly. London had been unusually unhelpful. The Chiefs of Staff seemed unable to grasp the simple fact that ships could not operate by day, nor soldiers move, without air cover. Neither did Their Lordships seem to realise that it wasn't the sacrifice of men or ships that the Navy resented, but that, after the inevitable collapse of Crete, if things continued as they were, there would be no fleet in existence to contain the enemy in the Mediterranean. A.B.C. nodded. 'Read it, please, Archie.'

'*To the Chiefs of Staff*,' Wavell recited, de-cyphering his handwriting.

Deeply regret to inform you that the Canea front collapsed in the early hours of this morning twenty-seventh, and that Souda Bay can only be covered for a further twenty-four hours. No possibility of hurling in reinforcements. I have therefore ordered evacuation to proceed as opportunity offers.

'I fully realise the grave effect this failure will have on other problems in the Middle East, but it is obvious that to prolong the defence of Crete now will merely exhaust the resources of three Services; this will compromise the defence of Middle East more gravely than would even the loss of Crete.'

Wavell sighed as he glanced upwards. His two companions nodded. The Commander-in-Chief initialled the signal and sent for his signals officer.

'Now,' Wavell said, leading the way to the Map Room. 'While we're waiting for London approval, let's get on with the business of planning the evacuation.'

In the adjoining room the three leaders peered once again at the vast maps of Crete.

'How many men to bring off, Archie?' A.B.C. asked.

'About 22,000.'

'That's a lot of men.'

'Can you do it, Andrew?'

Cunningham's forehead puckered. 'It's a question of how many of my ships are still operational,' he answered slowly. 'My ships have been continually at sea, some of them for nearly a month now. The ships' companies are exhausted and the strain is beginning to have serious consequences. They can't go on much longer — but they will.' He faced Wavell squarely. 'In eight days, Archie, I've lost two modern cruisers and four destroyers. Two battleships — *Barham* was hit yesterday, on her way back with Force A1 — our only aircraft carrier, a cruiser and a destroyer have all been so badly damaged that they are not operational. On top of that, five cruisers and four destroyers have also been damaged, although they can still fight.'

A.B.C. was prowling like a caged tiger up and down the Map Room, his hands clasped behind his back.

'Now that *Formidable* is out of action, the fleet has no fighter protection.' Cunningham paused to glance at Group Captain Pelly, the officer appointed by Tedder to liaise with the Navy. 'Thank you for the R.A.F.'s offer to help over the evacuation,' A.B.C. continued. 'We shall need every available machine to cover this lift.'

'We'll do everything we can, sir,' Pelly said quietly.

Cunningham nodded. 'This show's going to be worse than the evacuation from Greece.' He turned then towards Wavell. 'The Navy will bring off your soldiers, General, for as long as possible, regardless of losses to our ships. Now let's get down to the planning while we wait to hear from London.'

The Map Room hummed. The greatest difficulty was to estimate the number of troops that would be ready each night for evacuation from Sphakia, that tiny fishing village with only two hundred yards of beach. How could the garrisons at Retimo and Heraklion be taken off? Obviously, with the enemy mastering the air, embarkation could take place only at night: no plans could be cemented, until the answers to these queries were received from General Freyberg in Crete.

The day dragged on. By 1530 no reply had been received from London. W/T communication was sufficiently good to communicate with Freyberg, though the signals were taking longer to get through. Wavell, at 1550, without waiting for London, despatched the vital signal to the General Commanding in Crete: Freyberg was to evacuate his troops forthwith.

As dusk fell outside the windows of the Map Room, Cunningham squared his shoulders. He had never felt so proud of his ships. As he turned to leave, the Fleet Signals Office showed him a signal. Cunningham turned to face his staff:

'There's one ray of hope, gentlemen,' he said. 'The German battleship, *Bismarck*, has just been sunk in the Atlantic. *Hood* has been avenged.'

During the evening of Tuesday the 27th, General Freyberg received Wavell's order to evacuate Crete. For the last time from his Canea headquarters, Freyberg was struggling to maintain control of events. At 0824 that morning, he had signalled Churchill that Crete was no longer tenable, but that the Army would fight on if that sacrifice were required.

Now, however, the General had firm orders to evacuate his soldiers from the island. For the next few nights the Navy would be standing by to take off his army. It was up to Freyberg to plan the embarkation and to tell the Navy what he wanted.

First, he placed General Weston in command of all forces in the western sector of Crete, while he, General Freyberg, was moving his headquarters south to the Askifou plain above Sphakia.

Second, 1,000 men were to be taken off from Sphakia tomorrow night, Wednesday 28th/29th.

Third, 6,000 men were to be evacuated from Sphakia on Thursday night, 29th/30th.

Fourth, 3,000 men to be lifted from Sphakia on Friday night, 30th/31st.

Fifth, 3,000 men on 31st May/1st June from Sphakia.

The 5th and 19th Brigades of New Zealanders and Australians were to be the last to be taken off.

Sixth, Layforce and the Royal Marines were to be sacrificed and were to act as the final rearguard to hold off the enemy at the top of the Sphakia gorge. They were to take to the hills and surrender after the last ship had left.

Seventh, the Heraklion garrison of 4,000 would be evacuated by the Navy the next night, Wednesday 28th/29th of May.

Eighth, because Lieutenant-Colonel Campbell, the Commander who was so fiercely holding Retimo, had no cyphers, no signal could be passed to him to break out and march to Plaka. A Hurricane had been dispatched from Egypt to drop the orders over the Retimo garrison, but there had been no confirmation that Campbell had received it. Freyberg therefore gave orders that Lieutenant Haig, who was leaving Souda on his last provision run to Retimo, should pass the evacuation orders to Colonel Campbell.

As the final meeting broke up, a staff officer left the Headquarters to contact Haig.

The Army Captain stumbled through the rubble and in the darkness finally reached Souda waterfront. There was no ship alongside the quay; the port was deserted. The staff officer turned down the jetty but there was no sign of Haig or his trawler. Turning disconsolately away, the officer was about to leave when he bumped into a group of men standing by a wrecked crane. An R.N. Sub-Lieutenant (A) was talking to a dishevelled Army Captain, who was carrying a portable wireless transmitter upon his back.

'Haig left ten minutes ago,' the Sub replied to the staff officer's query.

The Captain swore. 'Retimo's lost, then,' he blurted. 'The poor devils will all be taken prisoner.'

The silence was broken by the Sub-Lieutenant.

'We've got nothing to lose, sir,' he said quietly. 'These chaps are what's left of a unit calling themselves "The Marauders". If they're game, we'll take the message through to Retimo.' He waved a hand towards the huddle of men lounging against the piles. There was a murmur of assent. 'You'll come along too, won't you, Mackie?' the Sub. added, addressing the Captain with the wireless set. 'We could do with your transmitter.'

The officer hesitated an instant. He nodded then, and his smile flashed, even in the darkness.

CHAPTER 16

Heraklion: Wednesday, 28th May

Alec Wright spent most of Wednesday in his cave overlooking the wadi. He could not emerge, for the Luftwaffe had been flying over in droves from dawn onwards. The sky had grown black over Heraklion: for eight hours bombs had been raining upon the town and the troop positions.

Alec Wright's W/T station had been busy. Cairo had been transmitting continually, until finally the last tragic signal had been received: the Heraklion garrison was to be evacuated from the harbour that night.

'Message ends,' growled Alec. He was disgusted, as was every man in that garrison. They felt cheated, for they had repulsed the worst the enemy could hurl at them and were in complete control of the situation. Now they had to quit, because the Souda front was crumbling.

Alec began wondering about the fate of Retimo as he and Knocker White started smashing their transmitters. He couldn't see how the Retimo garrison could be evacuated, poor beggars. If they, too, were catching the fury of the Luftwaffe, escape for them would be impossible.

After sunset, Wright led White, and Brander, the Snotty, whose wound was now practically healed, down to the harbour. Lines of men were also picking their way through the smouldering rubble, for this evacuation was to be conducted in complete silence and secrecy. The ships were to lift the whole garrison of 4,000 between 2330 and 0130. Anyone who missed the boat was lost, for at dawn the enemy would swoop into the empty town.

'Makes you sick, don't it, Shiner?' Knocker whispered.

Grunting acknowledgement, Alec held his handkerchief to his nose to reduce the stench pervading this stricken town. He had stumbled over something soft, and his heart had leapt into his mouth. The corpses had lain rotting in the sun for the past three days, neither side being able to bury their dead.

'Reckon things are ripe for a rattling good epidemic,' Brander muttered. 'Typhoid and all that.'

'Bubonic plague, too, with these rats about,' Knocker choked, as a dark shape scuttled between his feet.

'Thank Gawd we're getting out of here,' Alec said as the waterfront appeared through the smoke. 'The Black Death's one of the maladies not listed in my medical handbook.'

Platoons of men were marching in perfect order along the jetties. The embarkation was being organised by the N.O.I.C., Captain Macdonald, R.N., like a peacetime exercise: there was no noise, and perfect discipline. As each platoon marched into position along the jetty it turned towards the harbour, the troops standing at ease and unhitching their packs. There was no smoking, and the men spoke only in whispers.

It was 2330 exactly when the first shadow materialised from the darkness. A two-funnelled destroyer slid alongside and, astern of her, one of the new 'J's. Alec glanced at the first destroyer's pendant numbers as her wires swung across.

'*Hereward*, Knocker.'

'One of the 'H's, anyway. Could be *Hotspur*.'

A brow slid across and an Army Captain scrambled over to her iron deck. Wright was securing the gangway when a seaman from the destroyer came to help.

'Glad to see you, Jack,' Alec Wright said. 'What ship?'

'*Hereward*, P.O.,' the Able Seaman replied. 'What are you doing 'ere? Thought we were taking off bleedin' pongos.'

At that moment the Army officer aboard *Hereward* bellowed across in a stentorian whisper: 'All stretcher cases first, followed by walking wounded. Then the front platoons. Keep silence, keep moving, but don't rush.'

Alec, Brander and Knocker White watched in silence as the broken bodies were tenderly shipped aboard. The platoons on the jetty remained steady, waiting their turn.

'D'you reckon we count as a platoon, Shiner?' Knocker whispered. 'At least we're in the front rank.'

'Reckon so, but she's nearly full up now. Her upper deck's crammed.'

A voice was speaking calmly through a megaphone from the bridge:

'D'ye hear there? Captain speaking. We're coming back for another load, so don't feel you're being abandoned. There are seven of us ferrying you out to the cruisers, *Orion* and *Dido*, lying off in the harbour. I repeat, we're coming back. *Au revoir*.' The megaphone turned further aft: 'In brow. Let go aft.'

There was a murmur from the platoon as the plank was hoisted inboard.

'Room for two more if you're quick, mate,' *Hereward*'s Buffer hissed across at Alec.

Wright glanced helplessly at Brander. 'No,' he mumbled. 'Next…'

'Go on, Alec,' Brander said. 'For Pete's sake, you and Knocker nip aboard. I'll join you on her next trip.'

'Thanks.' Alec felt guilty as he leapt for *Hereward*'s guard-rail. He hauled Knocker after him, then turned to wave to the Midshipman staring up from the jetty. The P.O.Tel. raised his hand and Brander waved back.

'Good kid, that,' Knocker murmured at Alec's elbow.

The P.O.Tel. grunted. He hadn't liked quitting the Mid., but he knew Brander would be O.K.: *Hereward* would be returning after this trip and he'd get off in her. Already two other destroyers were manoeuvring alongside: *Jackal* and *Decoy*, by the look of them, and another 'K' lying off.

The breeze began to buffet Alec's face as *Hereward* went ahead. He inhaled deeply: it was grand to breathe again the clean night air.

'There they are, Shiner.'

A black shape loomed down their starboard side: a modern cruiser, with widely spaced, pugnacious funnels.

'Who is it, Jack?' a soldier asked in the darkness.

'*Dido*, mate,' Knocker said softly. 'She's the only one left of her class.'

Alec felt the propellers stop and then, on the starboard bow, the unmistakeable silhouette of a one-funnelled cruiser glided past.

'*Orion* or *Ajax*,' he murmured.

Ten minutes later Alec Wright found himself in *Orion*'s for'd mess decks. The troops were being squeezed in like sardines to allow for further loads. He glanced at his watch: it was already three quarters of an hour past midnight. Even the soldiers knew the urgency of the operation: the evacuation fleet *must* leave by 0130 in order to be clear of the Kaso Straits by dawn.

Jerry Phillips, Sub-Lieutenant of *Jackal*, liked feeling firm ground beneath his feet again, even if it was only the quay of Heraklion harbour. Number One had sent him ashore to hasten the embarkation. For the hundredth time Phillips glanced at his watch: 0115 on this Thursday morning of May 29th. Hell's teeth — only another quarter of an hour to go before the ships were due to leave!

He approached a bandaged face that belonged to an Army Lieutenant leaning against a bollard. The jetty was deserted except for a few silent Army officers.

'What's the delay, chum?' Jerry asked, trying to conceal his anxiety.

'The rearguard's been held up,' the Lieutenant said, fingering his filthy bandage. 'Sorry to keep you like this.'

''S all right, but we're pushed for time. We're supposed to leave in ten minutes.'

The Lieutenant shook his head. 'Not a chance,' he said apologetically. 'You'd better shove off with what you've got. The rearguard's only just disengaged: it will be at least an hour yet.'

Only the whine of *Jackal*'s boiler-room fans disturbed the long silence.

'Don't worry,' Jerry said. 'If we slip now, someone else will take off the rearguard. *Kimberley* and *Imperial* are lying off, waiting to come alongside.'

'Thanks. What sort of a trip have you had?' the Lieutenant asked, as if at a garden party. 'We knew you'd come.'

'Pretty lousy,' Phillips said. 'We were bombed during the dog-watches while passing through Kaso. They threw the lot at us: high-level, dive bombing and torpedo attacks.'

'Any of you hit?'

'*Ajax*, our third cruiser, was near-missed and had to return to Alex. *Imperial* bought a near one, too, but she seemed O.K. after a bit. She's out there now,' Phillips said, nodding towards the darkness. 'The day before, *Barham*, our third battle-wagon, was hit when covering *Abdiel*'s final trip home, so things are normal…'

A megaphone was trained down upon them from *Jackal*'s bridge.

'Stand by to slip,' the First Lieutenant called. 'Inform all troops that *Kimberley* and *Imperial* are coming alongside now to bring off the rearguard. This is the last lift. Speed is vital. I repeat, *speed is vital*.' There was a pause, and then came the final order: 'Let go aft.'

Phillips shook the soldier's hand.

'So long, chum,' he said. 'See you in Alex.'

The soldier smiled ruefully. The wires splashed into the water as Phillips scrambled aboard. The distance opened from the jetty, and, as *Jackal* moved out into the harbour, he watched *Kimberley* and *Imperial* nudging alongside. The time was already ten minutes to two.

Jackal stopped engines when clear of the harbour. It was cold and dark and Phillips could not control the trembling of his limbs as he waited amongst the troops packing the upper deck. When, for Pete's sake, was Force B going to get under way?

He glanced again at his watch: 0245 already, but mercifully the rearguard had arrived: he could hear soldiers clattering up the gangways of *Kimberley* and *Imperial*. Phillips left the iron deck and threaded his way to the bridge. A blue lantern was winking from the jetties.

'*Imperial*'s slipping now, sir,' the Yeoman reported to his Captain, Lieutenant-Commander Jonas. 'Embarkation completed.'

'Too blasted late,' Jonas grumbled. 'What's the time, Sub?'

Phillips glanced at the chart-table clock. Surely his own watch must have raced? His heart sank as he gave his answer: 'Three o'clock, sir.'

Jonas did not reply, his fingers drumming upon the lip of the bridge.

Twenty minutes more of agonising waiting, and then the two destroyers loomed out of the darkness. All eyes were now upon the flagship *Orion*, in which Rear-Admiral Rawlings was flying his flag. A phosphorescent gleam swirled at her stern. Force B was under way.

By 0320, the wind was streaming past Phillips's ears. Force B had worked up to full speed now, with 29 knots showing on the Chernikeefs.

'Thank God,' breathed *Jackal's* Sub as he took over Officer of the Watch from Number One. 'At last everything's going well.'

The First Lieutenant did not reply immediately. He was staring towards the eastern horizon. 'Even if Tedder's promise of aerial support materializes,' he said quietly, 'we are exactly an hour too late. We've evacuated the whole garrison of four thousand troops, but that ain't much help, Jerry, is it, if we're in the middle of the Kaso Straits at dawn?'

At that moment a destroyer's siren suddenly wailed from the darkness ahead: four short blasts.

'God!' Jonas exclaimed. *'Imperial's* out of control…'

Meanwhile, on the south coast, the first stage of the evacuation was proceeding according to plan.

For the first time in weeks Commander Geoffrey Robson was enjoying himself. He was wedged into his corner on *Kandahar's* bridge, the evening sun streaming warmly upon him. *Kandahar* formed part of Force C, a division of four destroyers under Captain Arliss in *Napier*, who, with *Nizam* and *Kelvin*, was steaming north from Alex to make a landfall at midnight off the south coast of Crete. This force had, remarkably, so far suffered scant attention from the Luftwaffe. Robson was chuckling to himself as he listened to the bridge loudspeaker which was relaying from the W/T office the voices of the German pilots squealing in protest to their Control. 'Headache', as the waveband was called, was always monitored by the devoted P.O.Tel., and this morning the German Control had boobed: it had supplied its pilots with the wrong square of their grid. Their aircraft were fruitlessly searching a barren area of sea and were being forced to return through lack of fuel to Scarpanto, their bombs unexploded. *Kandahar*'s bridge personnel were convulsed in merriment.

Dusk fell upon a serene sunset, streaked with pastel green, gold and orange; then night took over, an opaque darkness with, mercifully, no moon. A long, low swell ran beneath the glassy calm: if the weather held, it was going to be a good night for boatwork, but only a gale was needed now and twenty thousand troops would be lost...

At midnight, the division reduced speed and disposed in line abreast. At twenty minutes past midnight, Robson sighted a yellow light blinking from a deeper blackness ahead. At the same instant, *Napier* signalled to stop engines: carrying their way, the destroyers glided in while the soundings decreased rapidly.

'Right on the end of the knob,' Robson muttered. 'There's Sphakia.'

'*Napier*'s got a pretty good pilot, sir,' the First Lieutenant remarked, glancing at *Kandahar*'s Navigating Officer. The officers grinned in the darkness as *Kandahar*'s 'pilot' ground his teeth.

'By the mark five,' the leadsman's subdued hail floated up from the chains.

'Slow astern both,' Robson ordered. 'Away all boats.'

Leading Stoker Stevenson had taken over as Stoker of *Kandahar*'s first motor-cutter. His boat chugged at slow speed towards the white ribbon of surf, two whalers — loaded to the gunwales with provisions — lashed on either side to give added stability. Stevenson felt cold as the night air caught him when he stuck his head above the canopy. Then he sighted the beach: it was barely two hundred yards long, but already he could see lines of troops scuttling like ants across the sand towards the silver necklace of surf.

'Stop, Stokes...' The Coxswain was not using his whistle tonight.

'Slow astern... Stop...'

Stevenson jumped up from his engine and scrambled along the gunwale to help the motor-boat's bowman cast off the whaler's lines. Then he watched the whalers pulling towards the shore under muffled oars, flannel being wrapped around the looms. The boats grounded and the bowmen leapt into the surf.

The shore was a strange sight. From the heights above, little lights winked like glow-worms: either the flash from small-arms or torches signalling that there were plenty more troops to take off. On the beach, the sand crawled with men desperately trying to reach the boats. There seemed to be a cordon flung around one end of the beach and behind this a mass of men seethed. Occasionally an oath echoed across the water, and then the first loads shoved off in the whalers.

'Keep clear of the screw, mates,' the Coxswain whispered hoarsely. 'Don't want to spoil your chances now.'

The whalers were filled to capacity with all types: R.A.F., M.N.B.D.O., and wounded from all regiments. Clinging to the lifelines, men swam alongside the whalers on either side.

'Slow ahead, Stokes.'

Stevenson nursed the revs and gently let in the clutch. The little armada gathered way, five minutes later bumping alongside *Kandahar*. The first fifty-three men scrambled on board.

Stevenson's motorboat carried out nine such ferry services during the next two hours, each time landing precious rations and, on the return trip, bringing off over fifty exhausted soldiers.

When finally at 0300 the last boat had been hoisted, Force C had taken off 700 soldiers and landed rations for 65,000 men. The four destroyers then vanished into the darkness from which they had emerged.

CHAPTER 17

Retimo

'Try again, Mackie.'

Bill Tanner crouched over the Army Captain, who was wrestling with a wireless set. It was growing dark, and despair had begun to overwhelm this miscellaneous band of men who called themselves 'The Marauders'.

'For Pete's sake, stop breathing down my neck, will you?' Mackie retorted, glancing angrily up at Tanner. 'I'm doing my best.'

Bill stood back and stretched himself: he did not care much for this pongo. Mackie seemed to know all the answers but, when it came to the point, was singularly useless. They were all jaded after their day's march, however, which probably accounted for their irritability. All that long Wednesday May 28th, Tanner and his men had been cutting across country, south of the Germans whom they could watch streaming east along the coast road to Retimo. Late that night, hungry and exhausted, Tanner had been forced to call a halt. Though he could see the hills of Retimo and the clusters of white buildings, a ring of firing rattled ahead of them. He could see the flash of enemy mortars now, and the bursts where they exploded amongst the defenders of Retimo. The Germans were encircling their prey, and were between the Marauders and Retimo. Bill could see no way of carrying the message through to Colonel Campbell. Mackie's W/T set seemed the only solution.

The Army Captain wrenched off his headset and flung it down in disgust. 'Can't raise them, Tanner.' He stretched himself and stared antagonistically at the R.N. Sub-Lieutenant. 'Have a go if you like.'

Bill shook his head. 'What do we do now?' he asked, returning the Captain's gaze. He wished the man wouldn't grin like that: his flashy smile was irritating beyond endurance.

'There's only one thing for it,' Mackie said. 'We've got to get through. Follow me and I'll take you through the German lines.'

Bill hesitated. He glanced at his men slowly munching their meagre rations.

'I thought you were an intelligence officer, Mackie, not an infantryman.'

The Army officer bridled. 'We are all trained in field-craft. I could get you through.' He turned his back and took out his binoculars to peer into the gathering darkness. 'Dammit, Tanner, aren't you game?'

Bill did not reply at once. Distrust, that was the trouble. All through last night and this terrible day, there had been something about this soldier he didn't like. He'd evaded many of Bill's innocent enquiries and he'd been distinctly cool towards this enterprise. Bill usually got on well with pongos, but he had no confidence in this chap.

'Don't be stupid, Mackie,' he said placatingly. 'It's just that I can't see a snowball's chance in hell of our slipping through that lot…'

The whole front ahead of them had erupted into a long burst of firing, red flashes stabbing the gloom. In the lull, Bill heard grunts of assent from the eight men crouching around him.

'Halt!' one of them growled suddenly. 'Who goes there?'

The unit froze in the darkness as the scrub to their right rustled from several footsteps. Bill heard the click of safety catches being slipped off.

'Halt or I fire,' the man repeated.

Silence. A long silence in which Bill could hear only his breathing. Then, from out of the darkness, an Australian voice drawled:

'Friend, you Pommie baskets. Put away those shooting irons.'

'Advance and be recognised.'

A dark, dishevelled figure loomed from the scrub, hands above his head. 'Blimey, mate,' the Australian rasped. 'Thought we'd had it.'

Another man followed and a minute later the strangers had joined the bewildered band. They flopped to the ground and began munching their action rations. The Marauders regarded the newcomers with amused interest: the Australians seemed from another world.

'You cut off?' Stoker Petty Officer Renton, one of the Marauders asked, proffering his water-bottle.

'Yep,' the lanky Australian gulped. 'We've been told to make our way across the mountains if we're separated. Glad we bumped into you lot.'

The wide grin gleamed in the darkness. The two Australians pushed back their tin hats as they stretched their legs.

'It's been quite a fight, mates,' the tubby Australian growled. 'Jerry's thrown in everything he has, but the beggars are licked on the ground. The battle's swung backwards and forwards for a week, ever since the first paratroops landed on the twentieth.'

'We've got 'em taped here,' the tall Australian added. 'It makes us sick to have to quit.'

'Us too,' Renton added, turning on his elbow. 'But you can't do much if the Canea front has collapsed. Even Freyberg is moving south, they say.'

'That settles it then, cobbers. We've been given the chance to pack it in, but we'd like to make a break for it.'

The two Australians fell silent. They had escaped southwards rather than surrender.

'Can we get through?' Bill Tanner asked the taller of the two. 'We're trying to pass a message to Colonel Campbell.'

'Not a chance, cobber. Anyway the Colonel now knows about the evacuation. Lieutenant Haig was told to make for Sphakia: he's the Pommie who brings the stores by sea.'

'What will Campbell do?'

'He'll try to break out tonight and make for Sphakia.' The Australian scratched himself methodically. 'How long will the Navy wait, cobber?'

Bill felt all eyes upon him; he could hear the men's breathing as they awaited his answer.

'As long as it can remain afloat, Digger.'

A growl from the circle of men was interrupted by a string of Verey lights bursting to the northward of them, and the crackle of machine-gun fire.

'Let's get going for Sphakia,' said Bill quietly, looking at Mackie. 'We shan't be able to move much during daylight tomorrow. Captain Mackie's the only one amongst us with a map, so he and I will lead the way.'

The paper rustled as Mackie unfolded his pocket map and spread it out before them. 'Got it off a dead Hun,' he muttered. 'Now, if we march, let's see... yes, west-south-west, we should hit the Sphakia road.'

'Don't want to be caught behind the German lines, sir,' Bill said tactfully. 'Wouldn't it be better to march south-west?'

Then, as Mackie closed the map, Bill added quickly, 'Better to hit the coast road east of Sphakia and be faced with a few miles' tramp down the coast, than be put in the bag...'

'And miss the ships?' Mackie asked, an unpleasant edge to his voice. 'And be certain of capture?' He drew Bill to one side and spoke harshly in the shadows: 'Who's the senior officer here, Tanner, you or me?'

Bill felt the man's determination, and he bowed to Mackie's insistence. The Army Captain would lead the way and Bill would bring up the rear.

'We'll march till dawn,' Mackie said, smiling in the darkness. 'Then we'll lie up for an hour or so to gain our bearings. I'll try to contact our side on the radio when we get a bit nearer.'

Bill held out his hand. 'Sorry to be such an idiot,' he apologised. 'Press on and I'll carry your W/T set for an hour or two.' He reached out to ease Mackie's burden.

'That's all right,' the Captain replied curtly. 'I've managed it so far. I'll *keep right on to the end of the road.*' His smile flashed, but Bill felt irritated at the man's arrogance. As Mackie moved forwards in the darkness, Tanner tried once again to placate this prickly customer.

'What's the name of your fellow Scot?' he asked innocently. 'The one who's always singing that?'

Mackie hesitated an instant, then murmured over his shoulder, 'Lauder. Sir Harold Lauder.'

Tanner allowed the rest of the Marauders to trudge past him; then he brought up the rear and fell in behind Stoker Petty Officer Renton, who had also dropped back. As this file of men began its long march towards freedom, Bill felt fear striking deep inside him. Lost behind the enemy lines, twenty miles from that south coast and with a mountain ridge to cross; rations running out and no water; exhausted, and, led by someone he neither respected nor understood, it was no wonder that he was anxiously turning over the doubts in his mind. He was beginning to brood over the real meaning of capture, of being locked up for the rest of the war; or of being shot, if they missed the ships that surely must be lying there tomorrow night, the 29th of May.

What bothered him most, however, was his distrust of Mackie. What was there about the man that disturbed him so? Something was not quite right, apart from the mutual antagonism. He seemed insincere, bogus perhaps. But then several men he knew were, in some ways, acting a part…

'Sir,' Renton was whispering over his shoulder. 'Why did Captain Mackie call Harry Lauder *Sir Harold?* The officer's a Scot surely, ain't he, sir?'

Bill did not reply immediately. So, it was not only he who found Mackie a strange character… but discipline had to be upheld or they'd be in an unholy mess.

'I was wondering the same myself, Renton,' Bill said quietly. 'But it's our duty to follow Captain Mackie.'

'Yes, sir,' Renton replied. 'But I thought you'd better know, sir. It seemed queer, like…'

'All right, Renton. Thanks.'

As Tanner trudged in Renton's footsteps, his thoughts whirled in uncertainty. What, in the name of goodness, was he to do? It seemed that the Marauders were tactfully trying to tell him that they preferred to be led by one of their own kind. Yet Bill couldn't override his senior officer, even though Mackie belonged to another service…

Round and round revolved his thoughts as he marched painfully southwards. His boots were losing their soles: blisters burnt on either heel and on the ridge of his right big toe. The pain was numbing his feet now, but every step was taking them nearer the sea; every yard was closer to freedom, each pace further from the trap that was surely ensnaring them.

The hours dragged by, the march across the mountains becoming a nightmare of pain, thirst and hunger. Bill was numb with exhaustion when, in the early hours, he heard an order being passed down the line.

'We'll halt here.'

Tanner scarcely registered Mackie's order, he was so tired.

'Thank the Lord,' Renton muttered as he slowly collapsed to the ground. 'I'm all in.'

Bill staggered on a few paces until he reached Mackie at the head of the column. 'Well done, chum,' he croaked hoarsely. 'We've put some miles behind us.'

Mackie was pointing through the gloom to where a white ribbon wound round the side of the hill they were climbing.

'Here it is,' he said, glancing at his well-thumbed map. 'The track to Asfendhon.'

'Good-o, but where's that?'

'Next stop west is Imvros,' Mackie said.

'But we want to go south...'

Mackie threw down the map.

'God, Tanner, I've had enough. You take over,s then.' He lowered his wireless pack and stretched out on the ground. Within half a minute Bill heard his snores as oblivion overtook him. Already the rest of the little band was asleep, too exhausted even to place sentries.

Spreading his arms beneath his head, Bill gazed up at the stars whilst the fatigue oozed out through his toes. It was nearly five-thirty and first light was already stealing across the eastern shoulder of the hill. He closed his eyes, every muscle of his body aching with tiredness. After ten minutes' restlessness, he could endure no more. He rose without making a sound and tiptoed to explore the road ahead of them.

Around the western shoulder of the hill, the track curled in a hairpin bend, a precipice on its outer edge: he wouldn't care to drive round that. This must be the east-west road across the island: Imvros a few miles west, and the sea only seven miles over those hills to the south, if Mackie was correct. A thrill passed through him, for surely if they could slip through the German lines today, they ought to hit the coast by nightfall. If they didn't collapse from hunger…

He returned silently to his sleeping companions, and lay down again near Mackie. His eyes fell upon the field radio, now lying between Mackie and himself, where it had been dumped so angrily. Perhaps the Australians were within range? It would be grand to listen in to a friendly voice…

He picked up the headset and slipped it over his ears. He tried the switches and the middle one worked the oracle: the operator was talking in plain language and was coming through loud and clear. He was speaking in German.

Bill frowned as he sat upright. Maybe this was an Intelligence frequency? A ruse, maybe? But there was no British intonation in this operator's voice; it seemed gutturally Teutonic. Bill was thankful he'd learnt the lingo at school; he'd spent many holidays with his parents in the Black Forest and could speak the language well. Mackie was still snoring. Bill pressed the earphones hard, and listened, his heart thumping against his ribs.

The operator was losing patience: evidently he was trying to raise his addressee.

'H.Q. calling MECK. Come in, MECK, Come in, Meck. Can you hear me, Meck?'

Bill's thoughts raced. The operator was certainly German; but then who the devil was Meck? The innkeeper who used to accommodate the Tanner family in the Black Forest had a name that sounded the same, but he spelt it *Maeck*. Until the war broke out, he and Bill's father had always exchanged Christmas cards.

'Come in, Me-eck,' the operator was transmitting impatiently. 'What is the position of your force and where is eastern flank of British rearguard?' The restive German voice repeated its enquiry, but Bill flicked off the switch in the middle of the sentence. He took off the earphones, replacing them carefully by the set. He gazed upon the Army Captain lying turned towards him. He was still snoring and out to the wide. Bill lay on his back, his thoughts in a turmoil.

MACKIE; ME-ECK; MAECK. Preposterous... and yet?

Bill had been surprised when first he'd met Mackie down in the Canea area. The Army officer had been, so Bill thought, in a bit of a flap. The bombs were raining down upon the town, so who could blame the chap for shouting so loudly, for exhorting the civilians to flee? But, thinking back on it now, Mackie could have been whipping up terror, sowing panic and confusion in order to drive the refugees on to the roads. Madoc had remarked that a 'fifth column' was operating, was deliberately blocking the roads...

Bill leant on his elbow to take a hard look at the man. On careful scrutiny, even though his eyes were closed in sleep, Mackie's was a square face... yes, most definitely Teutonic. If he was a German agent, why had he left his set tuned into the German frequency? A careless slip? Or had he collapsed with anger and exhaustion, and fallen asleep before he could take precautions?

If he *was* an agent, what was he playing at? If Mackie had refused to join the Retimo excursion (Bill had been very insistent in the presence of another Army officer), surely everyone would have been suspicious? It was beginning to add up… Mackie (or Maeck), once he was committed, could be trying to make the best of a bad job: why else should he want to head west instead of south? Why else would hes insist upon leading the Marauders? Why spend so much time transmitting in solitude, particularly after last evening's halt to the south of Retimo? He could be passing on the information the Germans so urgently needed.

Bill subsided silently to the ground and stretched himself out. He must assume the worst, but before pouncing, he must somehow have undeniable confirmation of his doubts. He must discreetly warn Renton of his fears, but — whatever happened — he must not betray his suspicions to Mackie.

As he stared through the grey twilight of dawn, he began to feel the cold. Better get moving again; it would take hours to reach the coast through this country. Then he heard Mackie stirring. Through half-closed lids, Bill watched the Army Captain climb silently to his feet; he paused, peering long at Bill, then picked up the set and glided noiselessly towards the road.

Bill allowed him a few minutes, then roused the Marauders. As they buckled to, he took the opportunity of whispering his doubts to Renton.

'Don't tell the others yet.'

'Aye, aye, sir.'

'And keep close to him.'

'Right, sir,' Renton growled, tapping the pistol at his side. 'I'll be just behind him.'

CHAPTER 18

Small Mistakes…

Rear-Admiral Rawlinsgs was snoozing in the corner of *Orion*'s bridge when he heard four short blasts wailing fine on the starboard bow from a destroyer's siren: '*I am out of control. Keep out of my way; I cannot keep out of yours.*' Then, as he rose to his feet, the dim shape of a destroyer loomed down upon them from out of the darkness.

'Hard-a-port!'

Captain Back had leapt for the voicepipe and, at 29 knots, the cruiser swung savagely, heeling steeply to starboard as she wheeled.

Rawlings held his breath. *Imperial* lunged by, her bow wave gleaming in the darkness, her stern galloping rapidly towards *Orion*'s as the ships swung together.

'Hard-a-starboard!'

Back was reversing the wheel to avoid collision: a terrible disaster, if these two ships struck at this relative speed of nearly fifty knots. Their sterns were less than ten yards apart…

My rudder, Imperial's lantern winked as she flashed by.

'Well done,' Rawlings murmured to his Flag Captain, as the ships missed with only feet to spare. 'What the devil's happened to her?'

Before Back could reply, *Imperial* lunged towards *Dido* and, once again, collision seemed imminent. Rawlings dared not speak, nothing but the howl of the wind in the rigging disturbing those agonising seconds. *Dido* was hauling out of line to port… and then *Imperial* vanished astern, careering madly into the night.

'Phew!' Rawlings muttered. 'Flags, reduce the speed of the fleet to fifteen knots. We mustn't lose her.'

As the howl of the rigging decreased to a gentle thrumming, a blue light winked from the darkness astern.

'*From* Imperial *to Admiral, Force "B",*' the Yeoman shouted from the wings. '*Regret steering defective. Endeavouring to remedy fault.*'

'The result of yesterday's near-miss, sir, I expect.' Back was speaking from the compass platform.

'Would have to happen now,' Rawlings grumbled. 'We can't afford to lose a second.' He turned towards the Yeoman. 'Keep her in sight for as long as you can. We *mustn't* lose her now.'

As they waited upon *Orion*'s bridge, each man knew the decision their Admiral was pondering. As usual the Stukas would be waiting in the Kaso Straits. Dare Rawlings jeopardize his whole force for one laggard?

The alternative was to abandon *Imperial* to her fate. That meant the certain loss of the destroyer and the rearguard troops with which she bulged. This was the only sensible decision, yet Rawlings knew he could not so betray those gallant men. He slapped his thigh.

'Yeoman,' he snapped. 'Make the following signal to *Hotspur*: *Take off crew and sink Imperial.*' Then he added: '*Make for Alex.*'

The signal lantern clattered again, and then, as the executive signal was finally passed, a two-funnelled destroyer swung away to port and vanished into the darkness astern.

Hotspur was on her own now. The silence on *Orion*'s bridge indicated only too clearly the thoughts in all men's minds: *Hotspur*'s chances were nil.

Lieutenant Hugh Hodgkinson was First Lieutenant of *Hotspur*. He stood in the starboard wings of his beloved ship, watching the preparations he had instituted: in the darkness he could barely distinguish the blurred figures scrambling along the upper deck as they hurried about their business of providing grapnels, heaving lines and Coston line-throwing guns. Only the scraping of wires along the steel decks betrayed that *Hotspur* was ready to edge alongside the stopped and crippled *Imperial*.

The quarter-deck phone blared behind him: 'All ready on the quarter-deck, sir.'

Hodgkinson turned to his Captain. 'Ready to go alongside, sir.'

'Thank you, Number One. Stand by your Coston gun.' Lieutenant-Commander Brown, as imperturbable as ever, stood on the bridge seat: from here he could judge the distances better as *Imperial* drifted down upon *Hotspur*. A gentle crunch, and the two ships rolled together in the swell. The wires went across, the gangways were swung over, and the transfer began.

Hotspur's First Lieutenant watched impatiently as the first troops began jumping across the guard rails. *Imperial* had some six hundred men to transfer, and every ten minutes widened the gap from Force B by five miles. The soldiers were still drowsy from the deep sleep into which they had dropped as soon as they had boarded *Imperial*. They seemed not to realise the urgency… Hodgkinson picked up his megaphone.

At long last, the figure of *Imperial*'s Captain, Lieutenant-Commander Kitcat, finally followed his First Lieutenant across the plank. The destroyer was an empty hulk.

'Let go aft… let go for'd.'

Hodgkinson watched the sleek destroyer slide ahead as *Hotspur* went astern. Then, at a range of a thousand yards, *Hotspur* steamed slowly past.

'Fire one torpedo, starboard!'

A shining fish leapt from *Hotspur*'s tubes, and, aeons later, *Imperial* was struck amidships. A plume of water, and that beautiful, recently re-fitted destroyer slowly keeled over, but it took another torpedo to despatch her finally beneath the black waters.

Imperial's Captain saluted from *Hotspur*'s bridge. His men stood silently along *Hotspur*'s guardrails: they had not even had time to bring their personal belongings with them. Hodgkinson heard a terrible cry floating across the water: someone had been left behind.

Hours later, a demented Scottish soldier had unburdened himself to one of *Hotspur*'s Petty Officers.

'I just couldn't wake 'em. Two of 'em, there were: Aussies, just drunk as owls. I found 'em down a ladder in a wee space, after we got tae sea. "Just in time, Jock," said one of 'em, "for a drop o' home brew." I didn'a take much meself: I was too tired and I was soon asleep. Then out of my dreams came the yell. "Get away! Get away! Abandon ship! All men wake up…" And there they were, the two Aussies.

'I tried tae pull one up the ladder but he was too heavy, and then the shout came down tae me, "Hurry up. Anyone still below? We're leaving. The gangways are being pulled in."

'I ran on deck, just in time to board this ship. It was terrible to leave 'em there, but what could I do? No one on board listened to me. Och, man, I feel I've killed two men.'

'Port fifteen. Half-ahead both.'

With nine hundred men on board, Lieutenant-Commander Brown was chary of heeling his ship: with this extra weight crowding every inch of space on *Hotspur*'s upper deck, she could so easily capsize. Then, shortly after five o'clock, with first light streaking the eastern horizon, *Hotspur* worked up to full speed.

On the bridge the Captain, Hodgkinson and the Navigating Officer quietly discussed the position. All knew how slim were the chances for a lone destroyer: *Diamond* and *Wryneck* had been sunk in similar circumstances during the Greek evacuation only a month before.

The odds against reaching Alex direct with his cargo aboard were too slight for serious consideration. If, therefore, *Hotspur* succeeded in clearing Kaso, she would alter course to the westward and hug the coast of Crete before turning south for Alex. This might dilute the Stuka attacks by throwing them off the track; if the ship was hit, there might be a chance of beaching her; the human cargo would perhaps have a chance of reaching the shore. So it was decided, and in that silent hour before dawn, Hodgkinson left the bridge to deal with the problems facing him.

He went below, picking his way through the mess decks, which were packed with exhausted and bewildered troops. Crammed like sardines, they slept where they stood, their oblivion obliterating the fear of imminent death. Astonished by their calm acceptance of their fate, he returned to the upper deck.

Every square inch was crowded with men: sailors, soldiers, perfectly disciplined, ready for the ordeal ahead. Hugh Hodgkinson's heart sank as he watched them: the carnage would be indescribable should *Hotspur* be hit. Then, shortly before first light, the rattlers summoned them to action stations. His heart sank. He braced his shoulders and moved with the flood to inspect the mountings.

Silently the men were 'turning to', donning their asbestos anti-flash hoods, pulling on their long white gloves. Then, their tin hats atop the lot, they brought up every H.A. shell they could stack around the 4.7s and every case of ammunition they could muster for the eight 'point-fives'. The soldiers emerged from the mess decks to mount every conceivable gun upon the upper deck: Brens on H.A. tripods, Tommy-guns, anti-tank guns, and even captured automatic weapons. These were seasoned troops. They went about their preparations silently, professionally, realising the odds against them. Hodgkinson climbed slowly back to the bridge, knowing that the men were probably safer on the upper deck instead of being cooped below in the packed mess decks.

All was silent on the compass platform. Brown was leaning across the for'd screen, searching the north-east corner of Crete through his binoculars.

'We'll pass inside that islet, Pilot,' he said, turning to his Navigating Officer. 'It'll cut the corner a bit more.'

The First Lieutenant picked up his binoculars through force of habit and joined the officers peering into the gloom. Scarpanto airfield must be stirring to life at this minute: the Stukas would be checking their routines, testing their engines and warming up, the roar shattering the dawn; their bombs would already be armed and stowed in their racks... and here, out in the loneliness of another sunrise, their adversary was waiting, ready in all respects for battle as she scythed through the tranquil sea.

Hotspur had one chance: the R.A.F. had promised fighter support at 0530 — through no fault of theirs, the first such support they had been able to provide during the Crete campaign. A couple of Hurricanes overhead now would give *Hotspur* that precious cover she needed to elude her ruthless enemies.

Half-past five came and went; twilight merged into dawn. Hodgkinson's eyes ached with straining at the lightening horizon, but still no sign of friendly fighters. In half an hour it would be daylight, and then the Stukas would pounce. Despairingly he swept the horizon for the last time…

At first he did not register the faint blur in his circle of vision as he swept his binoculars across the horizon. His heart missed a beat, as he cut back to confirm that it could have been only his imagination. He stiffened as several grey shapes bore down upon *Hotspur* from out of the gloom. He held his breath. This was the end: the Italian fleet was waiting for them. *Hotspur* had steamed straight into the trap. He searched again, and then, suddenly, the leading ship's silhouette became more defined. She was a single-funnelled cruiser, with a junction at the base of her funnel. He'd recognise her anywhere. He could not conceal his emotion:

'It's *Orion*!' he yelled. 'My God, they've come back for us!'

The bridge sprang into life. Rawlings had turned back for them. *Good old Rawlings,* Hodgkinson thought. What a splendid man! Here he was to save them, just as he'd taken his battle squadron through Kithera to stand by King.

An Aldis was blinking from *Orion*'s bridge.

'Take station on the starboard wing of the screen, sir,' the Yeoman reported, unable to control the quaver in his voice.

'Port fifteen…'

Hotspur swung towards *Orion* as the squadron turned back to the southward. The Force was in the middle of the Kaso Strait, and in a few minutes *Hotspur* would be beneath the shelter of its A.A. umbrella.

The First Lieutenant glanced at the chart-table clock as the sun peeped above the horizon: six o'clock. They'd only just made it.

'Red warning, sir!' the Yeoman shouted from the wings.

A red flag was streaming from *Orion*'s yardarm, and answering pendants were fluttering upwards in all the ships.

From out of the dawn six Stukas hung, waiting for their prey, like vultures before a feast. The leader suddenly dipped, then down he plummeted, straight for the over-loaded destroyer still desperately clawing towards the shelter of the screen...

At 0624, Midshipman (A) Brander was manning a Bren on the after-control of the destroyer *Hereward*. When finally he had boarded her, on her second trip into Heraklion, he had been disappointed at not being transferred to *Dido*, for he would have liked to share this ordeal with Alec Wright: in spite of their disparity in age, they had learnt to respect each other. Now, on the port wing of the destroyer screen, *Hereward*, loaded to the gunwales with troops, was preparing to repel her foes.

Brander squinted beneath his bushy eyebrows at *Hotspur* who was taking station under *Dido*'s umbrella; twisting and turning with supreme skill, she had evaded the six Stukas who had tried to sink her before she gained safety.

'Alarm starboard... out of the sun!'

The warning was shouted by Captain Coates to his detachment of Royal Marines who had set up a veritable battery of Brens and rifles across the mounting of the after torpedo-tubes. At that instant, the first of the string of Stukas hurtled down upon them.

Brander heard the cacophony of guns blazing all around him. He was inured to action now, insensible to the fiendish din. All he craved was sleep, and Alex was a long way off.

He squeezed the trigger of his Bren, whilst a young Ordinary Seaman fed him with magazines. *Hereward* swung hard over when the 87s dived, the Captain forcing the pilots to dive steeper and steeper. The first two lost their nerve and let go their single thousand-pounders well above a thousand feet.

Then Brander noticed a third Stuka flashing across his sights… the gun juddered against his shoulder as he followed her all the way in. Down she screamed, growing larger at every second, her crooked black wings hideous and grotesque. She was immediately above now, at mast-head height; as she pulled out he heard her flaps shuddering and then, from her belly, there toppled not one huge egg, but five smaller bombs, twisting, plummeting, straight towards him. There was a blinding flash, a sickening jolt. Slowly *Hereward's* foremost funnel buckled drunkenly, with a tearing scrunch of metal, over the starboard side. A roar of steam, and clouds of vapour and black smoke streamed aft, choking all men abaft the funnel. *Hereward* lost way and, as the smoke cleared, Brander glimpsed *Dido's* stern growing smaller at every second.

At first, Brander felt no fear. The knowledge that *Hereward* was now left alone to her fate struck him as inevitable: he did not blame the squadron that still steamed at thirty knots away to the southward. Rawlings had no choice. His force was still in the Kaso Straits and the Stukas were merely returning to Scarpanto to bomb-up again before returning for further attacks.

It was the feeling of isolation that caused the terror. Out here, when the Stukas eventually hurtled downwards for the kill, when finally *Hereward* was to be sunk, Brander knew there could be no survivors. Those who managed to swim clear would be machine-gunned in the water. The coast of Crete seemed so close — yet, in reality, it was so far away. Brander surreptitiously puffed at his Mae West until it was fully inflated.

The guns blazed; the Stukas dived; the fountains of water from the near-misses drenched the men on *Hereward*'s upper deck. Brander ducked unashamedly from the bomb-splashes. Then suddenly he noticed that the coast of Crete seemed closer than when he had last looked: a ribbon of surf could already be seen, and the cliffs could now be distinguished. Lieutenant Munn, *Hereward*'s Captain, was edging cable by cable towards the coast where perhaps he could beach his crippled ship...

'Pretty grim, chum.' It was Coates, the Royal Marine Captain, who had come up from the tubes, the better to direct the fire of his detachment. Brander was taking a last look at the cruisers, now hull-down, a black cloud of aircraft swarming above them.

'Yep. D'you reckon we can swim for it from here, soldier?' Brandy asked, nodding at the coast ahead. He tried to conceal the terror in his voice.

The Captain of Marines did not reply.

At that moment *Hereward* was struck twice. Clouds of steam swirled across the upper deck, then within minutes she was gone. It all happened so quickly that Brander knew only that he was struggling in the sea, with men drowning around him. He tried to control the panic that swept over him. He knew that he was not the only man to be swimming for his life twice in one week; this thought steadied him until, his head bobbing above the swell, he sighted a beach, white with surf and barely a mile distant. He struck out frenziedly towards it, terror driving him onwards...

Brander never knew how long he was in the water. The coast came no closer, and soon he could swim no more. His Mae West supported him, but he was numb with exhaustion.

As despair swamped him, he heard men shouting ahead. Tears welled into his eyes as several motorboats chugged amongst the survivors. Encouraging cries in Italian forced him to control himself, and then, covered in oil, he was hauled to safety.

An hour later he, and those of *Hereward* who had survived, were landed at a fishing village a mile down the coast. The Italians treated them well. The villagers cleaned up the survivors and, after drying their clothes on the sun-baked rocks, the prisoners were dressed and fed. By evening the shock of the day's events gradually wore off. It was not until Brander, Coates and a dozen others were bundled into a dilapidated truck that Brandy realised with growing horror that he was a prisoner of war. He and many others from *Hereward* were miraculously alive: that was small comfort, for spending the rest of this war in a P.O.W. cage was not much of an alternative.

Brander sat dejectedly by the tailboard. As the truck bumped its way along the appalling track, the shadows streamed out directly behind them, throwing dancing patterns on the dusty road. They were driving west, away from those terrible Kaso Straits.

CHAPTER 19

… Cause Major Disasters

'Hell's bells!' Lieutenant Philip Cole ejaculated as he tumbled from his bunk in the darkness. 'We've been hit!'

A broad-shouldered, tough individual, he was not usually upset by alarms or excursions, but he was irritated by this temporary appointment to *Orion*. He'd just had his ship sunk under him and was longing for his next destroyer. He was no 'big ship' man, but at least he was at sea.

He grabbed his reefer from the foot of his bunk and lunged for the light switch. As he snatched his cap, the lights flickered, went out for a second, then came on again. He stabbed his feet into his shoes and flung back the curtain of the cabin, which was situated deep in the bowels of *Orion*. Still half asleep, he glanced at the clock in the after-cabin flat as he rushed along the passage to the ladder. ''Struth,' he muttered. 'Seven-thirty already.'

He reached the upper deck as the propellers stopped. He stood for a moment, dazzled by the sun; then hhe pulled himself together. Stumbling forward, he craned his neck to watch the clusters of bombers circling above. Stukas, 88s, ME 110s and 109s: the whole circus was there. He whistled, ducking from 'X' gun's blast as he scrambled along the upper deck.

'What's up, Sub?' he asked a pale-faced youth hurrying past him.

'Near miss, sir, alongside the engine room. The fo'c'sle's ablaze.'

On his way up to the bridge Philip Cole paused on the flag deck. Bunting was streaming from the yardarms as the signalmen scuttled to and fro. 'Speed of the fleet, 21 knots,' he muttered, decoding the signal. 'Damn! Just after Decoy's near miss, too, when we all had to reduce to 25 knots for her.' He glanced over the starboard quarter: the haze of Crete was still in sight and now their speed was being further reduced. There were hours of bombing yet to be endured before Force B could draw out of range of the Stukas. 21 knots: what a tragedy!

Cole stepped stealthily onto the port wing of the bridge. He had no duties to perform as yet, and from here he could watch events.

Commander C. Wynne was on the compass platform, and Rear-Admiral Rawlings was slumped into the port corner of the bridge. Cole could hear Wynne's voice crackling out orders to the fire parties for'd.

'Where's the Captain?' Cole asked a lookout.

'He was hit by an explosive bullet, sir,' the Able Seaman replied. 'He's hurt bad, sir. I carried him down to the sick bay. Commander Wynne's taken over the ship.'

Philip Cole felt shocked. Captain Back was an efficient and gallant Commanding Officer who had seen much action.

Then he heard raised voices from the Compass Platform.

'Where *are* those R.A.F. fighters?' Rawlings snapped impatiently, eyes roving the skies. 'Unless they get here, we're in for it, at this speed.'

Then, strangely, there was a lull: the bombers thinned out. Men snatched bites of food and gulped cups of tea while the gun barrels cooled. Spirits rose: perhaps the Luftwaffe had thrown in its hand? At that moment too, the fire for'd came under control.

As the call for the forenoon watch died away on the Tannoy, the alarm rattlers sounded again. Away to the east, wave upon wave of aircraft were approaching from Scarpanto. The enemy had evidently guessed the predicament in which Force B found itself; the Luftwaffe was now mustering every available aircraft for the *coup de grâce*. At three thousand feet, the armada split into groups, each concentrating upon its own target.

Every one of *Orion*'s 18 guns, both official and unofficial (the soldiers had mounted every conceivable automatic weapon upon the upper deck) suddenly opened up. Twelve Stukas peeled off from out of the sun, but the cruiser, weaving and listing, evaded the first attack. Cole breathed a sigh of relief and glanced to starboard at their consort.

Dido was a splendid sight. With all her turrets blazing, she was throwing herself about so effectively that eight Stukas had already missed wide of the mark. But a ninth was plummeting downwards and, at this instant, seemed inside *Dido*'s swing. Released at mast-head height, its bomb was plunging straight for the cruiser's vitals.

Captain McCall was a large man: he regretted his size as, standing squarely on *Dido*'s bridge, he conned her with uncanny skill to avoid yet another attack. This ninth bomber, the last one of the group, had him taped. He knew it, and he realised he could now do nothing about it, however accurately his guns continued to fire. The crooked-winged monster was now vertically above him and only *Dido*'s machine guns could reach it. The Stukas had dived at three-second intervals and this last of them had won...

He heard the Stuka's flaps shuddering above his masthead. Then he lost sight of it as his eyes riveted upon the thousand-pound bomb now toppling down upon him. A great black egg, arcing towards him…

'It's going to hit me in spite of my full rudder,' he muttered. 'It'll land right on top of me!'

He gripped the compass and squarely stood his ground, following the bomb all the way down. Then he began to feel it would miss the bridge; with luck it might even clear the ship. He ducked behind the splinter screen as it plunged from sight a few yards ahead of him. The ship shuddered, then trembled throughout her length.

He poked up his head and looked over the bridge screen. To his amazement, only one gun of 'B' turret remained amidst the tangled wreckage: its barrel was bent double. Yellow flames were licking round the gun deck twenty yards from him, but 'B' turret had vanished. Sickened by the carnage and choked by the fumes, he turned to face the next wave already hurtling downwards…

A surge of pride swept through him as he heard the rest of the armament blazing away, unaffected by the loss of 'B' turret. His heart ached, dreading the report on the casualties that the troops 'tween decks must have suffered. Yet the destruction could have been worse: if the bomb had not exploded on 'B' turret, it could well have burst in the packed mess decks; or in the magazine…

Alec Wright, Petty Officer Telegraphist, stood in *Dido*'s mess deck. For hours, it seemed, he had been standing there, looking upwards at the deck-head, waiting for the final stroke. All round him crouched, stood and lay hundreds of soldiers, silent, waiting, dreading the blow that must surely fall. These troops had got guts. *It's much worse just waiting for your lot without being able to hit back,* Alec thought. *Amazing what trust these soldiers have in us.* Worried the troops might be, but they didn't show it as they stood there silently waiting. They deserved medals, these lads who'd been fighting for ten days already — medals as big as bunker plates.

The bedlam down in the packed and stuffy mess decks was hellish. Above him thundered 'B' turret; Wright was almost swung off his feet as the cruiser heeled for the hundredth time under the skilful hands of their Captain.

Then there was a whoosh like a passing tube train; an ear-splitting crack that slapped his eardrums, and then a hideous explosion. *This, chum, is your lot,* flashed through his mind as the lights went out. *The flames next, and you'll be fried alive with the rest of these sardines...*

There was a long, terrible silence, and then, up for'd, he heard a man weeping softly. Then another sound, weird and strange: a dreadful clang, and then a *bonketty-bonk* sound, as if a bell were being rung.

At his feet at the bottom of the ladder landed the ship's enormous silver bell.

There was a momentary lull, and in the silence the Able Seaman next to him suddenly shouted at the top of his voice: 'EIGHT o'clock, sir — and ALL'S WELL...'

A cheer burst out, and laughter, and men's chi-akking voices as they buckled to, tending their wounded and dying comrades. Wright could do no more. He slid through the screen door to the upper deck. He wanted solitude: the courage of the Able Seaman had moved him, and he wanted to think things out.

The wind swept through his hair as he gazed out across the guard-rails. *Dido* still trembled from her guns, and she was still afloat. Soldiers had formed human chains and were feeding ammunition to the guns. What a spirit this ship had: there was no price on it. He wandered up towards 'B' gun, choking from the smoke, to see if he could do anything.

He helped to fight the fire and then he moved aft between the funnels. So far 60 dead had been counted: 30 soldiers and 30 seamen. The toll, he supposed, could have been much worse. He stood aft, between the funnels, away from the blast of the guns. He did not know how long he remained there, shocked by the appalling events. Only a week ago *Southampton* and *Fiji* had been sent to the bottom and they were efficient fighting ships. *Dido* had 1,500 exhausted soldiers on board and their presence inevitably affected efficiency. It was barely nine o'clock, and the battle hardly yet joined. He glanced to port, where *Orion* was fighting her way southwards.

A single 87 was diving upon her, a pilot of suicidal courage at the Stuka's control. Entirely on its own, the Stuka swooped on downwards, until surely it must dive straight into *Orion*'s fo'c'sle. Down it plummeted, the bomb spilling from the bomber's belly. The 87 plunged into the sea only feet ahead of the cruiser.

Alec Wright heard the cheers suddenly stilled. *Orion*'s 'A' turret had disappeared in a puff of smoke. When the flames had cleared away, the lid of the turret had gone, and both guns stuck, grotesquely twisted, into the air.

After 'A' turret had been hit, *Orion*'s lights went out. Philip Cole was helping to rig emergency lighting when the First Lieutenant passed him in the passage.

'For Pete's sake get rid of the free water in the sick bay. Cole,' he barked as he went by, 'take any men you can lay hands on.'

Choking and coughing through the smoke of the numerous fires, Cole struggled forward to the sick bay, collecting men as he went. He stumbled over the sill of the sick bay door and entered a compartment of indescribable confusion.

'Buckets,' Cole barked. 'Form a chain through the screen door to the upper deck.'

While this squad of helpers organised themselves, Cole stumbled through the two feet of water swilling about his legs. As the ship heeled, a wave of water surged up against the bulkhead. In this large area, all this free surface water could endanger the ship's stability. He groped forwards in the darkness, trying to distinguish the deeper end.

His feet stumbled into something soft. He froze where he was. He stooped down and gingerly felt for the dead man beneath the water.

'Lend me a hand, someone.'

Gently they raised the man's arms. Four gold stripes gleamed in the glimmer of the emergency lighting.

'It's the Captain,' Cole said quietly. 'Take him to the quarter-deck.' Thus Captain Back made the final rounds of his gallant ship.

It took Cole over an hour to bale out the sick bay. He glanced at his watch: 1045. Then, exhausted, he led his men back through the passage towards the upper deck. As he felt his way aft, an explosion rent the air about his head. A gout of flame and smoke spurted from somewhere for'd. He rushed through the screen door and gained the upper deck to discover what had happened.

The stricken ship had already begun to list, and in that moment Philip Cole knew terror. As he checked his Mae West, he learnt from one of the gun's crews that a dozen fresh 87s had dived upon *Orion* from aft. A bomb had gone through the bridge, down through the lower conning tower and into the bowels of the ship. The seaman was white-faced and did not know where the bomb had finally exploded.

Hesitating a moment, Cole watched the ships swinging past as *Orion* circled out of control and barely under way. Her steering had obviously gone; with a heavy list, she seemed to be turning completely round until she was heading back towards Scarpanto. He took a deep breath and forced himself back into the inferno 'tween decks.

It was the smoke swirling past him that gave him his sense of direction. Fighting his way through the filth and the fumes, he finally reached the for'd mess decks. Stretcher parties were already gathered there; he could see the surgeon being led down into the stokers' mess deck below. Cole hurried after him, dread swamping him at the carnage his eyes must endure...

There was complete silence down below, except for the whirring of the fire pumps. Lighting was already being rigged, and in its pale glimmer he saw hundreds of men staring at him. Their eyes were open and they were looking upwards, surprise on their faces. There was no mark upon them, for blast had done its work. All the men were dead.

In the shocked silence, Cole felt the surgeon gripping his elbow to lead him away. 'There's nothing we can do,' he said. 'Better close the hatch.'

Cole slowly regained the mess decks. There he helped to fight the fires raging next to the 6-inch and H.A. magazines. The heat became intense, and, when finally the flames were subdued, he picked his way aft until he reached the upper deck. He remained there awhile, drinking in the fresh air and discovering what had happened.

Orion was fighting for her life. Mercifully there had been no more Stuka attacks. Force B had closed around its flagship, protecting her as best it could. Thousands of men watched in suspense while she struggled to survive. Great gouts of yellow and black smoke guffed from her damaged boiler rooms, for sea water had percolated into the oil fuel tanks. She listed heavily to port, yet her remaining guns still fired while she gradually regained control. Sometimes making eleven knots, at others fifteen, her Chief valiantly and miraculously nursed his turbines and kept the power going, though his three Engineer Officers had been killed. Weaving wildly on either side of her course, she was steering in hand.

Rear-Admiral Rawlings, though wounded, had taken charge in the tiller-flat. They rigged tackles and sweated it out, hauling on the yokes of the rudder to obey the wheel orders that were passed by word of mouth from Commander Wynne, who was still conning her from the wreckage of the bridge.

At noon a cheer echoed across the blue waters. Rear-Admiral Boyd had dispatched his only two Fulmars from Alex to arrive over the Force at twelve o'clock. They arrived on the stroke, with orders to ditch alongside when their fuel ran out.

So when, at 1300 and 1330, further high-level attacks developed, the ships for the first time watched, in admiration and relief, the fighters scattering their enemy. Two against dozens, but the effect on morale was miraculous — and the bombs went wide. The final attack came at three o'clock, but by now the Luftwaffe was at extreme range and the ships were under the R.A.F. umbrella.

It was dusk when the ships of Force B limped into Alexandria. To welcome them, standing alone on the Mole, stood their Commander-in-Chief. As the bugles sounded and the bosun's calls shrilled, he slowly returned their salutes. He could barely distinguish his ships, for his eyes were blinded by unseen tears.

CHAPTER 20

In the Balance — The Second Night

After inspecting *Orion* and her men, Admiral Cunningham returned at once to his War Room. He had been shocked at the damage she had sustained, but, by God, he was proud of her. With only ten tons of fuel remaining, and only two rounds of 6-inch H.E. ammunition left, she had been a terrible sight as she slid slowly past him. The Squadron's entry into Alexandria had been a moving spectacle: the guns of the fore-turrets askew, barrels broken off, twisted and sticking grotesquely upwards; the ships' upper decks swarming with exhausted troops, the buckled plating gashed with splinter holes. Never had he felt so proud.

As Admiral Cunningham listened to his staff officers in the War Room, his worst fears were quickly realised. Out of 4,000 men who had been plucked so successfully from Heraklion, 800 had been killed on passage, wounded or captured. Even without the naval losses, was this evacuation of the soldiers justified, with these appalling losses?

In 24 hours, three cruisers (if he included *Ajax*) had been so badly damaged that they would be out of the war for months; two destroyers had been sunk and another damaged, out of a force of nine ships; and the ships' companies were out on their feet. Dare he continue the evacuation?

The Commander-in-Chief felt anxious, too, for Force D now on passage to Sphakia. Rear-Admiral King was to take off 6,000 men in his ships, the *Glengyle*, an assault ship with her own landing craft, being in the squadron. King had with him the cruisers *Phoebe,* his flagship, and *Perth; Glengyle;* the A.A. cruisers *Calcutta* and *Coventry,* and the destroyers *Jervis, Janus* and *Hasty.* The force would be reaching Sphakia in a few hours' time: was the risk justified if the casualties were to be similar to those suffered by the squadron which had just returned from Heraklion?

Clearly the Commander-in-Chief must consult Admiralty and General Wavell before such a momentous decision could be taken. Accordingly, he immediately dispatched a signal to Their Lordships asking whether he was justified in accepting the anticipated scale of loss and damage to the remnants of his Mediterranean Fleet. He stated also that he was ready and willing to continue the evacuation as long as any ship of his remained afloat, for he realised that it was against all tradition to leave troops deliberately in enemy hands.

As he looked up from drafting the vital signal, he turned to Commodore John H Edelsten, his Chief of Staff, and looked him squarely in the face:

'It takes the Navy three years to build a new ship, John,' he said slowly. 'It will take three hundred to build a new tradition. The evacuation will continue.'

Cunningham soon received Wavell's personal reply: *Glengyle* and the cruisers should not be risked further, but the destroyers should continue the evacuation. Later in the evening, Admiralty replied also, ordering *Glengyle to* turn back and the remainder of the force to carry on.

It was by now too late to recall *Glengyle,* so Cunningham immediately dispatched the destroyers *Jaguar, Defender,* and the Captain (D), Captain Waller, R.A.N., in *Stuart, to* act as additional support for King's force.

This night of Thursday 29th/30th May was to have been the last lift, but, acting on information given by survivors taken off by Captain Arliss's destroyers yesterday, Cunningham decided to risk one more embarkation from Sphakia. Tomorrow, on the night of Friday 30th/31st, Arliss and his destroyers would make the final lift.

Another of the Admiral's problems was how to evacuate the Retimo garrison when he did not know from which beach to embark them. He had organised ships to take them off from Plaka Bay, but he had no means of knowing whether Campbell had received the message to march south. Wavell stated that they had no supplies, so, in case they could reach Plaka, 1,200 rations were dropped there by the R.A.F. Finally it was agreed to abandon the Plaka plans and to send ships to Sphakia only.

Cunningham could do no more. He retired to bed in his inner office, there to snatch an hour or two of sleep. He was exhausted physically and mentally. He dared not dwell on the morrow.

Sergeant Hedges lay on the sand at the eastern end of Sphakia beach. Stretched on his back, he was looking up at the stars glittering in the indigo bowl above his head. Strangely, he felt no pain now, perhaps because at last he lay motionless. For the hundredth time, he gingerly pinched his thigh below the blood-soaked bandages: he was numb, he had to face it, unable to move his feet or legs. He'd been like that since that mortar got him in the olive grove.

'Fag, Sarge?'

He turned his eyes towards the stocky Yorkshireman squatting on his haunches next to him.

'Thanks, mate.'

As his companion stuck the Woodbine between his lips, Hedges saw that the crumpled packet was now empty.

'It's your last.'

'Garn, take it.'

The Sergeant closed his eyes. The Yorkshireman, and that tall Gunner standing on the far side, had dragged him all those hideous miles across the mountains. They had refused to abandon him and now, nearly mad with pain, hunger and thirst, they were waiting for the Navy. The nightmare was nearly over.

'Will they come, Sarge?' the man from the Dales asked yet again.

''Course they will. Haven't let us down yet, have they?' The tall Gunner walked down to where the waves lapped the beach. Slowly he returned, picking his way through the soldiers massed on the sand.

'Nothing,' he said. 'No bleedin' ships.'

'Wonder what the time is?' Hedges murmured.

'Half after…'

'Twelve?'

'No, Sarge. Eleven.'

Hedges sighed. Maybe he'd die in a German hospital tent after all?

Dimly he heard a murmur along the beach, and then the Yorkshireman jumped up as a cheer rolled softly across the sand.

'The Navy's here… they're back!'

From out of the darkness three landing craft were forging towards the beach. Hedges heard subdued orders and then the scraping of metal upon shingle. Painfully he raised himself on his elbows: he had a long wait in which to observe the scene.

As the landing craft grounded, the snaking lines of troops slowly began to inch forward like gigantic centipedes. When the craft were loaded to the gunwales they went astern, turned, then threshed into the darkness. Hedges learnt from his neighbours that the landing craft were ferrying to the three destroyers, *Jervis, Janus* and *Hasty*, who were closing the beach one at a time to embark their loads. Apparently the destroyers were not using their own boats because the beach was so cluttered. Hedges was not surprised: 15,000 men had to be taken off a strip of sand no longer than ten cricket pitches in length. Two of the craft seemed to be larger than the rest, and it was into one of these that Hedges finally was gently carried by his friends.

'Last trip, mateys,' a sailor said, barring entry to the press of men trying to board. 'We'll be back tomorrow.' The matelot turned to the crippled soldier. 'You're in luck, old son. This is our last trip tonight.'

'Thanks,' Hedges replied, 'but what are those other three L.C.I.s being left for?'

'To save time tomorrow. The final lift.'

Hedges smiled in the darkness. Though the pain was throbbing again, he was safe. The Navy would carry him back to Alex.

'How many've you taken off tonight, Jack?'

'Six thousand they reckon.' The seaman scratched his head. 'But there's a lot to take off yet.'

Hedges winced with pain as the landing craft bumped alongside a large ship. He looked up and saw *Perth* inscribed on the nameplate that swayed high above him in the darkness. They dragged him up the gangway, then took him for'd and laid him down at the end of the row of casualties waiting in the passage outside the sick bay.

The warmth, the smell of corticene and oilcloth, the glow of the lighting and the whine of electric motors swiftly lulled him into drowsiness. He closed his eyes to savour this most wonderful relaxing of tension: the Navy would care for him now.

He slept through the next morning's air raids: he did not stir even when a Stuka's bomb crashed through the galley to kill all the cooks, before exploding finally in Number One Boiler Room. Only when *Perth* finally reached Alexandria did the sick berth 'Tiffy' wake him. When originally he had landed in Crete he had weighed twelve stone: now he was eight and a half. For the last twenty-two days he had eaten nothing but bully beef and biscuits; even the thought of the stuff now made him retch. Of the 151 men in his troop, only 23 had survived.

CHAPTER 21

Dawn Encounter

'Come on, get cracking!' Tanner barked in the early dawn. 'We've a long haul yet. Renton, lead the way.'

'Aye, aye, sir.'

The Marauders slipped like shadows through the stunted cypresses; dawn was breaking upon this Friday, the 30th, but it was still dark and the Marauders could see only fifty yards ahead of them. As they neared the ditch beneath the road, they came upon the Army Captain packing up his portable wireless set. Bill went up to him.

'Me-eck,' he whispered suddenly.

The Captain's head jerked imperceptibly, then checked in the act of turning.

'Did you raise anybody?' Bill continued.

'My name's Donald, if you insist on using it,' the Captain snapped. 'I couldn't raise a peep out of our rearguard. We must be miles behind.'

'Sorry,' Bill said, rubbing his nose. 'Sure you're on the right frequency?'

Mackie spun round. For a second he searched the Sub-Lieutenant's face, long enough for Bill to detect fear lurking behind those ice-blue eyes.

This cut-and-thrust was interrupted by the tall Australian flinging himself flat. 'Down!' he whispered hoarsely. 'Someone's coming…'

The Marauders melted into the gloom at the edge of the track, their weapons at the ready. Bill cocked his Colt, Mackie being close on his right; to the left, Renton whispered as he slipped off the safety catch of his Bren: 'Fifteen-love to you, sir.'

Bill grinned in the half-light, but hell's teeth, what rotten luck to run into this lot… Thank God the side of the track was so sheer that the Marauders were invisible from the road above. The noise of lorry engines quickly grew louder, and then, down the road, roared the first truck of a small convoy.

Bill pressed himself into the scrub as the dilapidated transport rattled by. He could plainly see the driver and his mate staring through the open windscreen. As the lorry reached the sharp bend round the shoulder of the hill, the brakes squealed in the silence of the valley. The convoy concertina-ed upon its leader, the last of the seven trucks being reduced to a crawl. The lorries were packed with dishevelled men.

Its engine ticking over, the rear truck had stopped while the convoy negotiated the corner. Then its motor raced, the truck jerking forwards as the clutch was let in. At this instant a shadowy figure scrambled over the tailboard, dropped to the ground, then started racing back along the road. As the man rushed past the hidden Marauders, a shot rang out, ricocheting off the rocks and whining into the darkness. There was a scrabbling of earth as the fugitive flung himself over the edge of the track… then only the crickets disturbed the silence of the early morning.

Bill held his breath, his heart thumping against his ribs, as he listened to the footsteps of soldiers running back towards them. He pulled back the hammer of the Colt. Renton wriggled silently towards Mackie.

'He's gone,' a guttural German voice panted less than ten yards above their heads. 'We'll never find him in this country.'

'Is he armed?' another asked.

'*Nein, mein Leutnant.* We saw to that.'

The low voices were evidently consulting together…

'It's no use spreading out,' the officer growled. 'It would take too much time combing this cover. We can't hold up the convoy.'

'We had strict orders, *mein Leutnant.* We must not delay.'

The footsteps scrunched on the rocky track, then slowly receded whence they had come. An engine raced.

'A close shave,' Bill whispered. 'You O.K., Mackie?'

Bill could see the white face taut in the pale twilight. Before Mackie could reply, a Marauder growled from the left:

'We've got a prisoner, sir. He's English.'

'Good,' Bill whispered. 'I'll see him in a minute. Let's get out of here.' He scrambled up the bank, the Marauders stealthily following him. Keeping close to the far side of the track, they crept down the road towards the bend, Mackie following close behind Tanner. Bill halted them at the corner. He could hear the trucks clattering down the hairpins to the road which snaked up again on the side of the neighbouring hill, less than five hundred yards away.

'Let's have a look at the prisoner,' Bill whispered to Renton, who stood behind Mackie. 'Let that convoy get on a bit, Renton. Go ahead and keep an eye on it.' Bill watched the trucks jerking through the trees, while Renton reconnoitred round the corner, having handed his Bren to Tanner.

'He says he's British, sir,' a voice said gruffly from the scrub.

Bill turned round. A squat youth stood before him. He was in ragged peasants' clothes and his black hair was matted and filthy. He looked all in.

'Hullo, Bill.'

Tanner stared more closely. Then slowly he stretched out his hand. 'Brandy!'

The two men thumped each other, unable to speak. To hide his emotion, Bill turned towards Mackie to introduce his one-time observer. Mackie was standing motionless in front of the newcomer. For a long moment he stood there, his lips bared across his white teeth, like a wolf at bay.

Brander glanced at his old pilot. 'Bill,' he blurted, 'he's... Look out!'

Bill felt the pain in his elbow as Mackie wrenched the Bren from him. Leaping backwards, the Army Captain swung the barrel in front of him. 'If you lift a finger, any of you,' he shouted. 'I'll kill your Sub-Lieutenant...'

Bill saw murder in the man's eyes. The flame guard of the Bren's barrel pointed at Bill's stomach. Tanner stood transfixed, his men frozen behind him.

'Don't budge,' Brandy whispered behind him. 'I've met him already. He's a killer. He means what he says, Bill.'

Fascinated by the blue steel of the thin barrel, Bill stood rooted to the ground, like a rabbit mesmerised by a weasel. He felt his lips moving, then heard the strangled sound of his own words.

'If you shoot, Maeck, my men will get you.'

'Don't move, Tanner. I've drawn a bead on you and I mean to catch that convoy.'

Maeck was backing away from them, and had almost reached the curve of the hairpin. Already the whine of the lorries was echoing across the little valley as the convoy began climbing the neighbouring hill. If Maeck opened fire now, he'd scythe Bill in two and alert the convoy...

'Keep still, Bill, for God's sake,' Brandy hissed. 'We'll charge when he breaks for it.'

Maeck was inching backwards and nearing the inside of the bend that ran beneath an undercut of overhanging scree. He was already thirty yards away when the scrub above him suddenly quivered.

The German heard the cracking of a twig above his head. As he jerked the Bren barrel upwards, a flying jumble of arms and legs hurtled down upon him. As the impact of Renton's body sent Maeck flying, the Bren clattered to the ground. Jerking and kicking in the ditch, like a squib in the darkness, it sprayed the area until its magazine was empty. Bill dashed forwards through the indiscriminate hail of bullets, Brandy rushing up behind him.

Maeck was rising from the ground, his hands red with blood. He stood for a second looking down at Renton's body. As he turned to face his pursuers, a knife was in his hand, red and glinting in the half-light...

Bill continued his headlong rush, his eyes fixed on the crouching Hun. When Tanner was two yards off, he launched himself through the air in a flying tackle. Head down, arms outstretched, he groped for the contact with hard flesh... he felt the impact, grunted as the wind was knocked from his lungs. His arms threshed for the retreating body, but he felt it twist away. As he scraped across the dirt, he flinched from the steel poised above his shoulder-blades...

In that split second, Bill glanced upwards at his adversary. Maeck was toppling backwards, his knife arm swooping towards Bill's back. The German's heels struck the stone parapet; the sudden arrest of his retreating steps toppled him over, momentum carrying him backwards over the low wall. As the world spun around Bill, he heard a terrible scream.

Maeck toppled over the parapet and disappeared from sight.

CHAPTER 22

The Third Night — Friday, 30th May

The dawn of Thursday the 29th had brought hope to Major Madoc. As the warmth of the sun began to caress the shoulder of the mountain opposite, he had unravelled his tall frame from the rocks between which he had been lying all that long night. He stretched himself and moved to a cleft in the rock that overlooked the gorge. An overhanging ledge made excellent cover for his H.Q. perched here, on the edge of the precipice. He yawned, squared off his battle-dress, then went over to the Marine behind the anti-tank rifle which was sighted upon the road running to the left of the Company position.

'All well?'

'Nothing to report, sir.'

Madoc smiled to himself. His Royals were the salt of the earth: disciplined, efficient, tough.

The withdrawal southwards along the Sphakia road had been hell. It had been heartbreaking trying to hurry along that packed road. The worst section had been the climb through the passes and over the mountains. The difficulties had been immense, including the clearing of transport blockages by tumbling the trucks into the ravines. Thank God, he'd managed to collect last night the majority of his scattered units. Wednesday had been extremely trying, the longest Wednesday on record. At Imvros he had met Major Garrett and, as his Second-in-Command, Madoc acted as Movement Control Officer while Garrett formed the Composite Battalion. On a bend of the packed road, they had bumped into General

Weston and the Australian Brigadier, Vasey; from them Garrett and Madoc had received their orders.

The Royal Marines were to take up their final rearguard positions at the top of the pass, on the south side of the mountain and on the east side of the gorge. From here they must hold up the enemy while the remainder of the Army embarked at Sphakia. At the last moment the Royals were to disengage, scramble down the gorge, and jump into the waiting boats.

To allow Garrett time to organise his battalion's rearguard position on that Wednesday night, Madoc was to remain in a small village on the southern outskirts of Imvros. The New Zealanders were fighting to the north of the town and, to keep the road clear for their disengagement, no troops were to be allowed past the village until after 8 p.m.

When at dusk Madoc opened the floodgates, he and his men removed all weapons from the troops who would not be fighting again. As the New Zealanders finally came striding silently down the road, Madoc realised suddenly the grim truth: there was no one between him and the pursuing Germans. He felt an extreme loneliness in the silence of the darkness.

Captain Wilson, Madoc's driver, and his batman, had found in the village an empty cottage which was bulging with arms. After loading their van, Madoc drove off through the deserted hamlet. They passed an abandoned tank, which had been intended for use as a block-house, and drove south through the limping columns. When Madoc found his unit, he immediately resumed command: he had, however, few remaining officers and these he distributed sparingly. He appointed Wilson as his Second-in-Command, and Subalterns Hope, McPherson, Gale, Burton and Woods, Platoon Commanders.

By that Wednesday night, all units that had left Mournies had arrived. After distributing the weapons to his unit, Madoc struggled on down the pass to report the situation to Major Garrett who, with Major Sanders as his Second-in-Command, had set up his Battalion Headquarters in a culvert beneath the road. On returning to their Company, Madoc and Wilson stretched out to snatch a few hours' sleep. As they closed their eyes they heard the Sappers, under Colonel Parker and Captain Alabaster, blowing up the road to the north of them. The Germans had reached Imvros.

After clambering round his unit position on this morning of Thursday the 29th, Madoc once again went to visit Garrett in Battalion Headquarters. Major Sanders had been ordered by General Weston to evacuate that night, so Garrett had relieved Madoc of his unit and appointed him Second-in-Command of the Battalion. Gale took over from Wilson, who now commanded Madoc's unit. Once again during that long Thursday, the Germans lay low and did not attack.

At first light on Friday 30th, Madoc clambered from the sack on which he had been sleeping. He stretched himself, then left the culvert to inspect the battalion positions higher up the gorge. He felt jaded, his stomach ached with hunger, the roof of his mouth furred through thirst. Though the men seemed in good heart, it was obvious they could not hold on without rations and water. What kept them alive seemed to be the knowledge that they were to be taken off that night by the Navy. Only a few more hours…

Madoc knew that he must fetch rations and water up to his men. He grabbed Colour-Sergeant Fereday and set off down the pass in the van. Two-thirds of the way down, they were blocked by an inextricable tangle of transport. Three Australians were wrestling with the chaos: they reported that some trucks only needed starting to move them, but that the drivers had abandoned their vehicles and cleared off. Trucks had been run over the side of the road; some were burnt out, one of them with the charred remains of its inmates still in the cab.

Madoc jumped from his van. The abandoned vehicles would have to be blown up to clear the road. Defeated, he returned in the van to Battalion Headquarters to report the situation to Garrett.

Captain Pugsley stood at the entrance to the culvert, his arm soaked in blood. As Garrett's adjutant, he had been up in a van to visit Company Headquarters. He had been caught on the only straight stretch of the road, which the Germans were now shelling from the mountain slopes on the western side of the pass. Madoc could hear the swish of the mortar bombs even from this culvert. The enemy was encircling from the west. This explained why, for two days, the rearguard had not been molested. Now, from the higher slopes on the far side of the gorge, the enemy was pinpointing the Marines' positions.

During that long afternoon Madoc descended twice more to the road blockage. It was on his last visit that he encountered a party of sweating Australians struggling up through the wreckage of the transport. Grinning, they handed over the rations which they had lugged up with them. It wasn't much, but Madoc thankfully accepted them; then he returned with the food to Headquarters, where the rations were taken up through the shelling to the Companies fighting in the gorge.

'Rex,' Garrett said at dusk when they were alone, 'we're not embarking tonight.'

Squatting on his haunches, Madoc nodded, trying to conceal his bitter disappointment. His appendix scar was aching. He'd undergone the operation only eight weeks ago, when passing through Freetown on his way out from England. He felt whacked, and numb with astonishment and despair.

'Tomorrow, then?'

'Yes, so they tell us,' Garrett answered. 'Go down and reconnoitre the line of withdrawal, Rex. Leave at dawn; take two Company officers with you so they know their route blindfold.'

Rex Madoc nodded. So there was hope after all? Fifteen hundred troops were being taken off by two destroyers tonight. The troops were using the L.C.I.s left behind by *Glengyle,* he'd heard. Perhaps tomorrow there'd be room for the Royals after all?

Behind them, across the valley, was the swish of mortar bombs and the rattle of sporadic fire reverberating down the pass. In the darkness the echoes seemed to be closing in upon them...

There was a momentary lull. Madoc sighed, then sat up suddenly: the roar of heavy aircraft engines was drumming in his ears. He glanced at his Commanding Officer.

'That's the Sunderland, Rex,' Garrett said. 'It's taking off Freyberg, Morse and the staff. They've disobeyed orders for over twenty-four hours already.'

Madoc smiled ruefully. He felt lonely, abandoned. 'Who's in charge now?' he asked.

'General Weston.'

Madoc settled down for the long night. Weston was a Royal Marine.

CHAPTER 23

The Final Night — 31st May

'Sure you want to come?' Major Madoc asked the bearded Sub-Lieutenant standing before him at the entrance to the culvert of Battalion Headquarters. 'We could do with some help,' he added, buckling on the holster of his revolver.

'If you'll have us, sir. We've left our squad in the line with your ccompanies.' Tanner spoke also for Brandy who was standing beside him.

'Lucky you didn't get shot, bursting in on us like that in the dark.'

'We never knew you were Royal Marines, sir,' Bill grinned, 'or we shouldn't have dared.'

Madoc snorted. 'Come on,' he snapped, glancing at the two platoon cCommanders next to him. 'Better get going.' His batman was waiting outside the cave, and together they started scrambling down the gorge, Bill recounting the Marauders' adventures as they did so.

When Maeck had toppled over the edge of the precipice, Bill had been knocked out, but Brandy and the Marauders had quickly revived him. Dragging him with them, they had escaped through the scrub to the south, the lorry convoy having been alerted by the Bren that ran wild. After a nightmare trek across the mountains, they had left Asfendhon on their right, skirted round the eastern slopes of the mountain, and finally made contact with the right flank of the Royal Marines, who had opened fire. Only by singing 'Rule

Britannia' in the darkness had the Marauders persuaded the Royals to desist.

Madoc halted his recce party. 'We'll make this our covering position,' he said, indicating a huge rock which overlooked the narrow gully down which they were trudging. Above them was the filthy well which was their only water supply.

Madoc continued down the gully until they reached some open ground leading into a cobblestoned hamlet. On the seaward side of the houses, the path wound into a steep, narrow gorge, overhung with granite slabs. Underneath, the cliffs were honeycombed with caves and it was here that the majority of the troops were hiding during the day. Bill could see the caverns packed with the men, sitting, sleeping and feeding.

'Phew!' Brandy murmured. 'Don't 'arf pong.'

'Shut up, Brandy,' Bill said angrily. 'They've been here for two days already.'

Madoc's party crossed the gorge lower down and reached a path running parallel with the sea and across a coastal strip. For the night's withdrawal, Madoc selected another covering position on a small ridge. They marched on, until finally Sphakia lay below them.

'There it is, Brandy,' Bill whispered. 'The end of our road.'

The sea formed a blue wedge behind the huddle of stone houses, above which loomed the remains of a mediaeval castle.

They passed a cluster of wells in an olive grove stiff with troops, descending the cobbled path through the village until they reached a house overlooking the castle and the tiny sheltered bay of the fishing port.

'We'll take a breather here,' Madoc said. 'It's been much further than I expected.'

Bill saw that the Major was very grey with fatigue and pain, yet still he held himself erect. 'Colour-Sergeant,' Madoc told Fereday, the seasoned sergeant who stood by him, 'see if you can find the rations.'

The Colour-Sergeant saluted and disappeared into the village. He returned ten minutes later, a heap of tins cradled in his arms.

'It wasn't difficult, sir,' he grunted. 'The food store's wide open and everyone's helping 'isself. Some of 'em are even taking up the stuff in sandbags, back to the cave village.'

Madoc snorted. 'And we can't supply our fighting troops,' he said bitterly. 'Come on, get some food inside you and we'll organise things.'

Fereday had already jacked open the tins, which he handed round. Only the champing of jaws disturbed the silence.

'Best meal I've ever had,' Madoc said.

'Never realised bully beef and loganberries went so well together,' Bill murmured, savouring the mixture. Madoc was already on his feet.

They found chaos in Sphakia. This was hardly surprising, because the village was thronged with disorganised troops without leadership of any kind. Brigadier Hargest reported later:

There were hundreds of loose members... members of non-fighting units and all sorts of people about — no formation, no order, no cohesion. It was a ghastly mess: the men had straggled; small units like searchlight detachments had walked off when their job was done; isolated troops of gunners, engineers, field ambulance with no one to look after them. The stragglers were the worst, lawless and fear-stricken. At night they rushed for water and ravaged the food dumps and crept back into the caves at dawn — a hopeless lot — Greeks, Jews, Palestinians, Cypriots helped to swell the total…

In this confusion, unable to find volunteers to take food and water up to his Royals at the top of the pass, Madoc organised fifty Rangers to report to the store to take up the rations. They were told that the food had already gone up and that there was nothing for them. Madoc could find no one either to bring down his wounded or the wounded of the 2/7th Australians in the neighbouring pass. These two rearguards, therefore, would have to bring down their own wounded when they disengaged tonight, in their race to catch the ships.

In the village, Madoc found Colonel Jones of the M.N.B. and together they arranged that Sphakia should be cleared of all troops to allow the rearguards to pass through that night.

'It was a shambles last night,' Jones said. 'An Australian Major cleared the village, saying that anyone trying to enter Sphakia would be shot.'

'What happened?'

'There weren't enough troops to fill up the boats,' Jones said, rubbing his stubbly chin. 'The sailors were running up into the empty village, trying to find more men to embark.'

'We'll be here tonight, sir,' Madoc said grimly. He saluted and made off again up the village street. The sun was directly overhead: already sweat was pouring from their dehydrated bodies as they began their long haul back up the pass to Battalion Headquarters.

As they dragged themselves past the cave village, Madoc bumped into a Signals Company Officer of the M.N.B.

'Stinking hot, sir.'

Madoc nodded. 'Any more news?' he asked, saving his breath and trying to ignore the stench.

'The Navy have replied to Creforce's signal which General Freyberg sent yesterday, sir.'

'What did he say?'

'Requested a last lift tonight for 3,000, sir.'

'Are the Navy coming?'

'Yes, sir. Captain Arliss reported the situation on his way back with his destroyers last night. He signalled there were still 6,500 to take off. They're sending an extra cruiser.'

'Good. Who are going to be the lucky ones?'

'They've already been selected, sir.' The Signals Officer swept his hand towards the cave village. 'The Movement Control officer is organising them now.'

Madoc showed no emotion; he did not flinch. Squaring his shoulders, his eyes hard in the grey face, he turned resolutely towards the mountainous track. Bill followed at the tail of the line, a couple of sacks bulging with rations, slung across his back. So, after all the punishment, the Royal Marines, the New Zealanders and the Australians were being sacrificed: six thousand of them…

Bill stopped when Madoc halted to talk to a Maori at the top of the village. A huge man with an infectious grin, he sported an Iron Cross around his neck.

'Where did you win that?' Madoc asked, his mouth twitching.

'Over there, sir, in that western ravine.'

'How'd you get it?'

'Bayonet charge, sir. We caught 'em napping.'

Madoc looked worried. He'd heard loud mortar fire earlier that morning; it looked as if the Germans might cut them off from the coastal plain. He smiled at the Maori and moved upwards, collecting his batman en route, before deviating to find a well.

Bill was streaming with sweat. His legs ached, his eyes swam and he was nauseated by lack of food. Madoc staggered in front of him, iron discipline forcing him upwards. He looked as if he'd pass out at any moment from the pain of his recent operation. They'd never reach the top. Anyway, what was the point? They had to stand firm to allow that mob down below to escape…

As he clambered upwards, his feet dragging in the dust, Bill began to wonder what being a prisoner would be like. The enemy had found some of their own troops mutilated, their eyes gouged out by the Cretans, and the Germans were taking revenge on their prisoners. Bill smothered his fear. These rations had to be taken to those brave men at the top. Barely conscious, he struggled up the last and steepest section of the pass. When they flopped down in Battalion Headquarters, Bill listened through the haze of his consciousness to Garrett's decisive words:

'Thanks, Rex. Your journey was wasted, though, I'm afraid.'

'Why, for Pete's sake?'

'Just received orders that we are not to embark tonight.' Garrett looked round at the group of exhausted men. 'We are to hold this position until Monday.'

Madoc looked up, his eyes questioning.

'We're to escape to the east, along the coast,' Garrett continued. 'The Navy will take us off in some deserted bay to be detailed later.'

The silence expressed the thoughts of these worn-out men. *Two more days of this hell…* Mercifully, they'd be dead of thirst and starvation before then. Bill had seen men already, down the pass, who'd put a bullet through their own skulls rather than endure further agony.

As evening fell, so their spirits flagged. *It seems utterly remote up here,* Bill thought. *While we fight it out beneath the stars, the ships will edge into the bay for the last time. Then, by dawn, only the survivors of our rearguard will be left in Crete.*

He watched the sun setting, an angry blood-red orb in a crimson sky. He was sucking a pebble, trying to quench his burning thirst, when at eight o'clock the Australian, Brigadier Vasey, clambered up from below to talk to Garrett. As they conversed in low tones by the culvert, a runner appeared with a message from General Weston: the Royal Marines were to embark that night after all. They were to begin their withdrawal at 2030, in half an hour's time. They were to muster at Area Headquarters, in the caves north-east of Sphakia, which were up a gorge above the village.

'Get cracking, Rex,' Garrett barked. 'I'll meet you there.'

Bill and Brandy, who were now acting as Madoc's 'doggies' or messengers, scrambled after the Major, who was already jumping into the van. Away it bounced down the track until it reached the transport block.

'Shove her over,' Madoc ordered. They watched the stalwart little van, which had done such yeoman service, toppling over into the ravine where it landed alongside the wrecked car of the General. Leaving Colour-Sergeant Jones as a guide, they hustled on down to General Weston's cave, where Madoc met Colonel Wills and the General. Bill left Brandy outside, then followed Madoc discreetly inside the cave; there, unobtrusively, he witnessed the final drama.

Madoc saluted and stood, as straight as a ramrod, in front of his General. From the yellow light of the only lantern, the austere, clean-cut face of Weston was throwing a shadow upon the wall of the cave.

'These are your orders, Major Madoc,' General Weston said. 'This is the last night of the evacuation. Because both Major Garrett and yourself are specialists, you are to embark tonight. You are to take one hundred Royal Marine ranks with you.'

Bill watched Madoc. He stood motionless for a moment, stunned by the order.

'What, sir,' he asked quietly, 'about the rest of the Battalion?'

'They are to bivouac in the caves and wait for instructions.'

'Very good, sir.'

'That's all. No one is to enter my cave until further orders: I've an important signal to draft to Middle East.'

Colonel Hely, acting as the General's Quartermaster-General, handed Madoc a pass to allow his party through the beach cordon.

Madoc saluted and turned on his heel, Tanner following him outside into the half-light. There they sat down next to Brigadier Vasey's staff, who were also resting in the gloom.

'I'm stunned,' Madoc was whispering to himself. 'It's not possible...'

Bill turned away, ashamed at witnessing the man's agony. In the gorge below, the lines of Marines were already winding down towards Sphakia.

As darkness fell, Major Garrett arrived with the Battalion: one company was absent, having taken the wrong route down.

'What's the news, Rex?' Garrett asked, taking Madoc to one side.

'Only one hundred men and two officers are to embark tonight. This is the final embarkation.'

'Who are the officers?'

'You and me.'

Bill watched Garrett. He had turned and was looking out to sea, where the reflection of the stars danced upon the quicksilver.

'I refuse to go,' Garrett said.

'Better tell the General.'

Garrett strode into the cave. Bill could see him standing stiffly to attention. His face was drained of colour when he returned.

'Well?' asked Madoc.

'He repeated the order,' Garrett said softly. 'We'll have to go, Rex.'

They moved to one side, looking down upon their battalion stretched on the ground below them.

'Let's get it over with,' Madoc said. 'Here, Tanner, lend me a pencil.'

By the light of the lantern hanging at the entrance to Area Headquarters, the names of the hundred men were selected. Then Madoc went down to the Battalion to choose the one officer who was to go with the men. His Second-in-Command of yesterday rose to meet him.

'Hullo, sir,' Wilson greeted him, rising to his feet. 'What's up? You look all in.'

Bill watched the two men conferring in undertones. He saw Wilson's head jerk in anger, his face contorted with horror.

'I don't believe it, sir,' Wilson whispered. 'What's to become of the remainder of our battalion?'

'It's true, Wilson,' Madoc said, taking him by the arm. 'Come and help me draw lots for the officer who's to go.'

The two men climbed slowly back to the entrance of the cave. There, by the light of the guttering lantern, Madoc conducted the draw. Bill wrote the names of the Company officers on slips of signal pad, then tipped them into a tin hat.

Wilson stirred the pieces of paper. Then Bill held out the helmet.

For a long moment all eyes stared at Madoc's fingers as they unfolded the chit. He leant towards the lantern.

'Lieutenant Gale.'

There was a momentary silence; someone put his arm across Gale's shoulder. Then the officers dispersed for the heart-rending duty of detailing the men who were to leave.

'Tanner,' said Madoc quietly, 'muster the officers here. I want a word with them.'

A few minutes later Bill stood apart in the darkness as Madoc made his farewell. True to himself, he said little. He dismissed them, then silently they joined their men. Madoc went to the head of his column and started to march down to Sphakia, Major Garrett bringing up the rear. They overtook the Australians on the coastal strip and there the pace slowed down with frequent halts, as the crocodile crawled slowly towards Sphakia.

They had just halted for the hundredth time, when Bill heard the deep roar of aircraft engines echoing from the direction of the bay. Madoc was pointing seawards to where they could all see a white slick disappearing across the sea.

'The last Sunderland,' Madoc said, 'taking off General Weston and his staff.'

The column crawled like a snail down towards Sphakia. Tanner wanted to yell crazily in the darkness; his nerves were strained to breaking point. If only they could run, there'd be just a chance he could get off with Madoc... *Hurry, for God's sake,* his mind clamoured. He glanced at the disciplined men around him: steady as a rock they were, their trust in their Major. They did not know that Madoc was forbidden to inform them they were to be abandoned… Bill could not see for the tears welling into his eyes.

'Make way for Layforce!'

The head of another column was pushing past them in the darkness. As they jostled past, Madoc asked a Commando what they thought they were doing.

'We've orders to form a beach defensive line, sir.'

The Commandos jostled past them and into the darkness. When they had disappeared, Madoc halted his column near the house where earlier that day Bill had indulged in the bully and loganberries.

When he reached the head of the line, Bill looked down upon the fishing village of Sphakia. Behind the silhouette of the old castle, the sea was dancing and sparkling beneath the stars.

There, rolling gently in the swell, were the outlines of two darkened destroyers.

CHAPTER 24

Honour the Brave

Leonard Kent was Coxswain of *Kimberley*'s second whaler, which wallowed in the swell astern of the motor cutter. A burst of fire had brought them up sharply, but then the torch started flashing again, further down the coast to the east.

'I'll make over to starboard,' the Coxswain of the motor cutter called softly over his shoulder. 'Watch your painter!'

Kent pushed the tiller of the whaler over with his knee, and the little convoy swooped off to starboard. Five minutes later Sphakia Bay appeared in the darkness, the outline of cottages standing up against the mountains behind. 'Stand by to slip,' the Coxswain called.

'Slip!'

The bowman cast off the painter and as the whaler scrunched on the shingle, dark figures loomed out of the gloom to grab the whaler's bows. The time, Kent noticed by his watch, was half past eleven: dead on time. He nipped forward to help the bowman haul the soldiers aboard.

'Thank God we have a Navy,' a voice croaked from the beach. There was a low cheer, and then the flood broke. A mass of men milled around the whaler.

'Some of you hold on to the lifelines on each side of the boat. Hold on, and swim alongside,' Kent said. 'Come on, mateys, chop-chop!' He glanced round: the gunwales were barely above the water. As he leant down to haul the last man aboard, a voice spoke confidently beneath him:

'Skipper, will you take two Greek girls with you?'

Kent was dumbfounded, but before he could reply, the earnest pleading continued:

'For four days and nights they've fed, watered and shown us the way to this beach…'

Kent hardened his heart.

'Sorry, mate: no refugees. Strict orders from my captain.' He scrambled aft, shouting over his shoulder: 'Shove off, bowman.'

The motor cutter was already lying off. She manoeuvred carefully towards the whaler and took her on the port side, having already secured another on her starboard side. Thus the makeshift raft slowly chugged seawards, over a hundred men being borne off with it. In the darkness, three empty motor landing craft threshed past them, dashing for the shore. Fully loaded with troops, they had swept alongside the moment the anchors of the ships had plumped into the sea.

Kent glanced towards the dark shapes in the bay: Vice-Admiral King (he had recently been promoted) was wearing his flag in the cruiser *Phoebe,* who was rolling across the swell, her raked and widely-spaced funnels easily recognisable in the half-light; close to her lay the fast, three-funnelled mine-layer, *Abdiel,* and inshore of them the destroyers *Hotspur, Jackal,* and, right ahead, his own ship, *Kimberley.*

The whalers were slipped and Kent steered his boat alongside the after jumping-ladder.

'Shove off, bowman…'

So the ferrying continued. At each landfall, Kent could not but wonder at the discipline of these troops: they were fallen-in along the beach, a cordon of seasoned troops being flung around the edge of the bay to hold back the mass of waiting men by the rocks. All was order and silence on this last tragic night.

'Skipper, take these two girls off…'

'Sorry, no dice… but there are ways and means of getting 'em on board. Shove off, bowman.'

So throughout that long night Kent persevered in his work of mercy, the thought of the two Greek girls nagging in his mind. At two-forty-five a.m., Kent shoved off once again from *Kimberley*'s side.

'Last trip,' the First Lieutenant called down from the Iron Deck.

Kent's heart was heavy when he touched ground for the final lift. He realised full well why the squadron could wait no longer: if it failed to sail by 0300, it would be within the Stukas' danger area at dawn.

'Fill her right up, mateys,' the Coxswain growled in the darkness as he nipped for'd to help his bowman. His arms ached, his muscles strained by the continuous exertion of hauling limp men over the gunwales. He was surprised that the invisible soldier was no longer repeating his plea. He bent down for the last two hauls and grabbed a couple of arms clutching the gunwale. As he yanked upwards his hands clasped two tiny wrists…

'C'mon, me hearty…' Then, once again, he grasped the last pair of arms, which again tapered to those slender wrists. 'Go aft,' he whispered. His whaler was now nearly awash. Abruptly he turned his back on the lines of men filing imperceptibly towards his boats. He could not tear himself away.

'Shove off, bowman,' he growled angrily.

These magnificent troops, Australians and Marines now, obediently stepped back.

'Don't be long, Jack,' someone called.

The line of surf receded in the darkness as, for the last time, the motor cutter plugged seawards. Kent took the tiller and stared down at the two diminutive soldiers huddled in the stern sheets.

'Thanks, Skipper,' a Lancashire voice said from the thwarts.

'How'd you get the British uniforms?'

'Stripped a couple of our lads who'd shot themselves.'

'Ah...'

Kent sighed. God, what a terrible night!

'Listen, Bill.'

Tanner felt Brandy tug at his arm as they waited by the house beneath the castle. The unmistakable sound of cable clanking through hawse-pipes echoed across the bay from seaward.

'They're weighing, aren't they?' Brander murmured.

Madoc had climbed to his feet. 'Come on,' he called. 'We haven't much time.'

They never moved so fast in their lives. Clattering and clambering down the cobbled streets, Madoc exhorted his men to further efforts.

'Have they gone, sir?' Tanner panted in the darkness when finally they stumbled on to the beach road.

'They're making way,' Madoc said as he halted the column, 'for the ships lying further out to approach the shore.'

Bill watched the wavelets lapping the sand; lines of men stood there, staring out to sea.

'All senior officers are to report in the village, sir.' Madoc returned the messenger's salute, then followed Garrett up the narrow street.

In the darkness, the wait for Madoc's return seemed interminable. Eyes glued on the horizon, men stood silent, each with his own thoughts. Bill turned as a man's boots slipped on the cobbles behind them.

'All troops are to muster by the ruined castle,' someone ordered. 'Shake it up!'

They raced up the street to arrive gasping on a small ledge. There stood Major Madoc, the silhouette of the battlements jagged behind him. When the last man had mustered, Madoc addressed them. He talked haltingly, in sharp, jerking sentences.

'I've just seen Major Wolstenholme of the Gunners, and this is what I have been told…'

Bill had stopped breathing, knowing in his heart what he had been dreading for so long. He watched the strong grey face that looked down upon them.

'It's all up,' Madoc said quietly. 'The last ship has sailed.'

Bill did not trust his ears. It was over, finished…

'A party with a white flag will go out at dawn tomorrow to surrender Crete to the Germans.'

A long sigh escaped the cluster of men standing tensely in the half-light. Bill turned away, unable longer to watch their magnificent leader. Dimly he heard Madoc issuing his orders:

'I'm going to reconnoitre the village. I expect the Stukas to return at first light, and I want you to disperse.' He paused before giving the last, cruel command: 'You are immediately to smash on the rocks all your rifles and small arms. Then tear up and destroy your identity books. The Royal Marines have done well. I'm proud of you.'

Bill followed as the Major moved off into the night. They marched down to the shore, where men lay numb with despair. Climbing upwards, Madoc reached the houses. A stench of death wreathed the village, where the dead lay rotting in the cellars from the heat of the previous days.

Through this horror they stalked, until Madoc reached a small house overlooking the beach. Bill helped him to stow his equipment inside the house, then, still in silence, they walked down to the sand, past a beached landing craft and back to the troops. Madoc ordered them to disperse around the rocks and into the caves. He then went round to ensure that his men were properly concealed. Madoc, his task finished, walked slowly down to the shore, where he stood on the sand, gazing out to sea. A man came running along the beach towards them.

'Major Madoc, sir?' The soldier saluted: he seemed in a hurry and anxious to be off.

'Major Garrett's compliments, sir: there's a landing craft leaving now to get away to Africa.'

The Major turned away and looked out to sea. For half a minute he stood motionless, hands clasped behind his back. Then the tall figure half-turned towards the impatient messenger.

'Very good,' Madoc said softly. 'Carry on, please.'

The man hesitated. 'What shall I tell Major Garrett, sir?'

'I have fought through the whole of this campaign with my men,' Madoc said quietly, glancing up at the mountains. 'I shall stay with them.'

The man hurried off down the beach. Madoc turned to the Sub-Lieutenant standing behind him.

'Take my place, Tanner,' he ordered, holding out his hand. 'I'll look after Brander.'

Speechless, Bill saluted. He hesitated, then turned away. He stumbled blindly along the sand towards the M.L.C. wallowing in the surf.

CHAPTER 25

Tragic Voyage

Major Garrett had swum out to the landing craft which was drifting two hundred yards offshore. Though its propeller was fouled by wire, he found the craft in working order; he swam back for volunteers to help him clear the screw and bring the M.L.C. back to the beach.

As the craft threshed astern at 03.55 to leave the beach, Bill scrambled on board. Aboard this little craft were five officers and 136 men, including 56 Marines. Coughing and spluttering, the landing craft chugged at full speed to the southward — away from Sphakia which, within the hour, must again fall victim to the enemy. Even as they struggled to lift the fuel cans aboard the M.L.C., the Stukas had arrived, bombing and machine-gunning the little village. When dawn broke, the Australian mechanic on the engine pointed over the stern.

'Poor devils,' he whispered. 'They haven't got a chance on that crowded beach.'

In the twilight Bill could see the flash of bombs and then, over the cliffs of Crete where Sphakia nestled, black mushrooms of smoke.

'I can't look,' Major Garrett said. 'Cox'n, steer for that bay.'

For the last three hours they had been making for an islet called Gavdopoula which had come up over the horizon. If they could reach the island before the Luftwaffe spotted them, they could hide up during the day before setting forth again that night. Anxiously searching the horizon while the sun climbed into the blue, Bill sighed with relief as they rounded the easternmost point. Crete slipped from view behind the island and then a small bay opened up, in which they anchored.

'We'll lie here until dusk,' Garrett said. 'I want the engineer to overhaul the engines while parties search the island for water. Then we'll go ashore.'

They slept all that afternoon, dead to the wide, in the shade beneath the cliffs. The company was divided into watches, and rations for two meals were issued. An Australian kindled a fire and the first tea was brewed, the best Bill was ever to enjoy.

By dusk everyone's spirits had revived and, when the anchor was weighed, no one doubted for a moment that they would reach the north African coast, a hundred and forty miles to the south.

Bill sat on the bottom-boards, his back against the craft's port quarter. The stars waltzed crazily in the vault of the night sky: the seas had begun to rise, and white horses flecked on the starboard beam. At this moment the starboard engine spluttered, coughed and died.

'I shouldn't have let you put in that Dieselite, Chief,' Garrett apologised to the Australian mechanic, a tall, gangling man with wrinkled crow's feet at the corners of his eyes.

'Nothing like trying, sir,' the Australian replied. 'Any port in a storm, as you might say, when we've got no juice.'

'What d'you suggest?'

'Reckon we better strip her down,' the Chief said. 'We can flog on with the port engine.'

So, as she pitched and yawed, the mechanics, with only one adjustable spanner, took the engine apart. Bill felt his eyelids drooping, and he dozed fitfully for he knew not how long.

He was awoken by the silence: he could hear nothing but the swilling of water in the bilges and the groans of men vomiting over the side, as their rectangular tin can wallowed in the seas.

'Can you rig a sail on her, do you think, Buffer?' Garrett asked a burly Petty Officer named Dykes, the unofficial Chief Bo'sun's Mate.

'No sooner asked than done, sir.'

Half an hour later, with three oars lashed as a jury mast, the winch canvas was flapping aloft. Bill helped to secure the sheets and then the makeshift sail billowed and filled. Slatting and banging, it had an immediate effect on the motion of the craft: she steadied, but then turned full circle out of control before Garrett managed to head her south again.

'Keep a log for me, will you, Tanner?' Garrett asked. 'Reckon we're making a good three knots, with a knot leeway.'

'Aye, aye, sir. How far d'you reckon we are from the islet now?'

Garrett hesitated. 'About eighteen miles, I should think. Course due south.'

Bill completed the entries and marked off the dead reckoning on the army map of the Mediterranean that someone had found. At four o'clock the Chief swung the starboard engine. To everyone's amazement it roared into life. Men's spirits rose again as the landing craft surged once more to the southward. Their hopes were soon dashed, however, for the engine slowly died. The last drop of petrol was finished.

The jury sail was again hoisted. The sun peeped above the horizon; it climbed above the M.L.C. which was now wallowing sickeningly in the running sea. Then the port engine stopped.

'How far have we come, Tanner?'

'Eighty miles, sir,' Bill replied, the figures indelibly etched into his mind. 'Only 110 miles to Tobruk!'

'Roll on,' Marine Whittle growled from the bottom-boards. 'Hope Jerry's not captured it yet.'

A chuckle greeted the irrepressible Royal, and then they hoisted the makeshift sail. The M.L.C. immediately turned to port, and nothing that Garrett could do would hold her. She gybed, then turned full circle.

'Wish she was a sailing boat,' Garrett panted as he wrestled with the wheel. 'I'd know how to handle her.' After steering crazily downwind, he shook his head. 'There's nothing for it, Buffer,' he said, 'but to send six men over the side. They must try to keep her head up.'

Petty Officer Dykes called for volunteers. Stripping off, Colour-Sergeant Colwill and six men clambered over the side. By scrambling to the port bow and kicking with their legs, they managed to hold up her head. Garrett grinned. 'That's better, Buffer. Keep a watch going like this.'

By now, half a gale was blowing: if any of the human tugs slipped their grasp there could be no hope of rescue, for she could not manoeuvre when running before the wind.

'Reckon we're making one knot leeway to the east,' Garrett shouted above the rising wind. 'Allow for that, Sub.'

'Aye, aye, sir.'

Though the M.L.C.'s motion was horrible (she slid sideways down the waves like a flat pebble skimming across the water), she rarely took it green. The 139 souls kept dry, but the majority were seasick. The deck soon became indescribably filthy: if a man had earlier felt unaffected, he must own a cast-iron stomach now to escape the nausea.

'Take round the rations.' Garrett nodded at Colour-Sergeant Dean. 'Change the watches.'

Bill glanced with disgust at his water ration: a sixteenth of a pint which hardly covered the bottom of his mug; and half a biscuit. He spun out his breakfast and was still munching his biscuit when the sun eventually disappeared behind the scudding clouds.

Whittle looked across at him, his mouth twitching. 'You looked as if you enjoyed that, sir.'

'I did,' Bill said. 'When's the next meal?'

'Goodness knows.'

Though many men grumbled at their hunger, they were treated to another similar banquet when the sun sank upon that second day, the 2nd of June. On the next day, however, they realised how lucky they had been: the ration was now reduced to one meal a day, to be consumed in the evening, before the long night began.

By Thursday the 3rd of June, the company had settled into a routine. The watches were changed regularly, one-in-four for the officers, one-in-ten for the troops. Bill began to look forward to his watch on the wheel: the monotony was broken and he had little time to think. The sun had passed its zenith when Bill turned over his watch. He settled down in the bilges to the half-sleep that was their rest.

Bill felt despair gnawing at his spirit. The gale had now blown itself out; the sea was a flat calm, its surface streaked with silver and aquamarine, but the long swell which the storm had left in its trail rendered the M.L.C.'s motion more impossible than before. The slatting of the sail against the oars and the fretting of the sheets began to chafe his nerves… he couldn't sleep with this thirst, this pain clutching at his stomach. He began to long for the gale that at least drove them forwards, even if in the wrong direction.

'Sir,' a voice called suddenly from for'd. 'There's some petrol in this locker. It's not water after all.'

'How d'you know?' Garrett shouted. 'You must have tried it.'

There was a murmur from the men and someone laughed; then two jerry cans were passed aft from hand to hand.

'Put it in the starboard engine, Chief.'

There was silence while all eyes watched the precious liquid slopping into the tank: a difficult operation in this wallowing junk. The Chief swung the handle and, with a cheer from the company, the starboard engine roared into life.

It was grand to hear again the water slicking along the sides. At eight knots, assuming that she was consuming a gallon per hour, sixty-four miles would soon be rubbed out... With the joy of this thought singing in his mind, Bill dozed off.

He was woken suddenly by a very special Marine oath. The engine was roaring but, whatever the Chief tried, still the propeller raced.

'Clutch has gone, sir,' the Chief said, sweat pouring from his brow. 'I'm beat.'

Garrett looked to seaward, his face gaunt with anxiety. He turned slowly to Petty Officer Dykes. 'No point in wasting petrol, Buffer. Think you can distil water by using the petrol to boil it?'

Dykes shrugged his shoulders. 'Better than wasting the petrol on this engine, sir.'

The daily ration was issued, and then the twilight of the third night slowly descended.

Bill slept restlessly, but when he woke at first light on the fourth day, he knew by the slatting canvas that another windless day had dawned. The sun climbed into the sky and once again the battle became one of endurance versus thirst. It was during this day that time became meaningless, the hours merging one into the other in an eternal nightmare. During that afternoon the port lookout suddenly pointed across the port quarter:

'Sail ho!' he yelled. 'Coming up astern, sir.'

Delirious: another man going off his rocker, Bill thought. He climbed to his feet to peer where the man's arm pointed. There, a bone in her teeth, was an M.L.C., rapidly overhauling them. As she careered past them, Bill saw an officer in khaki hailing through cupped hands:

'We're running out of petrol. I'll go on and report your position.' He held up his thumb.

Garrett waved back and a cheer rang across the water. The noise of her fruity engines quickly faded as she disappeared swiftly over the horizon. Dejectedly, Garrett's company subsided again into their cramped quarters; hardly had they done so when an aircraft dived low upon them from out of the sun. From habit the men flattened themselves, covering their heads with their arms.

'One of ours!' Garrett shouted, waving frenziedly. 'She's one of ours, boys! Try to catch her attention!'

Shaving mirrors were hurriedly produced, their owners trying to heliograph the Blenheim which was turning to circle round them. The men waved, whirling towels as they jumped up and down. She flew off.

'She *must* have seen us,' Garrett said. 'Don't worry, lads; this is our lucky day.'

But the fourth day dragged into night and then, on the fifth, a gentle breeze shimmered with the dawn of another scorching day. It was on this day that Corporal Nugent, Private Legge and Marine Yeo went into the sail-making business: by using blankets sewed together with boot-laces, they fashioned a jib.

At last the craft became more manageable, being able to keep off the wind.

On the sixth day, by also enlarging the mainsail with more blankets, Garrett was able to hold her on a broad reach and even, if the strength of the wind was not too fierce, to sail close-hauled. She could not go about, however, and whenever Garrett wished to tack, Colour-Sergeant Colwill would go over the side with his six stalwarts. Then, by putting the wheel down at the identical moment when Colwill's party pushed as hard as they swam, Garrett managed to 'wear' ship. Though this manoeuvre was utterly exhausting in the men's flagging condition, an attempt was made at fashioning extra oars and to make an additional rudder; but even though Garrett moved the men aft, this proved fruitless — and, what was worse, exhausting.

One scheme was successful, however: Marines Harding and Booth managed to create a distiller from petrol tins and rubber hosing. By using the precious drops of petrol, they distilled 4½ gallons of drinking water during the next few terrible days. For, on the eighth day, the company was in desperate straits. Bill's tongue was swollen and black; his throat was raw, his head splitting as his mind began to wander. It was all he could do to keep a record of their position. The pains of hunger gnawed at his innards, until the agony became unbearable. Men groaned all about him and, as they slept, nightmares would convulse the contorted figures into gibbering, grotesque animals. Only discipline was now holding them together...

'Make a raft by lashing those empty diesel tins together,' Garrett ordered. 'A party must sail on ahead to fetch help.'

As they toiled beneath the blazing sun all that afternoon of the 8th, each man knew in his heart that they were finished. It was after the daily meal in the evening that Colour-Sergeant Dean whispered in Garrett's ear:

'Gunner Black's dead, sir.'

The man had died uncomplainingly; his neighbours had thought him asleep. They slipped the corpse over the side and Garrett held a short service. In the cool of the evening his simple words brought comfort to the silent company. Men braced themselves and reacted in different ways: some bowed their heads, others stared upwards at the cloudlets drifting across the blue heavens.

'*O most glorious and gracious Lord God,*' Garrett read from a dog-eared prayer book, '*who dwellest in heaven, but beholdest all things below; look down, we beseech Thee, and hear us, calling out of the depth of misery, and out of the jaws of this death, which is ready now to swallow us up: Save, Lord, or else we perish…*'

His voice cracked and, as he paused, a low 'Amen' whispered through the craft. Garrett returned to the wheel, his eyes distant as he gazed ahead.

The daily meal, the agony of digestion, the torment of the water ration… weaker, weaker…

A shot rang out suddenly from somewhere amidships. Bill could smell the cordite and the stench of burnt flesh.

'A Cypriot's shot 'isself, sir,' a Marine shouted in the shocked silence. 'Stoopid, ain't it?'

'Pipe down,' Garrett snapped. 'Is he dead?'

'He is, sir.'

'Put him over the side, then.'

Bill averted his eyes from the shocking sight. He heard the splash and tried to wrench away his thoughts.

Brander, how was he getting on? And Madoc? Poor devils: probably shot by now to add to the stench of Sphakia. Out of the frying pan…? But perhaps being in this M.L.C. was better

235

than being a prisoner — to be marched again, at the end of their tether, up that dreadful gorge, past the Australian dead who lay in the ditches where they fell, facing the enemy, their bayonets bloodied. *Why does Man cause such inhumanity to Man? What is the point of it all, dear God? There must be easier ways of defending decency and truth?*

A red mist swam across the retina of his closed eyes as the afternoon sun blistered from the glassy surface of the sea. His head kept slumping across his chest as he swam into semi-consciousness. Dimly he heard the squeal of the steering wheel in its bearings, registered the slatting of the sails that filled not... Only the helmsman and the lookout were on watch now.

'Land ahoy... Land... Land!'

The cry floated down the landing-craft. Men, interrupted in their several nightmares, twisted on their sides, cursing softly...

'Land ahoy, sir... there's flaming AFRICA!'

Bill jerked to consciousness. There was a roaring about his ears; a murmuring and a throbbing surge of life amongst these dying men. God, if this were a hoax, or a madman's hallucination? A mirage, so common at sea...? *Dear God, spare us that now... Let it be land, Christ... please...*

'It's land all right.'

The excitement trembled even in Major Garrett's words. He had climbed up on to the bow sponson and, steadied by the score of hands, in the awful silence he had gazed long at the blurred horizon ahead.

'That's Africa!'

A cheer quavered from one hundred and thirty-seven parched and swollen throats. Men laughed hysterically, slapping each other on the back. Garrett was carried aft to the throaty chorus of 'He's a jolly good fellow.'

The next eight hours were the longest the men were ever to endure. Imperceptibly, the yellow strand of low-lying coast enlarged, to disappear into the dusk of evening twilight. Night watches were set, but hope faded as men realised they could not survive another day: the sail flapped uselessly, the phosphorescence sparkled alongside. Midnight came and went; then at one o'clock on Monday morning, 9th June:

'Land dead ahead, sir.'

Bill hauled himself to his feet and stood swaying over the gunwale. Peering like an aged owl, he glimpsed a white ribbon of surf splashing upon a darkened shore.

At half-past one, the anchor plopped over the side in three fathoms of water.

CHAPTER 26

On the Road to Tobruk

The plume of yellow dust swirled behind the Bedford truck bouncing its way along the coastal road seventeen miles from Sidi Barrani. Driver Collett's thoughts languished on the green dales of his beloved Westmorland: those pastures where his father's fat sheep grazed beside the sparkling trout streams chuckling down to Ullswater…

He pulled himself together, wondering how many miles he had been trundling down this straight, unending road to the beleaguered garrison of Tobruk. His mate was nodding with sleep beside him, and if he, Collett, did not watch out, they'd both be asleep; at this speed, they'd never wake again.

He braced himself and gripped the wheel more firmly, but soon the whine of the governor caused his thoughts to drift again…

''Struth,' he muttered. 'What, for Pete's sake, is this?'

A column was staggering down the road towards him. Reeling in the heat that shimmered from the dusty surface, their leader was throwing up his hands as he staggered down the centre of the road. Collett grabbed the handbrake as the bearded lunatic flopped against the off-side wing.

The man's clothes were in tatters. His sunken eyes burnt above the hollow cheeks matted with grime and beard. He tried to speak, but no words would come from the lolling black tongue.

'Steady, mate,' Collett muttered as he opened his door. 'What's up?'

The column of ragged vagabonds had staggered to a halt. They stood pathetically to attention, propping up each other. As Collett jumped out, he heard the strains of 'A Life on the Ocean Wave' croaking from the swaying ranks.

'Water!' gasped the man. On the only remaining shoulder of his shirt was the faded insignia of a Major's crown. 'For God's sake, give us water.'

The driver stepped forward as the Major swayed in front of him.

'Quick, man, fetch help,' the officer was gasping. 'We've come from Crete.'

Collett caught him as he fell.

EPILOGUE

The Mediterranean Fleet was to suffer one more loss before the curtain fell on the Crete campaign: the anti-aircraft cruiser *Calcutta*, acting as cover for Vice-Admiral King's last evacuation force, was bombed by two JU 88s from out of the sun. She sank immediately at 0920 on the first of June.

In his dispatch, Admiral Sir Andrew Cunningham wrote:

It is not easy to convey how heavy was the strain that men and ships sustained. Apart from the cumulative effect of prolonged seagoing over extended periods, it has to be remembered that in this last instance ships' companies had none of the inspiration of battle with the enemy to bear them up. Instead, they had the increasing anxiety of the task of trying to bring away in safety thousands of their own countrymen, many of whom were in an exhausted and dispirited condition, in ships necessarily so overcrowded that even when there was opportunity to relax, conditions made this impossible. They had started the evacuation already overtired, and they had to carry it through under conditions of savage air attack, such as had only recently caused grievous losses to the Fleet...

It is perhaps even now not realised how nearly the breaking point was reached, but that these men struggled through is the measure of their achievement, and I trust that it will not lightly be forgotten.' (Author's emphasis)

THE VERDICT OF HISTORY

It is fitting, perhaps, that I lay down my pen on the day that Freedom's great architect of victory, Sir Winston Churchill, started on his last Great Adventure. Without his inflexible will to uphold our promise to Greece, it is doubtful whether Crete would have been defended.

Many of those who were sacrificed in Crete must have, during their long years in captivity, pondered why, up to the last minute, troops were still being poured into the Island? Why was Crete defended at all? The bereaved, too, must often have wondered why an island which was indefensible without air cover was ever defended. In the agony, history has proved Churchill right.

Hitler lost six thousand of his crack and irreplaceable parachutists. Suffering these appalling casualties, he could not immediately exploit his success in Crete by attacking Cyprus and thereby win the Middle East. The stubborn defence of Crete delayed Hitler's timetable: the German attack upon Russia was launched five weeks late. Caught by the Russian winter before it had consolidated its fronts, the Wehrmacht was halted, held, then hurled back by the Red Army.

For those who suffered and whose lives were scarred by those terrible ten days in May 1941, it must be no small comfort to realise that from the disaster of Crete were born the first stirrings of Victory.

JOHN WINGATE.

A NOTE TO THE READER

Dear Reader,

If you have enjoyed the novel enough to leave a review on **Amazon** and **Goodreads**, then we would be truly grateful.

Sapere Books is an exciting new publisher of brilliant fiction and popular history.

To find out more about our latest releases and our monthly bargain books visit our website:
saperebooks.com

Printed in Great Britain
by Amazon